Susan -
Thank you for your contribution to making this possible
Love,

THE 3 MARIAS

Visit my new blog at
donnadarlingauthor.blogspot.com

Cover photo: Coffee tree, Vicki Sutton-Beattie

Other photos by Donna Darling, unless otherwise credited

First Edition

ISBN: 9798849889726

Book Design: Brian Shea

BOOK ONE: PUERTO RICO

THE 3 MARIAS

Donna Darling

Maria Fina

Maria Celia

Maria Martina

Dedicated to
my father,
who told me I could write
&
Camille Minichino,
who taught me how

Thank you to Jo Mele, Brian Shea, Billie Dupree,
Ann Damaschino, Susan Lawson, David Flower,
Nancy Kors, Judith Overmier, and Lyn Roberts,
for without our amazing writers
group, this book would not
have been finished.

Special thank-you to my husband,
Dan, who has always supported
and believed in me.

My deepest gratitude and thanks to my
primos. Discovering our ancestry became
a history lesson about Puerto Rico,
and captured my heart.

Courtesy of the Kansas Historical Society

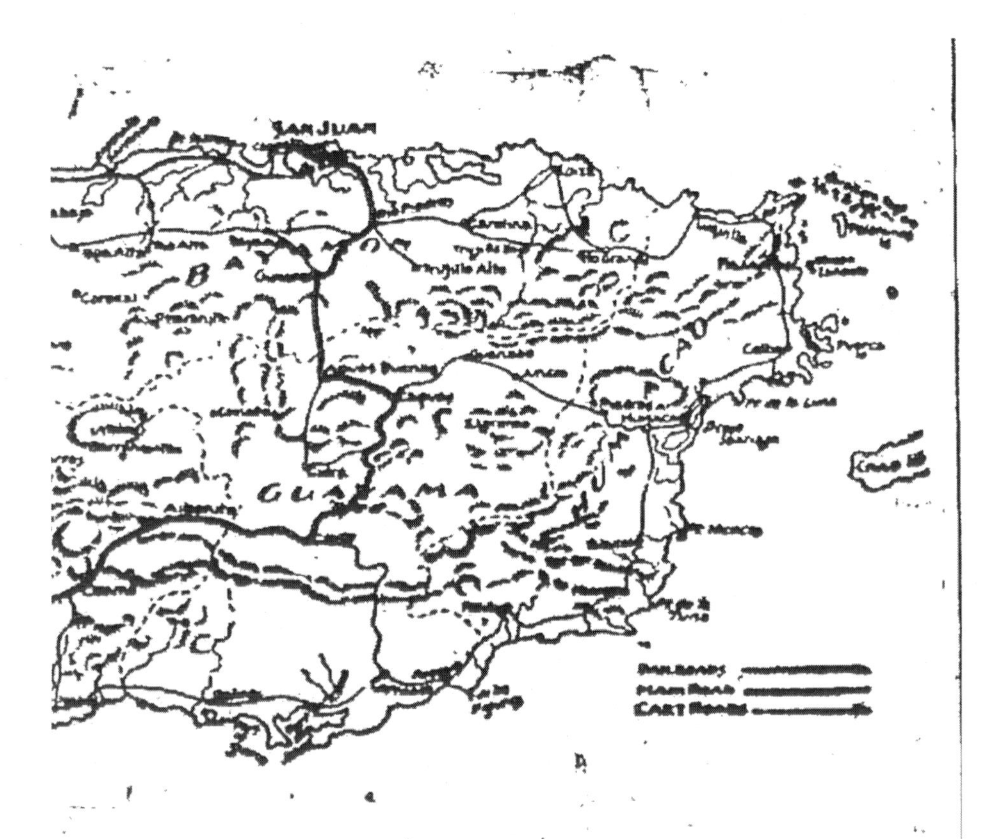

ISLAND OF PUERTO RICO.

Fina

By the age of 20, I'd lived two lifetimes.

My family lived a life of privilege, where to me everything was perfect. We had private teachers and servants. I thought I would become a nun and dedicate my life to the church.

Just before my 14th birthday, in the summer of 1895, there began a wave of change that swept Mama away, setting me adrift in my faith.

For those who survived the next five years, the taste of freedom was replaced with bitterness and desperation. My prayers went unanswered. I stopped asking God's forgiveness and did what I needed to survive.

The Three Marias
1895
Adjuntas, Puerto Rico

IN THE STEEP HILLS ABOVE the coastal town of Ponce was Adjuntas, a place touched by heaven and cursed by hell. We lived there, where coffee and sugar plantations dotted the lush, green Puerto Rican mountainside populated by many Corsicans, including my father, Guillermo Paoli.

Papa steered off the main road and turned up the narrow, one-lane road toward our hacienda. A sprawling, two-story house on our own coffee plantation. I was very proud of the strong wooden house that Papa built with help from local laborers. Some of the surrounding haciendas were made of brick, but our rustic house sat majestically in the tall trees as if it sprouted from the earth.

Banana and coconut trees grew plentiful in the cooler climate of the mountains, where we got much more rain than in the flatlands, and we thought made it the perfect place to live. The many rivers and streams flowed all the way to the Caribbean Sea.

It was a lush, tropical dream life, but the roads were treacherous. There was no way to see a cart coming toward you on the twisting, narrow road, so locals took up the use of a whistle to alert oncoming riders. Papa pulled the whistle from around his neck and clenched it between his teeth. He whistled at every turn, so that any rider coming down the hill would be alerted to our wagon coming up. The downhill riders leaned into the grade and rode fast and wild, without fear, taking blind turns and skirting the edge of the road, flirting with danger. If they slipped off the edge, a fall down a steep ravine would mean certain death. Their only weapon was the whistle clenched between their teeth which screamed in an alert while they rode a donkey, pony or horse with frightful intensity.

Riding uphill was a much more relaxed experience. My brother, Victor rode beside Papa and leaned with the turns. Victor was a serious man. Not to be crossed, but fiercely loyal to family.

My brother, Ursulo, who we called Lolo, picked up his four-string tiple and somehow managed to strum along despite the bumpy ride, while we clapped and sang a hollow tune.

"That's a song about heartbreak," Papa complained. "Play The Blue, Blue Sea." He always had a cheerful disposition and was the one to lift our spirits. "Fina, sing for us," he said. My given name was Maria Josefina, but they called me Fina.

Mama had the most beautiful voice in our family. Some of us kids liked to think we got her voice. Since she was at home, I led us in chorus, "Will you meet me at the blue, blue sea?" I sang.

Lolo was my playful brother, always ready with a joke. He took after Papa. I hoped he would meet a girl who would be kind to him.

Lolo was sensitive, and a strong woman like Mama might be too hard on him. He was born with a withered leg and Mama said it made him more determined. He was small and crawled on is belly as a baby, using his arms to pull his body. He got so strong, he pulled himself up on everything. When we were younger, he couldn't run and keep up, but he could climb almost any tree like a monkey. We always called for Lolo to get the highest fruit. He built a lookout, high up in a banana tree, where he perched for hours watching over everyone's comings and goings on the property. He was our little spy.

Lolo made the ride home enjoyable by playing his tiple. We all sang along and my eleven-year-old sister, Maria Celia laughed at the silly lyrics. Even my oldest brother, Victor's mood was light and he sang along too.

"Where's Rio?" Celia said.

Our family dog was always at the edge of our property when we arrived home. He sat at the bottom of the road to our house. Papa trained him to never leave the property, and he wouldn't put one paw over the line.

"Mama's home. He must be on the porch," Victor said.

Papa stopped the wagon in front of the house. "I'll get out here," he said and hopped out. "You pull around back and unload the supplies. I'll be out in a minute to help with the horses." Papa's long legs took the porch steps with one stride. Victor brought the wagon around to the side of the house, to the kitchen door where we began to unload supplies.

"Hijo de puta!" Papa's voice boomed like thunder and echoed in the trees.

My brothers and I turned to see Papa storm out of

the house and sprint to the barn. "I've never heard Papa swear in my life," I said.

"Mama must've been very angry," Celia said.

Victor set down the flour sack and ran to the barn. Papa erupted from the barn on horseback and raced down the hill, blasting his whistle.

"Where's Papa off to in such a hurry?" Celia asked. My little sister reported everyone's business in our family. "There goes Victor," Celia sighed.

Victor disappeared on horseback down the hill in a cloud of dust.

"Now we only have Lolo to help us unload the wagon," Celia complained.

I gave Lolo a look of concern. Panic grew within me.

LOLO REACHED INTO THE WAGON and pulled his pistol from the holster. He cocked the trigger and walked toward the front of the house.

"Carry things inside, I'll be right back," I said to Celia. I stepped into the mudroom where Isabella, more like family than a domestic servant, blocked my entrance into the kitchen. "Hola, Isabella—" My smile faded when I saw her usually pleasant face looking very grim.

"Isabella?"

"Give him a few minutes Josefina," she said.

Isabella never called me by my formal name. Everyone called me Fina and reserved Josefina for trouble.

"Is Mama mad? What happened?"

I heard Lolo's wail coming from Mama's bedroom, just off the front room. He'd entered through the front door. He sounded like a wounded animal. Isabella turned and hurried back to Mama's room. I followed behind her. Mama lay in her bed, face swollen and head bloodied. Her eyes barely able to open, she mumbled something and extended her hand toward mine. Her mouth was swollen and it was painful for her to speak. Isabella placed a wet cloth on her head and mouth. Mama moaned in pain. My God, she's got teeth missing, I thought. I covered my mouth to contain my sobs.

"What happened?" I asked.

Isabella motioned for us to move to the corner of the room. "She was alone," she said. "I heard Rio barking, and I ran to the house. I saw them ride off. There was four of them."

"When did this happen? How long has she been like this?" I rattled on. "What happened?"

Lolo interrupted, "Where is the doctor? And where is the dog?"

"Rio is in the barn. He is injured. Badly. He is a good guard dog, but—" Isabella spoke in a low voice, "I sent Basilio to the city for the doctor—"

"Why not get help from Adjuntas?" I began. "Why not send somebody for us?"

"She needs a city doctor from Ponce," Lolo said. "Not our country doctor."

"Oh, my God," I looked at Mama in her bed.

"The bandits came right after you left. I tried to help Senora Paoli," Isabella mumbled. "Then I ran for help. Jose said he looked for you in town, but didn't see you."

"We stopped at a friend's farm," I said. "Papa was talking."

"I told your Papa everything. He muttered something, said he knew who would have done this. Then he ran out of here like a rooster," Isabella said.

"Do you have any idea who he has gone after?" She looked at Lolo.

"No."

"Hey, why did you leave me to do all the work?"

Celia stomped in from the back porch. "Mama!" she called out.

I got up to stop her at the doorway and prevent her from seeing our mother. "Shhh, Mama fell from a ladder, and hit her head. She's not feeling well. Let's be very quiet for her, Mejia."

Lolo, Celia, Isabella and I sat with Mama all afternoon, taking turns checking on Rio.

Dr. Torres arrived before supper, around 6:00pm. The doctor said the swelling is very serious, and we needed to watch her. He very kindly treated Rio, and stayed as long as he could, but the hour was getting late. He left and said he'd be back in the morning.

Isabella reminded us to eat something, and at supper time Papa and Victor came home. They took care of the horses then washed up outside at the water pump, soaking themselves from head to toe. Celia reported from the window, "They're getting their clothes all wet! Rio is up! He's out there with them. I'm going outside."

"No, you stay inside," Lolo said and he walked out the door.

Celia pressed her nose to the glass and watched our brothers and Papa talk. I picked at my nails and wished they would hurry up and come in the house.

"I'm just dying to know what they were saying," Celia said.

"Come away from the window. Let's see what needs to be done in the kitchen." I tugged at Celia's elbow.

Papa and my brothers stepped into the mud porch off the kitchen, and changed out of their wet clothes. Papa and Victor sat with Mama for an hour, then we all talked. Papa explained that Mama was climbing on the roof to make a repair when she fell and was badly hurt. Celia had a few questions but was satisfied, and Papa sent her upstairs to bed.

"Papa, we know what really happened," I said.

Papa kept his gaze downward and paused, then answered. "Isabella told me she heard screams and ran to the house. She saw the bandits, maybe four of them. They wore masks and dressed in black. They rode off on horseback. Isabella came inside and found Mama." He shook his head. "She must have fought the robbers off, trying to save our money. I found her broken broom." He held his head in his hands and mumbled, "They beat her." Papa broke down and cried.

I sobbed. "Poor Mama. I can't believe this."

"Isabella thought you might know who did this!" Lolo said, She said they tore the house apart. She cleaned everything up before we came home."

"I've heard a couple of rumors about other attacks. I wasn't sure if it was a bad debt, or family squabble," Papa explained, "Now, I know."

Victor pounded his fist on the chair and snorted. "I'll find out who they are. I'll take care of them."

"No, you won't, Victor. They're going after progressives. Anyone involved in working for an Independent Puerto Rico," Papa said.

"Where did you go?" I asked. "Papa rode off like he was chasing after someone, and you rode after him.

Do you know who did this? Did Mama tell you?"

"I don't know who, but I know their intention. We went to see Dino," Papa said. "He knows about what's been going on."

Our neighbor, and fellow Corsican Dino Cesari owned a large plantation and several businesses in Ponce. When Papa came to Puerto Rico in 1853, he settled in Guayanilla, then moved to Adjuntas, where they met Dino, who helped Papa get his start in the coffee business. Dino was confident enough to know Papa would never be a competitor. Dino's plantation was equipped with elaborate aqueducts and irrigation, and a mill which is critical for producing fine coffee. Dino sold his coffee in the European market. Strapped for money, Papa borrowed from the banks to get his farm started, with simple wooden irrigation ducts and sold his coffee in the local market. When profits began to flow, he used all is profits and borrowed again to build a mill, and began to sell in the European market on a small scale.

They both knew that Dino would never allow Papa to gain an edge in business. As long as Papa maintained a small farm, Dino allowed it.

"I'll get some men together and we'll take care of these locals who think they're going to threaten us," Victor said. "We'll get these bandits."

"That's enough," Papa said. He turned to me and said, "You are not to be at home alone. From now on, there will be one of us here. The attacks on other farms happened at night. This was during the day." Papa's face showed his concern. "Very bold." He shook his head.

"I'll post a guard outside to watch the property."

We joined hands and Papa led us in prayer. The

house fell silent except for the sound of the clock ticking in the background. Papa said, "Let us now say the Rosary."

A knock at the door made us all jump. Lolo pulled his pistol from his holster. Victor ran to the door and stood beside it, with his gun drawn. Another knock and a deep voice called out, "Guillermo, it's Dr. Torres."

There was a collective exhale in the room. Victor opened the door. "I've come back to sit with Dona Paoli," Dr. Torres said. "I thought I'd stay through the night." He came in and set his doctor's bag on the chair.

I could see that he was worried and felt relieved to have him here, but if he was worried, we all worried.

"Celia will be up early. Someone needs to get some rest tonight. I will stay with Dr. Torres and Mama," Papa said. "Why don't you all get some sleep. I'll need you tomorrow."

Victor and I went upstairs to bed.

✡ ✡ ✡

Victor woke me with a nudge on the shoulder. I was slow to wake, as if all my senses came back to consciousness one at a time. I sat up and stared at him for a moment, his unmistakable boney cheeks gradually came into focus. He held his finger over his lips and motioned to me to follow him out of the bedroom. He was still dressed in his day clothes. I tip-toed out, careful not to wake Celia, who was asleep in her bedroom next to mine.

"She's gone," he said.

"What?" I burst into tears. My mind raced to catch

up with what I'd just heard.

"Quiet, don't wake Celia yet." He took me by the arm and walked me to the stairs in my nightclothes. "Papa is with her. Do you want to see her and say good-bye?"

"I don't know." I wiped my tears. "Are you coming too? Where's Lolo?"

"We've been in already. Dr. Torres went home."

"Yes, I want to see her, but with Papa," I said. "Oh, my God. Martina, she's — we have to send for her."

"We already did," Victor said and cleared his throat.

Victor assisted me down the staircase, as if I was feeble and might fall down. The floor creaked. I stopped. "Are you awake?" he asked.

"I don't want to wake Celia," I whispered. I crept down the stairs. Before I stepped into Mama's room I turned back and said, "Listen for Celia, she'll be up soon."

I'd never seen a dead body before. Papa's parents lived in Corsica. We received letters with photos from them, but had never met them. Mama's parents were gone before I was born. My baby brother died from pneumonia when I was five, and our parents never let us see him. I don't remember what he looked like except that he had black curly hair.

I stepped into the room and couldn't move closer to her. I froze. Mama lay in her bed, her face was swollen and bruised. Large patches of purple, black and red covered her cheeks, eyes and mouth. Her hair was loose and combed back from her face. Mama always wore her hair pinned up on her head. She combed it loose when she went to bed. She didn't look right. As much as I wanted to see her to say good-bye, I fought the urge and allowed fear to take me over.

"It's okay if you don't come to her," Papa said.

Tears streaked my face. "I want to touch her, but I can't," I sobbed.

"I know," he said.

Papa rose from his bedside chair and walked to me. He held me, and together we cried. "Good-bye, Mama," I said. He turned me around and walked me out of the room.

MY OLDER SISTER, MARIA MARTINA came home from school in San Juan the next day. I always looked forward to her visit but his time would be different. Our mother was dead.

Victor answered the door and went outside to say goodbye to Dino.

"Martina," I managed to get her name out before I crumbled into tears. I raced downstairs and into her arms. "I can't believe this," I said.

"I know," she said with a hug. "I got here as fast as I could."

"We need you."

"I felt so far from home when I got the news," she said. "I couldn't wait to get here."

We cried and shared a warm hug. Martina wiped her face and said, "She's really gone?"

I nodded.

"They will be caught and hanged," she said.

I sniffed and wiped my face. "Let's get you settled," I said and picked up her satchel.

Martina had matured in the months since I'd last seen her, and there was something else. She carried herself with the elegance and sophistication of a lady from the city. San Juan had influenced her.

"Your hair is different," I blurted out my words. "Oh, my! Turn around. I want to see your hair."

"It's not so different."

"Your hair is brushed upward and piled on top of your head like a cake, in a braided twist." I examined her coiffure. "But you've added little tendrils of hair at the neckline. It's very sophisticated."

"My God, Fina. You're concerned about my hairstyle now? I just walked in the door."

"Sorry. Let's go upstairs."

She stood taller, straighter and something was different about the way she spoke but I couldn't figure out what it was. Did she speak more slowly or had her accent changed? That school has changed her. She was fifteen but looked twenty.

"How did you get word?" I asked and started up the stairs with one of Martina's bags.

"The Sister of the school told me, and Dino Cesari sent one of his men for me as soon as Papa told him what happened. When I arrived, Dino drove me up to the house himself." Martina followed, dragging a large satchel.

"That was kind of him," I said. "We're hearing from everyone around Adjuntas. People are scared, but everyone wants to help. There are constant knocks on the door with someone bringing food or flowers."

Martina and I went to our bedroom. I moved my clothes into one half of the dresser. “I’m so glad you’re here,” I said.

“I’m glad to be home.” Martina looked around the room. “Sorry to crowd you. You had your own room for a while. I’ll bet you liked that.” She unpacked her bag and placed her things in the other half of the dresser. “I won’t take up too much space.” She placed her empty satchel under the bed. “But this, how could this have happened? I don’t know how to go on without her.” Martina began to cry. “Tell me what you know.”

I filled her in on the few details we knew about Mama’s murder. “I can’t imagine us without her either. What will we do?” I fell into her arms and we both sobbed.

✡ ✡ ✡

Mama was laid out in a pine coffin that Papa made. Her Sunday head scarf was veiled over her face and her hands were folded neatly on her chest with her rosary placed in her fingers. I never heard who arranged her that way. Things just seemed to happen all around me. Papa said there would not be a viewing; instead, he would hold her funeral immediately. I was relieved. The thought of her in the living room, with visitors passing through, disturbed me.

We started early the next morning. The twenty-mile ride down the mountain road to the city of Ponce was slow, with a coffin in the wagon. I didn’t understand why Papa didn’t want to bury Mama in our town of Adjuntas. Our hometown had grown, we had stores, a casino, hotel, a sheriff’s office and a telegraph office. Our local Padre was a compassionate man and I felt comfortable with him. Mama was traditional in many ways, and loved the city. Perhaps Papa wanted to honor her, with services at the church in Ponce.

Each bump in the road rattled the pine box and I feared the ropes would give way and release our precious cargo. Celia and I had to ride in the wagon with Papa, and I was nervous the entire way. Victor and Lolo rode ahead of us on horseback. The whistle blowing made me jump and my stomach ached all the way down the mountain road. Our funeral procession stopped a few times on our way down the road, a neighbor would step out from their humble wooden house with an armful of roses and a heartful of love. We received the gift, placed the flowers on the coffin and continued on our way.

We reached the Cathedral de Nuestra Señora de Guadalupe, the church in Ponce with a wagonful of roses. Father Taliaferro was out front. He was prepared, and we held the service on Tuesday morning at 9:00 a.m. Mama's sister in Ponce, Tia Lottie, cousins, friends, and a few of Papa's friends who we didn't know came. Our Aunt and Uncle from the farm lived too far and couldn't come. Papa had one cousin from Corsica who lived in Ponce who was there with his wife and children. We never saw these family members and it struck me that they showed up for funerals or baptisms. The women dressed in European fine silk, leather shoes and carried small draw string bags. The man carried a cane, but I didn't notice a need for it. I think it was for fashion. They were small in stature, but made a large presence. His shoes had a heel that gave him a little height and I tried to see if there was a dance sole on his shoe. They moved with grace and seemed to soak up the attention. They liked to be seen around Ponce and I guessed Mama's funeral was an occasion for them to be seen. I ran my palm over my dress to smooth any wrinkles and wondered if it was time to get something new.

The cousins made me feel like the rest of us were simple country folks. Mama would have worn a black mourning dress if Papa had died, but Papa wore his only suit. A white striped linen suit and straw hat that he purchased from our town. We each wore a simple dress, and the crosses that Papa had carved for of us. Our brothers dressed in their linen suits for church. Everyone shared kind words of comfort and offered food. Aunt Lottie slipped me a few pesos to keep for myself, she said, "Just in case."

The cemetery in Ponce would have been a great honor, but for some reason, unexplained to me, Mama was not buried there. Instead, we loaded her coffin back into the wagon and carried her back up the mountain.

I wondered if Father Taliaferro had explained this to Papa in advance, or if it was a surprise, sprung on him at the worse moment. Mama was buried at home, in our small mountain town of Adjuntas, in the tiny cemetery. Her cousin hand carved her stone.

She was forty-four years old.

Papa

I BECAME A PRISONER OF TIME. With each breath I took I prayed to reverse the minutes, hours that pained me, or move forward and free me from my grief. Each morning I rose and walked to the kitchen to see the calendar that hung on the wall, and was reminded that for us, it was forever July 1895. Mama's handwritten notes hung, abandoned and clipped to a wire strung across the wall. Reminders for Papa to get this or that from town, and a list of chores for us kids. One ignored note had been there for months, a reminder to fix the broken cabinet door in the kitchen that fell open and appeared to annoy only the women in the house. Papa never seemed to get that chore done. I wanted to turn the calendar page, but couldn't leave Mama behind. Each day the sun rose, and time took care of that for us.

With August came the rainy season, and the first appearance of cherry colored coffee berries in the fields. It was the first showing of what the season might be like for us.

With Mama's passing it didn't feel right to shift the focus from her to the harvest season. But the first berries would soon be ready for picking. Table conversation turned to running the plantation and the family was hesitant to bring up her name. She was all I wanted to talk about.

Papa returned to visits with his friend and neighbor, Dino Cesari. They spent hours in our barn, or Papa wandered across the road to Dino's farm where they sat and discussed things that bored me. Coffee prices in the European market, complaints about taxes, and they debated about who made the best pitorro.

One Sunday evening Papa invited Dino to dinner at our house. His wife had died of pneumonia six years earlier, leaving him to raise four children, a job he mostly left to his servants. The Cesari kids had played at our house, or we were at their house throughout our childhood. They were like family to us.

Dino was obsessed with work and I seldom saw him discuss anything that didn't relate to coffee or one of his other businesses in Ponce. When paying a social visit, he was friendly but somehow always brought the conversation around to business. As one of the wealthiest men on the southern coast, and certainly one of the most handsome, women of all ages laughed at his jokes and giggled nervously around him. He spent most of his time in a circle of businessmen, playing cards or attending political meetings. Dino kept his dalliances with the ladies discreet, and never allowed himself to be seen in public with any one particular woman, preferring to be seen as a grieving widower. But we knew what happened behind the walls of his hacienda, and who visited. I remember thinking, as Dino sat at our humble table, that now our Papa would be like Dino. I hoped not. He was very attractive, and his voice flowed like Trembleque, a sweet, warm pudding.

Papa sat at the head of the table and led the dinner conversation. The two men competing for who would be the rooster and who would be the hen. Papa clucked, crowed and danced around the conversation. At least a rooster's job is to protect the hen house.

I picked up my fork and my mind wandered. I thought of what a fine house the Cesari's had. Dino had a table shipped all the way from Spain for his wife. It was so long, he added onto the house to accommodate it. With seating for twelve, they entertained often. Local plantation owners, business owners from Ponce or out of town guests often gathered for meals or intimate gatherings and private concerts. I admired them, as if they were local royalty. Dino's mahogany table glowed with a rich luster, maintained daily by his domestic staff.

Our childhoods were imprinted onto our table, with a burn mark from a hot pot in the center where Martina forgot to place a pot holder. My oldest brother, Victor had carved his initials at his seat when he got his first knife, for which he received a whipping. The leg next to my chair was worn from my foot repeatedly kicking it. I could not seem to sit still at mealtime and Mama called me her little pollo escapado, or escapee chicken, because I would hop out of my chair and run around the room. She tied me into my seat with a dish cloth across my lap until I was old enough to sit still. But my feet kept moving, kicking the table leg. Candle wax and other scars completed the finish on the table.

Victor brought up discussion about work on the coffee plantation. Papa interrupted, "Look at us," his arms outstretched, "all of my children under one roof again." He nodded toward Victor seated next to him and

Lolo on the other side, then he looked at me and my sisters seated at the end, close to the kitchen. Papa never saw the marks on the table or things we broke around the house. He always saw us. His eyes pooled with water and glistened in the candlelight. "My three Marias," he said and pointed his finger. "Martina, tell us about your life at school."

"School is going very well, Papa," Martina interrupted her thought to fill her plate. "S'il vous plait passer les petits pois," she used the French Papa taught us, which always pleased him. He spoke French and Italian, from his homeland of Corsica. Mama was native Puerto Rican and preferred speaking Spanish. Papa insisted we learn to read and write all three languages. My younger sister, Celia, reached for the peas and spilled her glass of milk.

"Estupida!" Victor shouted. "Clean it up." He pulled his chair back from the table to avoid the milky puddle headed his way.

I used my napkin to sop up the milk. Celia burst into tears and scurried to her bedroom. I looked at Victor, cocked my head as Mama would have done and said, "She's only eleven. She was trying to pass the peas."

"That's enough," Papa said in a firm tone. He kept his eyes down and pushed his fork around his plate.

We finished our meal in silence. After dinner the men had drinks in the front room and I tucked Celia into bed. "I'll keep the window open for a bit," I said as I fastened the wood shutters in the opened position. I looked down from the second story window to see the armed men posted outside that Papa had hired to protect us.

The mountain air was cool in the evenings. Days were warm, and I was grateful to not have to lock up the windows. "It's going to be hard to sleep. The coqui frogs will keep you company."

Celia lay on top of the covers. Her legs reached more than half the length of the bed now. Her unbraided, long hair reminded me of mine. Thin and wispy. Papa had a full, thick head of hair but we got our mother's hair, straight as a stick.

"Fina, did you listen to the chirping frogs sing ko-kee, ko-kee when you were little?" Celia asked. "I think they talk in their own language."

I sat in the chair beside her bed and watched out the window at the stars above. "Yes, they are your friends. I think they're singing a song too. Some people don't like the coqui's noise, but I love it." A stream of memories flowed through my mind. Thoughts of my sister, Maria Martina and me as we lay awake, listening to the coquis. In the evening we'd listen to the sounds of the coqui frogs, and in the mornings the cheerful song of the birds. We talked about everything in the world until we fell asleep. Now, Celia had only the coqui to keep her company. I knelt down and kissed her goodnight. "Sleep well."

Celia snuggled into her pillow, damp from her tears. "Close the window."

"It's too hot. The air is nice and you like the coquis," I said.

"I'm afraid someone might come."

I closed the window. She'd overheard something, I thought. I decided to stay with her. This night she needed her sister. "Go to sleep." I reached for her scrapbook and flipped through each page, remembering our life together through her young eyes. A poem, pressed flowers, a letter from our grandmother in Corsica. Then I turned the page to see a sketch she had drawn of our house. Celia had always liked to draw and sometimes got into trouble for taking Papa's papers to scribble on. But this sketch was extraordinary in detail and depth. Every pail, board, and fence post were exact in dimension and perspective. Then I noticed Mama sketched in the window. I looked over at Celia to ask about her book. Exhausted, she had fallen asleep to the sounds of the Caribbean night.

"Goodnight, Celia," I whispered. I moved a tiny painted, wooden coqui frog from the shelf to the bedside table, shut off the kerosene lamp and left the room.

THE KITCHEN IS THE ONLY PLACE you can have a private conversation in this house," I whispered. "Because after dinner the boys avoid this room like a disease."

"Nothing changes. Mama never trained them to do dishes. That was our work on the maid's day off." Martina sneered. "Victor and Lolo sit with their feet propped up while they read."

Tidying up the kitchen brought a sense of order and calm which I needed. "I don't mind." I picked up a dish to dry. "The boys work hard in the fields, you know. The coffee harvest looks good this year. I pray every night for a good crop." I lowered my voice and looked toward the door to see if anyone heard us. "We need it. I think Papa has heavy debts."

Martina shook her head. "Like I said, some things never change. Is Celia all right?" Martina asked.

"She overheard something. We'll have to be more careful."

"I see," Martina said as she washed a pot.

"Things are different," I explained. "Papa sits with Mama's picture at his bedside when he gets home from work and all the boys do is read in the evenings." I dried a dish and placed it in the cabinet. "Victor's nose is always buried in some book about time travel. He daydreams about a crazy machine that takes you to another land in a distant time." I wiped a knife and put it away in a drawer, "I do my best to keep up the house, but we don't have as much help these days." I slammed the open cabinet door shut.

Martina watched me and said, "I understand."

"We must take care of Papa," I walked back and forth in the kitchen. "But this is too much for Celia."

Martina nodded, "I'm here now."

I rattled on, "Isabella comes in and cooks. She took it hard, bless her heart." I poured a pot of hot water into the dish pan and grabbed a platter.

"Fina, stop!" Martina grabbed my wrist.

The platter crashed on the tile floor and shattered into pieces. "Why did you do that?" I yelled. "Look what you made me do! Mama's favorite piece." I sat on the floor and held back my tears. I started to pick up the pieces of broken porcelain, took a deep breath and exhaled. "Martina, why did Papa want to bury Mama in Ponce? We carried her body all the way to the city, then all the way back home. That didn't make sense. We like Father Millan in Adjuntas. I don't understand why Papa would take her to Father Taliaferro for the service."

Martina took a piece of broken china from my hand. "Fina, we've never buried a family member before Mama. Have you ever heard how they bury the dead here?"

"What do you mean?"

"Our little cemetery — how do I say this? Many of our locals don't have money for a casket or pine box. They dump the bodies in a grave, with other bodies, no casket." Martina cringed. "The wealthy get a wooden box, but it's not a grand affair. The cemetery in Ponce is traditional and there's a better chance the body will be undisturbed."

"Undisturbed?"

Martina took a deep breath. "The ones without a pine box? They open the graves, to make room for new bodies. They raise the oldest and bury the new one underneath. Finally, the oldest body is removed and placed in a pile of bones in the corner of the cemetery. I'm sorry to tell you this." She knelt down and picked up a piece of china. "Why didn't you send for me sooner?"

I dropped my pieces of china on the floor. "What do you mean? Dino sent for you right away."

"I'm not talking about Mama. Things aren't going well here. You should have written to me."

"I don't want to think about Mama buried." I wiped my face. "I've never heard that, about how the dead are buried. I assumed everyone had a pine casket. Now I know why Papa took her all the way to Ponce. He must be so angry at Father Taliaferro for turning him away."

"I think that it had something to do with the Church cemetery not accepting more for burial. Papa didn't make proper arrangements. There's also a cost involved. Maybe he couldn't pay the fee. What's going on with him? That's what I meant, when I said why didn't you send for me sooner. What happened to all the help? The private teachers? Papa is operating this place on almost no help and you're not getting an education."

"Everything was wonderful. We had maids and teachers, then we heard Mama and Papa argue about money. Victor and Lolo didn't return to school. They stayed home to work the plantation and said it was because they were going to take it over one day." I took a deep breath and sighed, releasing my troubles. "I wanted to come to school with you Martina. I really did."

Martina patted my hand and said, "It's going to be all right."

"I kept hoping, but it didn't get better. I thought the new moon would renew his spirit."

"I don't think it's his spirit. His business is down. I felt something was wrong when you didn't start school." Martina looked me square in the eyes. "Fina, don't lie to me. You're not going to school anymore. You're too old for our local school."

"Don't," I said and closed my eyes to shut her out.

"I didn't know Papa was in debt or that bandits were roaming at night. Fina, you were supposed to join me in San Juan months ago. You're almost fourteen." She shook her head.

"Papa let Celia's and my teacher go and he told us to study at home with what we have."

"How did I not know?" Martina said. "I'm not going back to San Juan."

"What do you mean?" I asked.

"I'm not going back to school at El Convento. I'm needed here, I'm staying in Adjuntas. I will teach you and Celia. Victor and Lolo studied at home. Papa can't afford to send me away to school."

"Oh! What did Papa say?"

After getting no response I asked, “He doesn’t know yet?”

“Fina, you must not tell him,” Martina shook her finger. “I’ll speak to him soon. Don’t worry, everything will be fine. I will try to stay with you.”

Paolo

A COOL BREEZE DRIFTED IN through the open bedroom window. Martina and I sat in a patch of moonlight on the bed. "Time to close the windows," I said. I stepped to the open window, breathed in the fresh air and gazed at the star-filled sky outside. "I think I see a falling star!" I said, and pointed toward the sky.

"Wait!" Martina joined me at the window. "Make a wish," she said.

I closed my eyes and thought hard about what I wanted. My usual wish was for true love but tonight I wished for something I couldn't have. To go back in time, like in Victor's book by H.G. Wells. Back when Papa and Mama took us to the sea and we played in the sand. We often took the ponies down the mountain road to Ponce, then to the shore for a picnic. I wished for a time when life was trouble free. Then I opened my eyes.

"Okay! You got tonight's wish," Martina said with a giggle and fell back on the bed.

I closed the window, plopped onto the bed. "Tell me about El Convento. What did you do after school? Did you get outside to see the young men in town?"

"Oh, yes! I have a beautiful lace dress from Aunt Lottie. It is blue, like the sea. We attend dances every Saturday. The young men line up on one side and we stand on the other side. The boys wear white gloves so they never touch our skin. It is all very proper," she sat up straight and smiled. "But we learned how to use our eyes."

"Show me," I begged.

"Like this," she gazed into my eyes seductively.

"Martina!" I gasped.

"It is in the dance," she stood and swayed. "I met a boy." Her eyes nearly rolled back into her head. "His name is Paulo. I knew the first night we danced..."

I noticed a glow to Martina's face, as if she was in a dream.

She continued, "My heart raced and I felt my body flush with heat. I thought I would faint. I've never felt this heat before," she twirled around once on the wooden floor. "I stopped the dance and raced to the powder room from embarrassment." She plopped down on the bed and covered her face with her hands. "I was sure he saw the red in my face!"

I leaned in, eager for more. "What happened?"

"Nothing. I collected myself and came back inside. He was dancing with another. My heart sank," Martina's voice trailed off.

"That's the end of the story?" I said. "What a terrible story."

Martina continued, "The next week I returned.

Paulo was there and once again he asked me to dance. This time I did not allow the uncontrollable flush prevent me from being near him."

"Oh, no!"

"I felt his hand on my back, gently pressing on my skin through his glove," she placed her hand on my back. "His other hand held mine tenderly as we danced through three songs."

"Three songs?" I asked. Why didn't I join her at school in San Juan, I thought.

Martina stood up again and said, "Each week I returned to the dance. We spoke about school, our families, and made plans for the future. He is bright and captivating." She sat and looked me in the eye. "Together we mastered the art of embracing through the eyes." Martina fell back and melted into the bed.

"Martina! You are in love!"

"Yes, Fina, I am! Paulo is too. We cannot wait to marry," Martina sat up and whispered. "But you cannot tell a living soul. Paulo's family is very influential and he must finish school before such an announcement is made. He wants to be an officer in the military. Do you understand?"

"I understand. I'm so happy for you. But how can you leave San Juan? Don't you want to get back to Paulo? You can't stay here with us."

"I do love him. But I love my family too. With Mama gone, I will stay here to help." Martina stood and looked out the window. She turned back and said, "There will come a time for me to return to San Juan. Paulo will understand."

She wiped her eyes. "We will write and I'll find a

way to make a visit to San Juan."

"I love you, dear sister."

Martina said, "I love you too."

We hugged and cried together. Sadness exhausted me.

DREAD REPLACED OPTIMISM in the New Year 1896. It was another reminder that Mama would never grow old. I will not make her a grandmother, or learn another thing from her. The start of a new year brought sorrow, and the refusal of time to stand still was especially twisted and cruel.

Our once vibrant two-story home was quiet, and all color had faded from life. I longed to hear the sound of Mama's voice and I closed my eyes, but had no recollection. She would come to me at odd times. I would hear her voice in my head when my brothers irritated me, or when I needed a reminder to do something. I remembered how she would bark at the boys and sweep them out of the house with her broom, and I smiled at the memory. The moment would pass, and once again I was left without her. Each tick of the clock echoed through the house, like a hollow beating heart.

Papa numbed his grief over the year since Mama passed with rum, visited friends or extended his work

ONE SUNDAY IN JANUARY 1897, we were leaving morning Mass in town when Dino pulled Papa aside. Martina, Celia and I were already in the wagon, waiting for Papa and the boys. Sitting up high, we had a view over the crowd. I wasn't able to hear what they said, with the ringing church bells and rushing river nearby, but I watched carefully. I saw that Dino had clenched fists and he looked angry.

I nudged Martina. "Look, something is going on."

She adjusted her hat to block the sun and joined my spy team. "Papa looks upset."

"Yes," I said. "Dino has his arm around Papa's shoulder, patting his back. Like he's reassuring him."

"Or calming him down," Martina added.

Celia and Lolo approached. "What's going on?" Celia said. Lolo had bought her a fistful of candies. He was soft hearted, a push over. Celia had him wrapped around her little finger.

"Get in the wagon, Celia," Martina ordered.

"I'm going to see what's going on." Lolo said, and walked over to Papa and Dino.

Celia stepped up and took a seat in the wagon. We watched Papa, and scanned the crowd. Victor was talking with some hired men from Dino's plantation and seemed to react to whatever news they were giving him. He moved like a man in charge. Victor knew many of the locals, having worked with them in the fields. He was steward over Papa's farm and worked for Dino too. Victor slapped a young man on the back of the head and looked around to be sure they weren't being overheard. I was familiar with Victor's head slapping move, having grown up on the receiving end. He quickly walked over to Papa and seemed to be reporting what he'd heard.

"Victor look's angry," Celia said.

Martina, Celia and I watched and didn't dare leave the wagon. Papa grabbed Victor's arm and looked around. They talked for a few minutes. I was growing impatient, waiting and watching the crowd.

Dino's sister, Juana Cesari, approached with her driver and said with her usually stern voice, "I'm going to take you girls home. Come with me," she ordered, "we'll go in my carriage."

Papa suddenly appeared, "Go with Juana. I'll see you later." He looked at the driver, "Take good care of them." He tried to hand the driver a pistol discreetly, but I saw it. Juana glared at us. Without a word we climbed into the back of the carriage. Juana stepped up in the front and took a seat beside her driver. He lit a cigarette and handed it to her. I'd never seen prune-faced Auntie Juana smoke in public before. Many women smoked cigarettes or cigars in public, but they were peasants.

Such a thing would be looked down upon for an affluent woman. Juana puffed on her cigarette all the way from town, and up the mountain road to our plantation. She was a property owner, with a small business in Ponce and didn't hide her smoking habit. There was something about Juana that I admired. She commanded respect and was fearless. After an uncomfortably silent ride, we arrived at our hacienda.

We rode past the abandoned servant huts on our property to our house. Juana sent Celia inside for a glass of water. I think she wanted to talk to us alone. Her deep-set dark eyes, caressed by wrinkles, were filled with pity. She said, "Lock the doors." Looking us directly in the eye, she added, "and keep a weapon at your bedside."

"What happened?" I said.

"Adults will take care of things," she said. She waved her hand for her driver to nudge the horses.

"Wait!" Martina yelled.

The carriage stopped. Juana looked back in surprise.

"Something happened, and you warned us to keep a weapon at our bedside," Martina said. "But you drop us off alone? I'm seventeen. What's going on?"

Juana drew a deep breath and slowly exhaled. "Jose and Anastasia Perez' farm was attacked last night."

"Were the attackers dressed in black?" Martina asked.

Juana snapped her head around as if we were the attackers, "How did you know?"

Martina's eyes squinted. "After what happened to our Mama?" She turned to me and continued, "We know there are bandits, men dressed in black. They've been attacking farmers. We know they killed our Mama." She stuck her chin out and bravely asked, "What happened to the Perezs'?"

Juana caught a tear with her handkerchief, "I cannot repeat." She waved her hand for her driver to flick the reins.

Martina and I watched them disappear down the hill. I looked around at our slice of heaven atop the mountain, and realized how isolated we were. "I've never felt so frightened and alone," I said.

"Let's go inside," Martina said and hurried to the kitchen door.

I followed, nervous and afraid. "Martina, wait," I said. Martina stepped inside and closed the door behind me. I tugged at her sleeve. "Talk to me!"

"Fina!" Martina pulled her arm back. She slid a board across the door while she spoke. "Don't you understand? Have you heard anything that Papa and Victor have been talking about? Or read the newspaper? We both know about the attacks at night. They're not common robbers. They rape the women and mutilate the men. They're brutal."

"I've read the papers and heard the stories. Some say they're bandits and are working for Spain. There's something I could never explain," I argued. "Why? Papa said that Mama fought to save our money. But Papa was in debt. Do you think they were collecting on a debt? Or threatening him by attacking Mama?"

"I think Dino paid all of Papa's debts," Martina said. "Taking our farm wasn't the only debt relief from Dino."

"It wasn't exactly debt relief," I said. "We all work for him now."

"He pays us, and we have a house to live in. Our house. So, Dino owns it now. At least we're still together." Martina's eyed filled with tears.

"Papa lost the house, and plantation to Dino, but Dino doesn't own us," I said. "Spain won't own Puerto Rico either. We're going to be independent."

Martina stepped inside the kitchen.

I followed, "Spain's grip on our country, bandits lurking in the night. But they came during the day. What really happened?"

She shook her head. "Poor, Mama."

"We'll find out," Celia said from the hallway. She stepped into the kitchen holding a glass of water. "I started to bring Juana her glass of water, but figured out she didn't want it."

"Oh, Celia dear. I'm so sorry," I said.

"Don't be sorry. I've been sneaking out and watching like a spy. Dino has something going on in the fields at his plantation. It's a secret," she said. "Hidden in the middle of his coffee plantation is an open field where men shoot rifles and train like an army. They're training to fight against Spain."

"Shhh, Celia, keep your mouth shut." Martina looked around and pulled a large knife from the kitchen drawer. "Oh, my God! How do you know about this?"

"You think because I'm only thirteen, that I don't understand. I hear you talking and I get around Dino's plantation. I see more than you do. But why do we want to fight against Spain?"

Martina looked at me and turned to Celia. "Thirteen... things have changed. Spain is strangling our island and Cuba too. They don't care about us, only what they can take from us. The United States President, Grover Cleveland announced he might take action in Cuba if Spain doesn't resolve the crisis there. Some of our men are fighting back against Spain's rule. They want to free Puerto Rico."

"I'm afraid," Celia said. "What's happening to Puerto Rico? What happened to our family?"

"The United States will soon have a new President, William McKinley. Things are changing." I paced the kitchen, then walked to Papa's desk and let out a groan. "We've been suffocating in grief since Mama died. I feel like we're bound in chains. It's been almost a year since Papa lost the plantation." I raised my voice, "Now look at us, working as domestics for Dino Cesari and Victor is probably involved in Dino's secret camp. Can you believe it?" I cried. "Victor working as steward over what used to be our own plantation?" I pounded my chest. "We had maids and private teachers. We grew up with something. We had our own land and the coffee farm. Now? We have nothing." I shook my head. "Martina, you were in school in San Juan. Celia and I were supposed to follow." I stopped and remembered, "San Juan! Paulo, what about—"

"I haven't seen him since, forget him. Don't mention his name," she paused, then said, "Fina, it's not only Victor. Papa is steward over Dino's plantation too. Don't you think he knows about the secret camp?"

I opened the desk drawer and pulled out a pistol. "Do you think that's why the bandits came? Things have changed, and nobody can protect us."

10

PAPA WAS DISTRIBUTING the wages and plantation tokens to the laborers at the end of the day when Dino approached on horseback. Dino and Papa had a meeting earlier in the afternoon and already discussed business when Papa picked up the payroll.

"Hola, Dino," Papa said. "Did you forget something?"

Dino waited until Papa finished, then said, "I've come to discuss a matter man to man." He dismounted and tied his horse to a fence post. "I came after work so that we would have time alone." His chest puffed out, he said, "Walk with me."

Papa locked the door to the shed and the two men walked into the coffee fields.

Dino paused, picked a berry and sniffed it. "Guillermo, you, and your sons have done an excellent job for me. The plantation is thriving, and you have taught my workers well."

Papa's nostrils flared and his shoulders tensed.

Was he about to be fired?

"Do you miss having your own plantation?" Dino asked.

"Of course, but I appreciate the job, Dino," Papa said. "Are you not pleased?"

"I am getting on in my years now. I'm forty-seven. Since my wife died, I have been very lonely. My children are grown." Dino adjusted his hat. "Your daughters have been a great help. Martina has been an excellent housekeeper and I think she would make an exceptional wife."

Papa stopped and swallowed hard.

"Before you speak, please hear me out." Dino paced, with his chest puffed out. "I realize there is a great age difference between Martina and me, but I am a man of means. She will do well as my wife and I am prepared to offer a dowry gift to help your family. I would like to sign over the northwest parcel for the hand of your daughter. You will once again have your own coffee plantation." Dino stopped, faced Papa and said with a smile, "You and I will be in-laws."

"Martina is only seventeen years old," Papa protested. "And you're forty-seven."

"She will make someone a fine wife, and it will happen very soon. She can marry a young man with nothing to offer, or take my offer and help your family."

Papa paused, "Thirty years between you is a lot." He turned and took a few steps.

"Guillermo, this is not a poker hand. But very well, I'll include your home in the parcel." Dino stiffened and added in a firm voice, "My offer ends when this conversation is over."

Papa ran his fingers through his thick blonde hair

Isabella

I WOKE EARLY AFTER A FITFUL NIGHT, my mind-filled with thoughts about Martina. I eased out of bed, tip-toed across the room, paused at the door and looked back at Martina who was sprawled out, in a deep sleep. Her hair, usually groomed and in a thick braid on top of her head, was loose and blanketed the pillow. I grabbed my shoes and shawl and gently closed the bedroom door behind me.

I crept through the house, past the kitchen, skipped my morning coffee and slipped out the front door. The early morning hours were quiet. Darkness still ruled the sky and I had to watch my step. It felt refreshing to walk in the cool air and with each breath, my senses awoke.

Isabella's quarters were about two hundred feet up the hill, behind our hacienda. Her modest wooden shack, with a thatched roof overlooked the river. She enjoyed an expansive view across the gorge, showcasing peaks of green covered mountains as far as the eye could see. The base of the gorge was filled in with the lush greenery of banana and coconut trees. Her tiny house was built atop the slope of the mountainside. There was no formal entrance. The back of the house had a small sitting porch that extended beyond level ground, and was perched on stilts. We spent many hours talking and enjoying the view from that porch. It was my favorite place, and felt like a slice of paradise. Papa always said Isabella had the prime site on our land. On many occasions, you would find Mama or one of us sitting on Isabella's back porch. Sometimes, Mama and Isabella smoked cigars or cigarettes back there, believing they were being discreet. But we spied on them and Victor stole a few cigarettes for us kids to smoke, which we did behind the barn.

This morning was dark and I was sure Isabella would be asleep, but my news could not wait.

"Isabella!" I called out as I knocked on the simple wooden door frame.

"Who's dat?" Isabella said as she walked to the doorway. Her short, round silhouette was illuminated in the dim lamplight. Her hammock was still swinging in the background. I felt sorry for waking her. "Who come calling at this hour?"

"Isabella, it's Fina."

"Some tin' wrong?"

"I've come to talk to you. It's important."

"Well, it better be. You're up 'fore the chickens!" Isabella pulled back the simple curtain covering her doorway. "Come on in." Although her hair was graying, her skin still had a youthful glow. She shuffled around the small one-room shack in her bare feet. Her warm, brown skin and ready smile was a welcome sight. I'd spent my childhood nuzzled in her arms and I yearned for the comfort of her lap. I took a seat at a small table pushed up against the wall, and nervously fingered the colorfully embroidered tablecloth. Isabella started a flame in the belly of the stove. She reached into the open shelves, where a few dishes and pots were neatly stacked.

"No, Isabella, I don't need breakfast."

Isabella took two cups from the shelf. Her dish towel, with red and black embroidery hung beside the washing tub.

"Child, what is it?" Isabella asked.

"Isabella, it's about Papa — and Martina. Papa accepted a dowry from Dino Cesari. A parcel of land — our old plantation — for the hand of Martina."

"Oh, child! This is wonderful news!" Isabella said. "Have mercy on your family!"

"That's not why I came this morning." I reached into my skirt and pulled out a stack of letters. "I found these in Martina's bed." I leaned close and whispered, "She's been stealing your mail."

Isabella stared at the pile of letters on the table and took a deep breath. "Oh, child," she said.

"I — why would she do such a thing? They've all been opened," I said. "But I didn't read them. I brought them straight to you."

"No, child these aren't my letters. They belong to Martina." She shook her head and pushed the letters back at me. "Bring them back to her."

I was confused, "But they're addressed to you."

"Ask Martina about them," Isabella said. "They were addressed to me, but when they came, I gave them to her. That's all I can say."

"I don't understand." I looked at the return address and noted they came from San Juan. "Martina told me not to tell anyone, but she met a boy in San Juan; his name is Paulo. Are these letters from him?"

Isabella turned away to check the stove.

"I'm asking you because I need your help." I opened a letter and read it. Then I scanned the rest. A photo fell out and I saw Paulo for the first time. The photo showed him dressed in a military uniform. He stood tall and proud, and he was strikingly handsome. I turned the picture over and read the note. I will wait for you. Dearest Paulo.

Why did it take me so long to figure this out? Isabella had been Martina's accomplice. She was the carrier pigeon for their love letters.

"Holy Mary, they're in love and have been making plans for the future," I explained. "Isabella, you've been helping her? She can't marry Paulo; he's in the military. Our family resists Spain's military." I ran my fingers through my hair. "But Martina shouldn't marry Dino if she's in love with another. What a problem!"

Isabella poured two cups of coffee and took a seat at the table. She sat slowly, as if the news had poured over her like heavy mud. "Oh, child, this is not for you to decide. These things are bigger than you or Martina. The elders make these decisions. You must learn to accept what is best for the family. Martina will do well with Don Bernadino Cesari." Isabella placed her hand on mine. "What does Martina say about this?"

"She is very upset, but like you, says that the die is cast. She told me she hasn't spoken to Paulo in months." I looked straight into Isabella's tobacco eyes. "She never told Papa about Paulo. Did you know about him?"

Isabella stiffened and pulled her hand back. The warmth drained from her caramel face. She sat with eyes fixed, her mouth set. Her cheek twitched and she snorted her understanding.

I loved Isabella. I loved the feel of her soft skin and her smell. She was like a mother to me, having been my caregiver since birth. "Isabella, I didn't mean to upset you," I said. "I came to you for help. I'm sorry if I made you angry."

"I know that, and I love you child." She nodded. "Your Papa's been good to me too. But child, you got to understand some things," Isabella said. "I keep my mouth shut. Martina knows. You understand that too."

"I do," I said. I wrapped my arms around her and felt her soft cheek against mine. "I love you so much." I gave her a kiss.

She kissed my head and offered me comfort, as she always did, making me wish I could be a little girl once again, when she could make things better with a hug. Mama taught us that women could be strong in their own way. Martina did as Mama taught, and said it was her duty to marry Dino. I wondered how it felt for her heart to die a little for duty to her family. Isabella reminded me that the elders decide our future. I wiped a tear and realized at that moment that Martina was right.

I would be next.

✡ ✡ ✡

Martina was having coffee in the kitchen when I walked in. "You're up early," she said with an icy, cold glare.

"Want to bring your coffee upstairs?" I poured a cup and headed upstairs to our bedroom.

"Give them to me," Martina said sternly, and closed the bedroom door behind her.

"I thought you stole Isabella's mail." I tossed the letters on the bed. "I found them under the pillow last night. They're addressed to Isabella, so I brought them to her."

Martina took a deep breath, and sighed. "You went to Isabella?"

"You've been writing to Paulo all this time?" I whispered. "Martina, what are you thinking? He's training to be an officer. Papa rants about Spain's rule. My God, Papa was part of the Grito de Lares in '68."

"Enough!" Martina said. "Fina, you can't understand how I feel. You've never left home or been in love. Don't try to tell me." She paced the room, "I had a life. I was going to school, had friends and met Paulo. Then I came home to be with my family." She stopped and looked at me in despair. "It's been like a curse." Martina began to cry. "Now, Papa traded me off, like a piece of property in an arranged marriage to Don Bernadino Cesari. Our family will get a piece of our plantation back and what do I get back? A piece of my life?" She shook in anger. "I get nothing. It's my duty as a daughter to marry, and my husband has been chosen for me. Don't lecture me about who I love." She picked up the letters. "I'll burn the letters." Her hands shook. "Clearly it's over with him."

"I'm sorry, and I'm sorry that you didn't tell me. If I'd known, I would have understood," I said. "Please, let's not keep secrets from each other."

The room fell silent and I dared not speak the next

words. Finally, Martina spoke. "Fina, you know you will be next. Papa will sell you off in marriage."

I felt a jolt in my chest. "You don't think he would do it again—"

"Of course, he will," she said. Martina leaned forward. "We won't allow it. If I leave here and marry, I'm running my own house."

Martina gave a sly smile and I knew she had a plan.

I HAD PLANNED TO WEAR my Sunday dress for Martina's wedding in March 1897, then Papa said I could go to town with him, and he would buy Celia and me new ones. Mama always bought her clothes from town, preferring a more traditional style. She had two elegant dresses from Ponce, which she seldom wore. Our stores in Adjuntas sold grocery items and carried a full stock of liquor. For other purchases, vendors appeared on the streets of the town square, carrying baskets on their heads filled with toys, trinkets and dresses. Those dresses weren't as nice as my Sunday dress.

Isabella was making chicken stew for our Sunday dinner. I worked at the kitchen table, kneading dough for bread. "It's been a while since I've had your chicken stew," I said. "I need to learn how to make it."

"Well, I add a little seasoning." Isabella stirred the pot.

Martina walked in with a smile and pulled out a cup and saucer. She filled it with coffee and sat at the kitchen table. “I have exciting news.” She took a sip of coffee.

“What is that?” I pointed at her flowered teacup set.

“It’s English.” She drank again, holding the handle with her thumb and two fingers.

“Where did you get it?” I said with a laugh. “And you’re not drinking tea now, are you?”

“Dino bought it for me from the grocer in town.”

I couldn’t tell if Martina was defensive or embarrassed.

“That was very nice of him,” I said. “I’ve seen some of the things from England at the grocer’s. Of course, she would have tea cups.”

“And tea,” Celia said with a mouthful.

“I doubt she sells any tea around here,” I said.

“If you are finished, I was about to tell you that Dino has invited us to visit his store in Ponce and pick out dresses for the wedding.”

“Oh?” I wasn’t sure I heard her right. “Your wedding dress?”

“He said that you and Celia could each choose a dress from the catalog,” Martina said. “Or, he has a few dresses in stock.”

“Papa said he would take me to town—” I started.

Martina wrinkled her nose. “Fina, this is Ponce, not our little country town. Dino will include new leather shoes.”

“I can’t believe it!” Celia and Martina held hands and jumped up and down.

I smiled and said. “When do we go?”

Isabella looked over her shoulder at us.

"We'll go soon," Martina said. "Because if we order from the catalog it takes a month for the dresses to arrive. Dino has a tailor who can make the dresses for us in a week."

* * *

The wedding ceremony was performed on a Tuesday, at our local parish church. Everyone loved and respected Father Millan; although, they were careful around him because he sympathized with Spain. He was a kind man and much more approachable than Ponce's parish priest, Father Taliafaro. I was glad Dino and Martina didn't hold their wedding in Ponce. I preferred to stay home. This meant that family and friends traveled to us and filled the hotel in town. Close family stayed at Dino's house or at our house. We spent the entire week planning, cooking and preparing.

I was proud to serve as my sister's maid of honor, and floated through the smiling crowd at her wedding reception. It was held on the grounds of Dino's two-hundred-acre plantation. I felt like one of the women in the catalog at Dino's store. My dress was the most beautiful dress I'd ever owned. The pale blue satin shimmered softly, like sunlight on the sea. A crochet appliqued bodice with matching detail applied to the skirt gave it a high fashion style. The long sleeves came to a point at the back of my hands, with intricate crocheted detail. Martina, Celia and I had the servants do our hair in a sophisticated upward style, and added jeweled hair pins. It was the only jewelry Papa permitted, other than the cross of course.

Martina was a vision in white organza with flower

applique. She carried Mama's crocheted shawl and wore a large carved wooden cross pendant from Papa, which hung low on her bodice, creating a deep V. Her bouquet of pink Maga and greenery was a favorite local flower. Dino presented her with a delicate engraved gold band, adorned with a small emerald. It was exquisite, and she looked like a Queen.

Celia selected a soft pink satin dress with a lace collar. It suited her sweet personality. The skirt was draped in a lovely modern style, with lace pinned in tucks at the hem. She favored Papa, with her soft brown eyes, but had Mama's smile. When the sun shined on her hair, hints of red sparkled through, like strands of copper. With her hair pinned up, Celia looked older and quite beautiful.

We gathered in Dino's courtyard, attached to the brick house for the reception. It was open, with a view overlooking the canyon. The same view enjoyed from the house. Green peaked mountains, banana and coconut trees, and the coffee plantation on rolling hills as far as the eye could see. In the distance, a gray streak hung from the sky. Rain. Tables and chairs were arranged, with an open space for dancing. An enormous mango tree served as an umbrella over the band. The same mango tree we had climbed as children. The band, was dressed in black and played softly. The courtyard was surrounded by a short brick wall and several pillars, enclosing the area. Dino had built this area for his children to play when they were small. We played with them on many occasions. The bricks were now crusted and green, with broken edges. Flowers grew over to brighten the walls and created a lovely and welcoming patio. Thunder cracked in the distance.

I smiled and nodded at relatives as I made my

way to the kitchen to retrieve the Bride and Groom's goblets for the toast. Dino had courted Martina over the last six months and as Papa said, Martina grew to love him. We had escorted her during the courtship, walking along with them many times when they were together. She enjoyed many lovely gifts and fell under the spell of the lifestyle of a rich man's wife. Dino made sure he spoiled her well in advance of the marriage, with expensive dresses, jewelry and concerts. The couple was always accompanied by Dino's relatives, my Aunt Lottie, Papa or sometimes my brothers. In the beginning I resented Dino for his gifts, or bribes to my sister and noticed she spoke less and less of Paulo. When I saw her smile return, I realized she was happy and began to wonder if she was truly in love with Dino.

My mind returned to the crowd when I overheard a young man's voice speak in a loud whisper, "This cannot become another El Grito de Lares." I looked to see the voice was coming from a group nearby, "We must free Puerto Rico!" he said.

The voice stopped me cold. El Grito was a failed attempt at independence from Spain in 1868. I'd heard stories but much of it was not discussed and I knew many men died or were imprisoned. A neighbor had escaped and lived in exile in New York. I paused at a pillar for a moment to hear more.

"I understand," said another, "but you must be patient."

"The old men tell us to wait, wait. They are old and are losing their courage. We are ready now."

"Keep your voices down. Listen to me. Stay with the plan and together we will take over in Yauco. Be ready and don't let anyone follow you. Spain's rule will soon be over!"

Tingles of fear crawled down my spine as I overheard the conversation. I quickly moved on, careful not to be seen.

Presenting the goblets to the newly married couple was an honor reserved for the Maid of Honor while the Best Man gave the toast. I was thankful to not have to speak. I carried the goblets to the wedding table and turned back to see the table of young men. I noticed a man in a linen suit and straw hat standing behind a pillar, listening in on the group of young men discussing their plan. I swallowed hard and pushed through the guests.

Dino and Martina emerged from the reception line to take their place at the head table, adorned in ribbons of greenery with red and pink Magas. A large, silver candlestick centered the display, anchored with blood red tapers. Dino extended his arm to his new bride, like an angel, in her gorgeous white gown with puffed fabric at the shoulders and delicate pleats at the bodice. I fought tears. The couple took their seats to the applause of the crowd. I realized I felt happy for Martina for the first time. I could see the tenderness in Dino's eyes when he looked at her and I saw that my sister loved him.

Dino spared nothing and guests were indulged like royalty. He had his servants roast a pig and his full cooking staff was called in. Some cooks prepared dishes at Papa's house, some at a neighbor's farm and some in Dino's kitchen. Favorite dishes from Puerto Rico were served as well as his favorites from Corsica. Guests heaped their plates with Arroz Con Gandules (white rice with pigeon peas, olives, capers, tomato sauce, seasoning, sofrito and pork), Tostones (fried plantain slices), Alcapurries (fritters filled with beef, with yucca and plantains), Empandadillas (small meat pies), Mofongo (fried plantain dish) and Pasteles (similar to a tamale; meat wrapped in green plantain masa, encased in banana leaf). Dino's nod to Corsica was wild boar soup. The roasted pig was Dino's personal prize from a hunting expedition with his sons. Of course, there was plenty of wine for everyone.

After the wedding meal, guests socialized and danced. Celia and I sat together, watching and having more fun than we'd had in years. Papa enjoyed the wine and beamed with pride over the marriage of his daughter. Dino's sister, Juana, scowled at the new couple from across the crowd.

"My lace collar is scratching my neck," Celia said.

"You look pretty," I said. "Look at Auntie Juana," I whispered. "She has the face of a prune."

"I don't think she's going to be giving Martina the family china," Celia said with a snicker.

Dino, dressed in a white linen suit, led Martina to the patio dance floor. He slowly walked around her, as if worshiping his Queen. The band started to play a danza, slow and romantic dance music. The song began with passion then switched to a Caribbean beat. Martina smiled with her eyes fixed on Dino. His black and silver-streaked hair was combed straight back. He reached for his bride and she rested gently in his arms. He spun her around to the beat of the music. Her crocheted shawl twirled and her silky black hair glistened in the afternoon sunlight. Dino bowed on the final note and Martina laughed her contagious, joyful laugh. I'd forgotten how long it had been since we'd heard that sound.

Celia held her fan against her arm. "Does it go this way?"

I held my closed fan against my arm. "You hold

it like this, to let the man know you are available to dance." Then moved it gently in the air. I noticed Jorge was watching me. I snapped my fan closed and tucked it away. I felt my cheeks turn hot and said, "I'll show you later, Celia."

Dino's sons, Antonio and Jorge, were seated at the table next to Celia and me. We laughed and talked under the watchful eye of the elders. Prune-faced Auntie Juana stared at us from across the crowd. I felt like everyone's eyes were on me.

"Fina, may I have this dance?" Jorge asked.

Dino's sons were both handsome, but Jorge had grown up to become an elegant and charming young man. I forgot to take a breath. "Yes," I said.

I slowly rose, extended my gloved hand to Jorge and we joined the couples on the dance floor. The band was playing a quick folk song and I couldn't wait to feel Jorge's hand again. We kept in step with all of the couples in a circle, laughing and switching partners. The song ended and Jorge said, "You're very good at keeping up with the music."

His eyes are gorgeous.

The band played into a slow song. "May I have one more?" Jorge asked.

I hadn't seen Jorge since we all said goodbye when he left for school. He looked so young. We chased each other around the farm and pulled pranks growing up. I never saw him when he came home to visit. Since I'd been working at Jorge's father's home, I'd gotten reacquainted with Dino's family, but it was Jorge who interested me most.

Jorge walked me back to my table. My feet moved but my mind didn't follow. It was still somewhere on the

alone. "I don't think anyone should've overheard it."

"What did you hear?" Victor stopped and turned to me.

I took a deep breath and said, "First, I need to ask you something."

"What's going on?" Victor's voice raised. "Just tell me."

"Please, tell me about El Grito de Lares."

Veins bulged in Victor's forehead. "Fina, what did you hear at the wedding?" he asked.

"I was walking past a guest table to get the wedding goblets when I heard a group of young men talking. They said, 'This can't be another El Grito de Lares'. They were whispering loudly about something planned in Yauco and said Spain's rule will soon be over."

"Damn it!" Victor kicked the sand. "Who was it? Who did you hear saying this?"

"It was a group of locals. Horacio, and there were a couple that I didn't recognize. But what are they planning? Do you know?"

"Forget you ever heard anything. Don't speak to anyone, Fina. Do you hear me?" He stepped closer to me. "This is very serious. Do you know what's been going on in this country?"

"I'm not stupid. Men discuss government or business and don't include us, but women know what's going on. We don't know the details, but we understand. That's why I wanted to talk to you today."

"There's been a lot of things happening that you may not be aware of," Victor said.

"I'm telling you that I do know. The bandits that appear in the night, dressed in black. They rob farmers and rape their wives. They've killed, too. I talked to Anastasia Perez last year. She'll never forget the man with the scar on his lip. I think these are the men who attacked Mama." I stepped closer to Victor and said, "Why have your men not found him?" I shook my head. "That's right, I know you have some men and you go out to get justice for us." I touched my lip. "How many men have a scar on their lip? This man can't be hard to find. And I've seen the locked room at Dino's house. I went inside and saw all the weapons and ammunition. Guns, rifles, and piles of machetes. I know it's not for farming or coffee business." I leaned in. "I know about the secret field where your men train."

"Keep your mouth shut," Victor snapped. "If you talk about any of this you could get yourself killed or put in prison."

"Dino's running a rebel camp to free Puerto Rico, isn't he?" I asked.

"Don't ask questions. And don't poke around." Victor looked around and stepped away. "Shit."

"Tell me," I asked, "was Papa involved in Grito de Lares?" He turned and looked at me. I stared him in the eye and asked, "Did they kill Mama over this?"

"Fina, you are like a ...." Victor groaned. "I will talk to you because I want you to know the truth and not some strange story concocted in your head." He stepped closer. "Many men fought for change, including our father and Dino Cesari. They failed in 1868, but continue to work for change by being involved in business and politics." Victor's eyes lit up. "Yes, I have heard about the plans in Yauco and other plans too. Something big is planned. It's a rebellion and we will succeed. Hundreds of local men are involved." Victor's arms flew in the air. "Yes, we've been training, in a secret place in the fields.

You cannot tell Papa or Celia or anyone. Men will die if you talk."

"Men will die if they do something in Yauco," I said.

"Stay away from Yauco."

17

ISABELLA COOKED FOR DINO three days a week and I loved working in the kitchen with her. If I could go and live at her house I would, but living at Dino and Martina's house was a good plan.

"Get someone to help you; I need banana leaves for the pasteles." Isabella chopped the pork into small pieces and dropped it into a large pot on the stove.

"I'll tell you who we need, we need Lolo," I said. "Nobody climbs better than he does."

"I know, Mejia," Isabella said. "You miss your Papa and brothers. You'll see them Saturday." She shooed me out of the house. "Get going."

I paused for a moment, and grabbed a wicker basket on my way out the back door.

"Where you off to?" Jorge was sitting on a rail, scraping thick, dried mud from the sole of his shoe.

"Isabella needs banana leaves."

"I'll get you some," Jorge said.

Jorge was shorter than Papa, more like Lolo, about five foot-seven at most. I wondered if I needed a taller man for the job. He stepped to the porch where he picked up a machete. Hmm, wonder where he got that? I thought.

"I'll come along," I said. "To carry the leaves." I lifted my basket over my head, to show my worth.

We walked behind the house and stepped carefully down a steep hillside, where he began to whack at a tree and quickly tossed four banana leaves my way. "If I get you these leaves, then you'll have to save me some extra pasteles. Sometimes I get up for a midnight snack."

I laughed and said, "Of course, how many would you like?"

Jorge stepped close and dropped a handful of leaves into my basket. "Maybe you could meet me in the kitchen at midnight," he said.

His hand touched mine and I felt a tingle run through my arm. Our eyes met and I felt the same flutters I'd felt when we danced at the wedding.

"Yes," I said. "I can warm them for you or make coffee."

Jorge leaned in and kissed me, gently. I was nervous and turned to see if we were in view of the house.

"We're covered under a canopy of trees. No one can see us," Jorge said, and he took my hand. "Remember when we played hide-and-seek around this place when we were kids?"

I smiled and leaned in, signaling my acceptance. "Yes, who are we hiding from?" I had waited so long for his touch, to be kissed.

I never imagined it would be under the banana

tree, dressed in our work clothes. His lips were soft and full, his body warm. The tropical scent in the air mixed with his scent intoxicated me. He held me gently and kissed me passionately. My heart beat faster and I felt my temperature rise. I'd never kissed a man before and had only imagined the airy, dizzying feeling. I was on fire. Was it the grade of the hillside or was it my head spinning? The other sensations that stirred within me surprised me and I was physically drawn to him in ways I didn't want to control.

"I enjoyed being with you at the wedding," he said. "I wanted to see you again."

Jorge was all I'd been thinking of since Martina's wedding. I mumbled in agreement, unable to come up with any words. Then I leaned in and kissed him. I instantly regretted it and was embarrassed, ashamed. What had I done?

He embraced me and I dismissed all inhibitions.

"We'd better get these to Isabella," I said, lifting the basket.

Jorge looked around at the trees, covered with rain from the night before. "One minute." He took a banana leaf, curled it into a funnel cup and held it under a tree branch. He pulled on the branch to allow the water to run down the leaf, into the funnel cup. "Want a sip?"

I smiled and held his hands around the leaf cup. I took a drink of fresh rain water. Jorge took my hand and we walked back up the hill.

ON MARCH 24, 1897, the Paoli brothers, Victor and Lolo, and the Cesari brothers, Antonio and Jorge, gathered with a group of about 60 men armed with rifles and machetes who gathered outside the mountain town of Yauco. Other groups stood at the ready nearby. A Puerto Rican flag was revealed and displayed for the first time ever, and the crowd erupted in cheers. The handsewn flag fueled the men. A sky-blue triangle sat on its side, with a white star in the center flanked by red and white stripes set in a rectangular pattern. One rider held it high and the leader, Nieves, dismounted and stepped forward.

"Men, this flag represents our independence. The red stripes represent the blood of our brave warriors. The white stripes represent victory and peace, which will soon be ours. The white star is the island, and the blue represents the sky and sea. Let us offer a moment of silence to honor our beloved Puerto Rico."

Nieves placed his hand over his heart and hung

day in the coffee fields. He stayed late in the barn at the end of the day, preferring the company of Rio the dog over us. Sometimes he visited with Dino and sometimes he stayed out there alone. Always emerging and lumbering into the house with the sharp, sweet smell of pitorro on his breath. He may have been less cranky, with the edge softened by the rum, but his hearty laugh was a becoming faint memory. He was unaware of what was going on in our lives, our family and often could be found stretched out on the sofa, avoiding his lonely bed. He bathed less often, shaved rarely and his charisma was drained from his soul. He missed her.

We all missed her. My brother Victor's unpleasant disposition filled family mealtimes with tension. Lolo worked extra hours in the coffee fields and Papa escaped to play cards several nights a week at the casino in town. He never missed the Thursday night group. It was his favorite, when he played with old friends, mostly Corsicans. My older sister, Martina quietly cried herself to sleep too many nights, and I absorbed her pain knowing she gave up school and Paulo, the boy she loved, to stay at home with us. I missed the way Mama held our family together. Papa brought language and culture from Europe, but Mama brought tradition and family loyalty. She was fierce in her love of country and family. Martina and I tried to do what Mama would want and we became our family's mother.

After supper, Victor came to me and said, "Fina, we need to do something about Papa's gambling."

"What do you mean?" I asked. "You've been going to the casino since you were eight and I see you gambling on the roosters in town."

"Everyone gambles around here. Our good Padre has the best game in town. Hell, he usually wins,"

Victor smirked. "Papa has always played cards with his Corsican friends," Victor said. "He's losing money, lots of money. He's in too deep and they're telling him to pay up."

"I don't understand. Papa wouldn't—"

"What the hell don't you understand?" Victor raised his voice. "Papa's been gambling the family money away!" He shook his head. "Jesus Christ."

"What do you want me to do?" I asked and took a step back. I hated the way Victor yelled at me. He towered over me like a church steeple. He was too big to swat with a broom. I tried to chase him out of the kitchen with the broom.

Victor stood firm and said, "I need you to get into his desk. I can't because he's always home when I'm home. Tomorrow, when we leave for work, look at the books. Look for any notes or bills." Victor stared into my eyes. "We'll talk tomorrow night and then I'll confront Papa."

"Go through Papa's personal papers?" I whispered loudly. "We never touch his desk."

Victor took a deep breath and I could see he was about to throw a dish or yell.

"Okay." I answered and pulled my arms up, protecting my body. I justified spying on Papa because I didn't want Victor, with his hot temper, to confront him until we knew the truth.

Victor added, "And look for anything from Dino Cesari."

"Dino Cesari?" I raised my eyebrow. Papa's friend owned a three-hundred-acre coffee plantation next to ours. We grew up with Dino's children and they were like family to us.

"Don't ask. Do it." Victor turned and walked out.

✡ ✡ ✡

The next evening after dinner Victor came into the kitchen while Martina, Celia and I did the dishes.

"Well? What did you find?" He stood impatiently.

I handed Victor an envelope of papers that I found in Papa's desk.

He sat down at the kitchen table and went through the stack of troubles. "Oh, shit!" Victor studied the papers. "Papa is late on the loan payment to the bank. They'll take the plantation."

"There's more," I whispered. "There's a note in Papa's handwriting, men's names with an amount next to each. Dino Cesari is owed the largest sum but look at these figures next to their names." I pointed to the list and said, "These men are all in the Thursday night card club at the casino."

Victor grabbed the note from my hands and scanned it. "That's more than a year's earnings for us!" He pushed the kitchen door open, banging the plaster wall on the way out. I followed to see what he was going to do. Victor found Papa sipping from a glass in the front room. Lolo was stretched out on the sofa, reading a book.

Victor shouted, "Papa, we have to talk!"

Martina, Celia and I stood in the doorway. Lolo sat up straight and set his book down.

"What's going on?" Papa said as he set his glass down.

Victor slapped the note with Papa's debt list on the lamp table and said, "Let's start with this."

"You'd better back off son. Don't come in here, in my house, and take a position with me." Papa looked at the note. "You've been in my desk?" His voice incredulous, "Gone through my papers?"

"I would never intrude in your business but I heard you're gambling and you're in too deep." Victor shook his head. "How could you, Papa?"

"Get out!" Papa pointed to the door. "Get out of my house!"

Martina, Celia and I stepped back into the hallway, out of sight. Victor stomped out and slammed the front door, knocking over a vase. Papa went to his desk. My sisters and I retreated to the kitchen. "Oh, my God!" I said. "What do we do now?"

Celia sat in the chair, crying.

Martina looked at Celia and said, "Don't cry, it will be all right." Martina looked at me and said softly, "We need to find work."

Dino

THE NEXT DAY I BROUGHT LUNCH to Papa in the coffee fields. When I got to the top of the hill on the northwest parcel, I could see Papa and another man in the distance. I stopped and watched the two figures. They were having an animated conversation, arms waving in the air as if they were having an argument. I moved closer, careful to stay out of view. I could see that the other man was our neighbor, Dino. They spoke in raised voices, and it was clear they were in some sort of disagreement. Papa was angry and said something about being cheated. Dino demanded payment. Most of the conversation was too hard to hear, but I heard the words plantation and land as clear as a bell. I had never seen Señor Cesari so threatening and it frightened me. Rio was with Papa, and I prayed he didn't see me. I squatted low and crept close to the trees on the hillside. My dress caught and tore on a branch. I released my dress from the threatening branch and squatted in the dirt.

Please don't see me.

After a few minutes, Dino Cesari cursed and rode off. Papa stood; shoulders slumped in a cloud of dust. I waited until Dino was out of sight, then I came out of my concealed hideaway. I brushed myself off, walked with my usual stride, and put on a smile so Papa wouldn't suspect I'd heard a thing. Papa stood at the end of a long row of coffee trees. His head hung low, with the weight of the burden he carried. Not wanting to surprise him, I called out, "Hola, Papa! Good boy, Rio."

Papa looked up and gave me a weak wave. I approached with his lunch of fruit, bread and a small piece of chicken. He dusted off his sleeves and smacked his hands together. "Thank you, my girl. Let's sit together."

He seemed agitated but I didn't ask questions while we ate. I had no appetite after seeing Papa and Dino argue and I knew the fight had something to do with the note I found in the desk. Victor was right. I was so angry at Papa and wished that Mama was there to fix things.

After lunch I headed back to the house. Before I started up the road to our hacienda, I glanced across the road at the sprawling Cesari hacienda.

How was Victor going to fix this?

and briefly paced in the field. Dino turned to mount his horse.

Papa pivoted in the rich soil, waved his hand and said, "Dino my friend, what a fortunate man I would be to have you as husband to my daughter." He approached with extended hand and gave Dino a strong handshake. He said, "Your offer is most generous."

"Then it's done. Congratulations to us!" Dino gloated. "I'll draw papers in the morning." He mounted his horse and said, "I can offer her the protection she needs. Fina and Celia can work as domestics." He rode off, down the long row of berry covered coffee trees.

The anger toward Dino that had screamed in silent voices quieted to a whisper in Papa's head in that moment. He had been unable to protect his wife and feared for his daughters' safety against the masked bandits. The northwest parcel had been Papa's original coffee plantation. It was a hillside parcel, but he would once again dig his hands into his own soil. He had watched in bitterness as Dino profited from his plantation for twelve long months. This would be a fresh start.

Papa stopped by the shed before going home. He reached into his bucket for his bottle of rum. He took a drink and let the warmth coat his dry throat. He drank once more before replacing the plug, then locked the shed. His mind began to race with the possibilities the offer presented. There was no going back now.

This is my chance.

"The smell of Sopa de Pollo is in the air! I have an appetite tonight. I hope you made a large pot," Papa kissed Martina on the cheek.

Martina giggled. "I used Mama's recipe."

I was surprised to see Papa so happy. I looked up from my job of setting the table for six.

"Beautiful table, Fina." He kissed me on the cheek. "I'll wash up."

We gathered for our meal at the long wooden dining table that Papa made and we kids had branded over the years. I used Mama's hand embroidered table-cloth to cover all the burn marks and scars in the wood, and placed a vase of roses in the center. Papa sat at one end, with Mama's empty chair at the other. Papa was in an especially good mood and brought the full bottle of pitorro to the table, rather than his usual glass. I adored my father and thought he looked sophisticated, with his gray-streaked blonde hair. He led the grace in French, as he did each night with table conversation continuing in Spanish. Papa was fluent in four languages, French, Italian, Spanish and English with limited Taino language. He insisted we practice speaking and writing in French, while we used Spanish in our daily life.

Dressed in a white shirt and striped linen suit, Papa sat tall and straight in his chair, like he was ready to deal a card game. As supper came to an end Papa announced, “I am so proud of my beautiful family. Your mother and I had great plans for our family and you are all wonderful children. You know that blood is thicker than water, right?”

“Yes, Papa,” we echoed.

“We always stick together.”

“Papa,” Victor blurted out his concern. “Is something wrong?”

“Oh, no,” Papa laughed and waved his hands. “Victor, quite the contrary. Something very wonderful has happened. I have great news to share. An announcement for a member of our family — good news for our entire family!” Papa grinned so broadly he smiled with his eyes.

I leaned on my elbows, waiting for the news. Papa circled his hands in the air as if leading an orchestra, and with a raised voice he said, “Dino Cesari has asked for the hand of Martina, and his dowry gift is the northwest parcel of his coffee plantation. This parcel — our original parcel with the house! We won’t be living in this house as stewards. We will own it once again.”

I sat frozen in my chair and watched for Martina’s reaction. Her face grew red then a deep shade of magenta. For a moment, it appeared she had forgotten to breathe. Finally, she screamed out in a loud, guttural explosion of tears.

She flew from her chair and ran out of the room.

The small dining room filled with the sound of voices but they sounded like clashing cymbals rather than a symphony of celebration. Victor jumped from his seat and peppered our father with questions about who would run the plantation and would he continue to work for Dino?

"Our original parcel?" Victor asked. "What about all the land you added through the years? And the mill you added? That's on the new parcel. Will that stay with Dino?"

"Yes, it will." Papa wiped his mouth. "We will process our coffee the old way, and sell it in town."

"Papa, we'll lose the European market!" Victor said.

"This is our chance, Victor. We can sell local. It was a generous offer, and I knew Dino would have no further appetite for negotiation."

Lolo shoveled his meal into his mouth at a quickened pace. He always ate when he was nervous.

Celia sat quiet and listened.

We all paused and listened to the terrible noise of Martina's loud sobs coming from the upstairs bedroom.

"He's older," Papa murmured. "But Dino is a very wealthy man. He can offer protection from bandits or corrupt police that I can't. Our family will recover some of what we lost."

Papa shrugged. "She will grow to love him."

"You sold Martina to cover your gambling losses?" Lolo said. He stared at Papa and shook his head in disappointment.

Papa gulped down his glass of moonshine rum

and set his glass down firmly. The glass tipped over, spilling what was left onto Mama's tablecloth. He stood and marched out the front door.

"Martina's going to ruin everything!" Victor said. He pushed back from the table, stood and knocked his chair over. He followed Papa outside, slamming the wooden door behind him.

I left the table and went upstairs to my sister. Martina was stretched out on the bed. She sat up and looked at me through red, swollen eyes. Her face was puffed and her beautiful, braided hair style now looked like duck feathers sticking out of her head.

My perfectly put together sister had come undone. I sat beside her and gently stroked her arm. "It will be all right," I said. I wondered how it would.

Martina rejected my touch and jolted to a standing position. "How? How is this going to be all right Fina?"

"You must talk to Papa."

"Are you too dumb to understand? The dye is cast." Martina wiped her face and dropped on the bed beside me. "I am grateful that it's Dino and not the widower, Don Francisco Ortiz. He makes me uncomfortable." Martina pulled her skirt tight and folded the fabric over her lap. In San Juan, he watches from his horse. He knows when the young girls will be out of school. He never speaks a word. He leers from under the brim of his hat." She shivered. "We always walked quickly when we passed by him."

"Ewww!"

"At least I know Dino's family. We grew up with his children." Martina got up and walked around the room. "What will that make me? Their mother?" Her body shook. "I love Dino but never thought of him as a husband."

"You won't be home with us anymore. I'll miss you most on Saturdays and Sundays," I said.

Martina blew a strand of loose hanging hair from her face and said, "My life is over." She threw herself backward, onto the bed.

I wrapped my arms around Martina's trembling body and held her tight.

"You and Celia have got to come with me," she said. "You can't stay here, or you'll be next. As a wife, I can arrange for you to be full-time domestics. You already work at Dino's house." She looked at me with eyes wide. "He has plenty of room. You have to come with me. I can't do this alone."

Tears flowed like a soft rainfall down Martina's tired face. Huddled together, we fell asleep to the sound of the coqui frogs outside the bedroom window.

PAPA WAS PLAYING A HIGH STAKES GAME. He had his agreement to get the plantation back from Dino in exchange for Martina's hand in marriage. While he parlayed her into a winning hand for the pot, we sisters played another hand, and Martina shuffled the deck.

Dino courted Martina, and he was very charming, calling her his vibrant tropical flower. She began to plant the seed to save Celia and me from being next to be bargained off in marriage. He would come by the house for Martina, with two chaperones. Usually his sister, prune-faced Juana, and the second person rotated throughout his family or mine. They followed the couple on walks or accompanied them to Ponce for musical performances or social events once or twice a week. Martina listened to Dino and when the time was right, she let him know what was in her heart.

After one afternoon visit Dino came in the house to see Papa. Martina and I listened from the upstairs hallway. We had a full view.

Papa walked around the dining room.

"What's he doing?" I whispered.

The clink of glasses and the sound of a bottle being placed on the dining room table were familiar. A few sighs as if they were releasing the day's burdens and the sound of a chair scooting out from under the table signaled their conference was about to begin.

"They're not sitting in the front room," Martina whispered. "They want to stay near the bottle."

"Are they going to drink all afternoon?"

"Shhh," Martina held her finger over her lips.

"Did you get that fencing repaired?" Dino asked Papa. Dino sat in Victor's chair and had his back to us. He broke Papa's rule and leaned back, lifting the front legs off the floor. The old chair wobbled and creaked under the weight. Victor had broken that chair multiple times over the years and I prayed it would hold up.

I rolled my eyes and slowly crouched down on the floor, scooting closer to the stair railing. This was going to be a long conversation.

Martina settled on her knees and bowed over as if she were praying.

"Guillermo, I want you to know that everything is going well," Dino said. "Martina is lovely. I'm taking her to Ponce to get a dress for the wedding in March."

"Thank you, Dino," Papa said. He set his glass down with a knock. "She tells me things are going well." He poured another glass of rum. "I can't give my own daughter a wedding dress."

"You gave your daughters a good life. Fina and Celia are excellent workers and get along with my other domestics," Dino said. "I'd like them to stay on full time. We need the help."

Martina winked at me, and nodded yes.

"I don't know, they are young." Papa's words began to slur.

"Guillermo, your daughters are paid well. I will give them Saturdays off to be with you. They can stay at my home. You'll save on food."

I hung on every word. My knees were sore and I slowly lay down on the floor, keeping the dining room table in my sight. Martina shifted her body and hunched on all four, leaning forward. She listened with eyes wide.

"I need them here." Papa shook his head no.

Dino took a drink and set his glass down. "You are a tough businessman. I will give you access to the mill one day a week to process your coffee beans. This way, you can sell to the European market."

Papa used the voice he had when we were in trouble. There was no arguing when he was in this mood. "They will come home on Saturday mornings and return Sunday mornings."

"Very well, I need them by Sunday at 7:00 a.m." Dino's voice was quiet, agreeable, not the usual firm tone he used when doing business.

Papa nodded in agreement and his shoulders slumped. For some reason I felt sad for him. He looked defeated. I exhaled, relieved Papa no longer held us, for his next play.

Martina sat back, against the wall and looked exhausted. I looked at her and mouthed, "Thank you."

She reached out and took my hand.

CELIA AND I PREPARED FOR OUR MOVE into Dino's grand hacienda across the road from our house. Dino's sprawling brick and mortar house was built by Corsican laborers, in the Italian and French style. There were five bedrooms upstairs and four bedrooms downstairs by the kitchen, which served as the domestic's quarters. The cook showed us to our room. Celia and I shared the bedroom closest to the kitchen and heard the bang of the pots and pans when the cook started at about 5:00 a.m. We started work an hour later, and hoped to sleep a little longer, but quickly learned that was impossible.

One day, after being awoken early by loud pots banging, I decided to inspect the two unoccupied bedrooms in hopes of moving to a bedroom further from the kitchen. The doors had been kept locked and when I asked the cook about them, I was told they were for family use. That day I snuck a key from the drawer in Martina and Dino's bedroom. I opened the bedroom door and started to walk in. I stopped and caught my breath.

The small bedroom was filled with open crates of weapons. There were hand guns, rifles, machetes and many crates of ammunition. My God, I thought. He's got an ammunition bunker. I stood for a moment and scanned the room. Fearful that someone might see me, I closed the door and looked around. I opened the next locked door. It was the same, filled with ammunition, rifles and crates of machetes. This is a supply depot. But for what? My hands began to shake and I fumbled with the lock. I secured both doors and went to my room to gather myself. Surely others know about these rooms. Who can I trust?

The new bride-to-be, Martina, had some say in our appointment at the house. Celia was given the duty of cleaning the upstairs bedrooms, while I assisted the cook in the kitchen and served occasionally. I kept my eye on the back hallway and took note of who entered the two locked bedrooms. I told Martina about the rooms, but she insisted that was old business. It was from the El Grito de Lares in 1868, and that Papa and Dino had both been involved in the failed rebellion. They were old friends. Dino stored everything at his house as a favor to local farmers who didn't have room.

I didn't agree that the weapons were from Lares, but kept quiet about it.

dance floor. "Thank you, Fina," Jorge said.

"Yes," I said. The scent of his hair tonic was intoxicating and smelled like the white blossoms from the coffee tree.

Jorge returned to his table with his brothers. I heard them tease him about dancing with me.

Celia leaned in and whispered into my ear. "Yes? That's what you say to him after two dances? Yes?"

"Oh, it's nothing."

"You like him!" Celia smiled.

"Shhh! Quiet," I said.

"I can see it. I thought I could tell on the dance floor but now I know it."

"Celia, I couldn't think," I said. "I didn't know what to say to him. All I could think of was, yes." We giggled.

Celia and I both had a hand on our shoulders. It was Papa. "My girls, how are you? Isn't this a magnificent day?" He waved his wine glass in the air. "Doesn't our Martina look beautiful? You are beautiful too, my darling girls."

"Yes, Papa, I haven't seen you so happy in years," I said. "You even danced with sour Aunt Juana."

"Yes, I know she is bitter," Papa said, "but the two families must show her we are united as one."

"Papa, who is the man in the white linen suit?"

I asked.

Papa laughed a hardy laugh. "Nearly every man here is wearing a white linen suit." He looked in the direction I inquired and said, "Why, that's your new brother-in-law, Dino."

"No, I mean the man in the straw hat, with a glass

of red wine. I saw him standing behind the pillar earlier. He was listening in on a conversation that I'm sure was intended to be private," I said. "I noticed that you greeted and kissed nearly all the men, women and children today but I have not seen you speak to that man."

Papa sharpened his focus on the man then turned back. "Don't worry about that man." Papa stroked his beard. "And don't talk to him. He's involved in the government."

"My sweet Celia, how is my girl?" Papa kissed her on the cheek.

"I'm going to greet these gentlemen," Papa said as he motioned to a group of men. "Enjoy the celebration, my loves." He kissed Celia and me on the cheek.

I thought about the man involved in the government and the group of young men talking about the fall of Spain's rule. What were they planning in Yauco?

Jorge Cesari and his friends were sons of men who failed at the El Grito de Lares, the first major revolt in Puerto Rico in 1868. I don't think I was meant to overhear the eager young men discuss secret plans of the upcoming revolt.

✡ ✡ ✡

Dino watched his sons as he shared a drink with a guest. He overheard a few key words, "revolt ... Cuba ... ammunition and plantation camp." He felt his blood boil and hoped it didn't show in his face. Members of the Spanish Militia were also guests at the wedding and it was much too dangerous to have such a conversation.

"Excuse me, I must greet my sons," Dino said. As he moved toward the table he was stopped by another guest, the Mayor of Ponce. "Let's get a drink, to celebrate my wedding!" Dino said and placed his hand on the mayor's shoulder. Dino walked him across the courtyard to keep him from the discussion at his sons' table.

Dino was furious with his sons but it was too late.

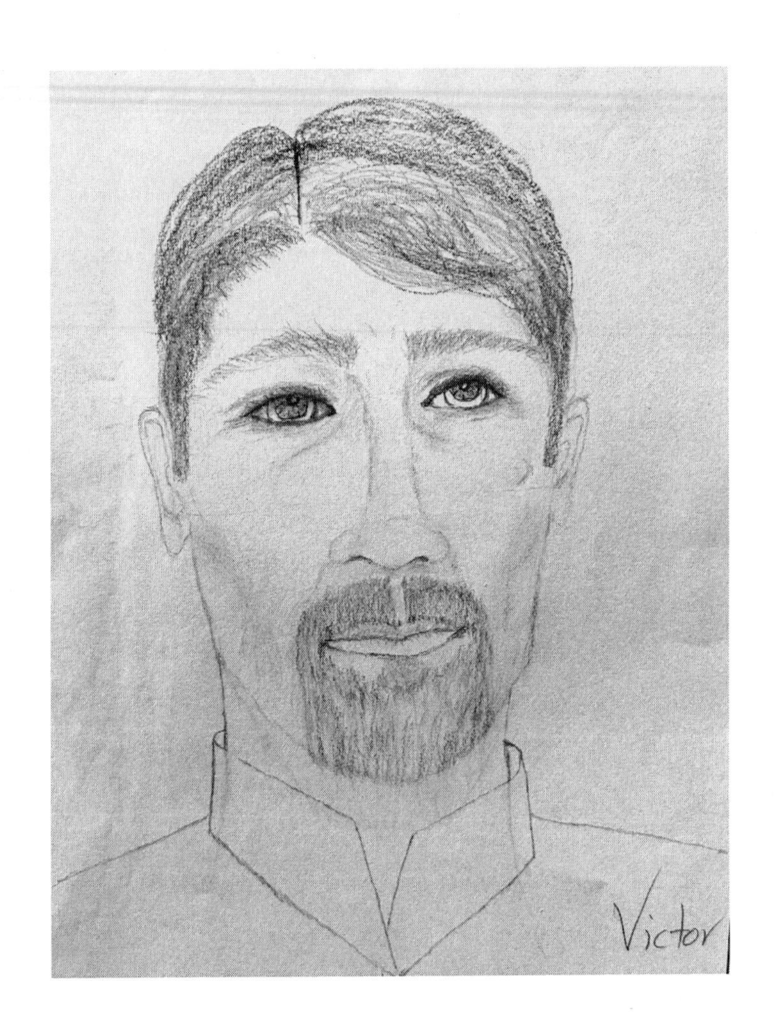

Victor

THE EXCITEMENT FROM THE WEDDING preoccupied my mind with thoughts about the man in the linen suit who was eavesdropping on the young men's conversation at the reception. I missed Martina and wanted to ask her about El Grito de Lares. We'd heard stories about our father being involved in secret revolution activities, but women were not included in such discussions. Because the Cesari's had family in town, Celia and I stayed at home with Papa for the night. It felt good to sleep in my old bed. I decided to speak to Victor in the morning about what I'd overheard at the wedding, then I relaxed and closed my eyes.

"Good morning," I said as I walked into the kitchen where I found Isabella cooking Sunday breakfast. Papa, my brothers and Celia were dressed and having coffee.

"You must be hungry after a big night, Señor Guillermo," Isabella heaped another scoop of beans onto Papa's plate.

I plucked a fresh pork pastelle from the neatly stacked platter and washed it down with black coffee.

"What are you drinking," I asked Celia.

"Coffee." Celia looked up over her floral English tea cup and saucer set.

I shook my head. "Another sale at the grocery store."

Victor said, "Lolo brought the carriage around, but he's not feeling too good this morning. I don't think he's going to be much help."

Papa sighed. "I can go with you."

"You're taking people back to Ponce?" I asked.

"Yes," Victor said, "and they're going to be outside in ten minutes."

"I can ride along so Papa doesn't have to go," I said. "I need to pick something up in Ponce. Let's go!"

"You — what help will you be?" Victor said.

"I'll let you drive the carriage," I said. "Do you want me to whistle for you? Or drive the ponies?"

"That's enough," Papa said. "Victor, she can go. Fina can shoot a bird from any distance and handle the carriage if you can't. Get going, so you can make it back before dark."

"Come on, Fina!" Victor said. He walked out the door.

I took a last sip of coffee and walked outside. I looked up at Victor, who was already seated in the carriage and had two passengers. I climbed into the front seat beside my very sullen brother. He grabbed the reins and said, "Hold on. Ready? Let's go!" He flicked the reins and the ponies trotted down the hill. We hit the mountain road, and they started their downhill run, with Victor blowing his whistle in frantic blasts to warn any oncoming riders. We were used to the wild ride, veering on the edge of steep canyons, on narrow turns. The ponies were trained and kept up the quick pace, to avoid being run over by the carriage behind them. They pulled the weight all the way to Ponce, where they got a well-deserved rest and drink of water. Our passengers departed, giving us a little time together.

"I don't really have an errand in Ponce," I said. "I wanted to talk to you alone."

"What's the problem?"

"The horses need to rest," I said. "Let's go to the sea. It's a good place to talk."

We went to my favorite place. The seashore calmed me and cleared my head. Papa took us there often when we were little. The water washed onto the beach in sparkling-white waves. The sea faded into shades of jewel blues. Many times, I tried to capture the teal-blue water into a cup and save it. The magic blue of the sea disappeared every time, leaving me with a cup of clear liquid. The magic of the island was beginning to feel the same.

When we were children, we played in the sand and Papa held our hands so we could splash and walk along the water. As we grew, we walked with him many times on the bright white beach and listened to him talk about the Isle of Corsica, his homeland. The sea was a good place to take my brother, where no one could hear us discuss Lares, or plans for Yauco. We walked along the shore.

"I need to talk to you about something," I said. "I overheard a conversation at Martina's wedding that I shouldn't have." I looked around to be sure we were his head in silence. His men followed.

Nieves spoke after a moment, and said, "To independence!" He hoisted his rifle into the air. "Let's take them, and raise our flag." He mounted his horse and said, "Line up."

"Who would have ever thought we'd be attacking Yauco," Lolo said.

"We're not attacking it," Victor said. "We're setting it free." He paused then said. "Lolo, stay on your horse. No matter what."

Lolo nodded. He looked left, then right at the line of men who flanked him on horseback. About ten or twenty others stood behind, with machetes and rifles. He adjusted his hat and held the reins tight.

Nieves sat atop his horse, and spoke to his men. "There are almost six-hundred of us here today. Each group has a mission. Once we take over Spain's militia barracks and we capture their ammunition, we will control this region," he said. He strode back and forth on his horse as he spoke. "Our ability to move up our attack will surprise them."

"We're prepared," Jorge said. He turned to Victor. "I'll take my men in from the East and meet you at the barracks."

"It's no problem," Victor said. "My men will come in from the West. This won't take long."

Nieves walked his horse up close and stopped. "What are you doing up front, Antonio?"

"I'm leading my men."

"No, you're not. Fall in line. You're in Jorge's group." Nieves pointed toward the crowd of men.

Antonio turned and whispered. "I didn't leak the

plans. Why am I demoted? Stupido." He walked away, with his arms in the air.

"Antonio," Nieves yelled. "This is not a time for insolence."

Antonio turned and said, "You take my men from me and want me to take orders from my brother? My father is Dino Cesari."

Nieves walked his horse up close to Antonio. "Do not test me. You are in my group because of a favor to your father." He spat in the dirt. "We are here today, months in advance of our plan because of your poor leadership, your men." He leaned forward in the saddle. "Or was it you who talked too much at your father's wedding?"

Antonio stiffened and looked surprised.

"You thought nobody knew you had a big mouth?" Nieves sat up straight in his saddle. "You won't listen to your brother? Take your orders from Victor. Fall in." Nieves turned his horse around.

Lolo pulled the reins, and moved his horse to make room for Antonio.

Victor motioned to Antonio. "Let's go."

"It wasn't me," Antonio said. "It was Horacio and his idiots who talked."

"Come on," Jorge said. He looked around. "They're moving."

"Come with me, Antonio, and don't be pissed off about it." Victor mounted his horse and waved to his men to follow.

Antonio mounted his horse and fell in line behind Victor. Jorge rode to the east, with his men.

The machete and rifle wielding rebellion approached Yauco, ready to free Puerto Rico from Spain. The new Puerto Rican flag painting the sky.

The ambush began immediately. Bullets rained from the sky. Dust clouds floated upward in tufts, clouding the virgin flag.

Screams of anguish and the smell of gunpowder filled the air, burning everyone's noses. Spanish soldiers had been lying in wait, and the rebels were outmatched. Within minutes, moans and cries pierced the sound of gunfire. They retreated. Lolo masterfully rode beside Nieves, shooting and protecting his leader. He leaned far forward and hugged his saddle with his knees, becoming one with the horse. Lolo's horse trusted him and together they rode wild and free, evading the enemy.

Victor raced for a building, firing his rifle.

Antonio followed, leaning deep into his saddle. He rode between a house and a fence.

"Shit," Victor muttered to himself. He would be like a caged animal, trapped between the fence and house. They had to get away.

Men were retreating and being arrested. Victor rode to Antonio's aide. When Victor approached, he saw Antonio shoot his handgun. His rifle lay on the ground, assumed empty. Victor dismounted and walked into the narrow opening. There were no soldiers in sight. He stepped slowly with his rifle ready. Antonio spun around, his pistol pointed and ready to fire. Victor held his hand out and Antonio drew down. The street beyond was quiet. Antonio dropped into a curled ball and began to cry. Victor inched forward to the edge of the building and risked a look around the corner into the street.

A girl in a white dress lay in the dirt road, bloodied.

Jorge rode in from the opposite side. He jumped off his horse. "Holy Mary, what have you done?"

"Not me," Victor pointed to Antonio.

Jorge knelt in the dust and weeds beside his brother. "Are you shot?"

Antonio shook his head, no. "She was chasing her dog," he mumbled. "It was an accident."

"She's a child." Jorge looked around the corner to view the scene. A dog barked in urgent yelps.

Victor and Jorge exchanged a quick glance and spoke through their eyes.

"Antonio, get on your horse. Now." Victor ordered. He grabbed his arm and pulled him to his feet. "The soldiers are on the other side, arresting the men who didn't get away. There's an opening in the fence. Let's go!"

Victor mounted his horse and rode out fast.

A small crowd began to gather around the body of the girl in the street. Cries and wails echoed in a cacophonous symphony. A dog whined, adding a top note. Jorge and Antonio rode swiftly after Victor.

Within minutes, the streets were cleared of all rebels and the chance for independence was lost for the second time.

Jorge

19

DINO CAME INTO THE KITCHEN early for coffee, skipped breakfast and went straight outside where he paced around like a bull. He walked to the back of the house, where the living room window faces the canyon, and the view cuts across the trees to the lush, green mountains. To the far right, there were glimpses between the trees of the winding road. We served him breakfast outdoors. Later, he took lunch in the same spot. Dino maintained his observation post all afternoon.

Martina stood in the living room. She motioned for me to come in. "Fina, something is wrong."

We stayed out of view of the window, but we could see Dino outside. "What is it?"

Martina whispered, "The rebellion."

"Oh, no!" I stepped closer.

"He was up half the night," Martina said. "Men came and emptied the downstairs rooms of weapons."

"I didn't hear a thing."

"There were about a dozen wagons up here," she said. "You sleep like a bear."

"My new room faces the canyon." My mind caught up. "Oh, God. Victor. Victor is with them."

"I think Jorge and Antonio are with them too," Martina said. "That's why Dino is so worried. They didn't come home."

"Lolo too?" I asked.

"I don't know," she said. "Why did you think Victor is with them? What do you know?"

"I heard they were planning something in Yauco."

"We looked out the window. Dino stood alone, at the edge of the patio. "What is he doing?" I asked.

"Praying."

✡ ✡ ✡

That evening Dino joined us in the dining room for a late supper. All the lights were lit, as we waited for the men to come home. Martina, Celia and I pushed our food around our plates, but managed to eat a little. There was no conversation. My stomach was twisted in knots.

The kitchen door opened. We all jumped from our chairs. Dino walked ahead of us and before he got to the kitchen Lolo walked in, covered in dust.

"Where are they?" Dino asked.

"They're not here?" Lolo asked.

"Come with me," Dino walked to his study. Lolo followed and Dino closed the door behind.

We listened at the double doors.

"What the hell happened?" Dino's voice rose.

"They ambushed us."

Martina covered her mouth to contain any sounds. I leaned against the door, to hear better. Celia squeezed in close to listen.

"Are they dead?" Dino asked.

"No. I don't know. I don't think so," Lolo said. "The Spanish soldiers were arresting many of our men. I rode away with Nieves and wanted to get him out safely. I saw Victor with Antonio."

"Where was Jorge?" Dino asked.

"He was with his men."

I held my breath. We stood like statues at the door.

Dino paused, "So, Victor and Antonio were together, but Jorge was not with them. Tomorrow we will try to get word," Dino said. "There will be a list of names of those arrested or killed. Thank you for coming by. Do you want something to eat? Please, sit with us and say hello to your sisters. But say nothing of this business."

"I need to get home to Papa," Lolo said. "I'm sure he's worried."

We hurried back to the table of cold food plates before the doors opened.

"Martina, where is Victor?" Celia asked. "Has something happened to him?"

"Shhh, we'll talk later," I said.

Lolo walked in, looking exhausted. I rose from my chair and gave him a grateful hug. One precious brother was safe. Martina and Celia gave him a kiss on the cheek.

"I'm going home," Lolo said.

"Give our love to Papa," I said.

Lolo walked out and I held my tears.

✡ ✡ ✡

After dinner, Celia and I cleared the dishes. We were alone in the kitchen. The cooks were all gone.

Martina walked in. "Dino went to bed." She spoke in a hushed voice. "Sit down."

We gathered around the kitchen table in the amber light of one lamp. "Listen," Martina looked directly at Celia. "You're only fourteen, too young to hear all of this, but I know that you've already seen and heard too much. It's important to know that you can be trusted."

"I won't say anything," Celia said. She stroked her braided hair.

Martina looked at me and said, "Remember the weapons you saw in the downstairs bedrooms?"

"Yes," Celia said.

"She saw them too?" My eyes darted back and forth from Martina to Celia.

Martina tucked her chin and looked up at me with the same look that Mama used to give me when she thought I should understand something, or I should know better.

I looked at Celia and said, "You never said anything to me about it."

Celia shrugged.

Martina looked at me with complete calm, and said, "What does it matter? I'm the oldest. She came to me." She looked at Celia and said, "Okay then, you can be trusted. There was an uprising today. You heard Lolo.

Dino said six hundred men were going to take Yauco today, but it was apparent the Spanish soldiers knew they were coming. Lolo told Dino they had no chance, and retreated immediately, but Victor, Jorge and Antonio didn't come back. We don't know if they've been arrested."

"Oh, God," Celia teared up. "What do we do?"

"Nothing," Martina said. "Act as if you know nothing. Do you understand?"

"Why did they attack Yauco?" Celia said. "Why not the capitol?"

"The Spanish Military has a stronghold at Yauco and a lot of ammunition there."

"Our cousins," Celia said. "Our friends in Yauco. I don't understand."

I placed my hand on Celia's. "I think the people there are safe," I said. "It's the rebels that will be punished." I looked at Martina. "I wonder if Dino let us move to the upstairs bedrooms to get us away from the ammunition rooms downstairs?"

"Yes, I think he was preparing for action," she said.

"And I thought he was treating us more like family," I said.

* * *

Antonio and Jorge came home the next morning, looking exhausted but unhurt. Celia cried when she laid eyes on them. Dino, Martina, Celia and I raced to the front porch to greet them.

Dino embraced his sons and kissed them. "And Victor?" he asked.

"He's fine," Jorge said. "He went home."

"Thank God," I said. I exhaled a breath I'd been holding for at least a day.

Martina wiped a tear from her eyes. "I'm so relieved," she said.

We all gave them hugs; then the men walked in together, arms around each other. They went to the study and closed the doors, leaving us behind.

"I don't know why we can't hear about it," Celia said. "We already know."

"Come on, Celia." Martina turned her shoulders around and marched her into the kitchen.

Martina laid a book on the table. "I'm the oldest, and it's up to me to see that you continue your education."

"I'm going away to school?" Celia asked.

"We're going to keep up on our lessons while you live here." Martina opened her school book to the desired page. "It will help to understand what's happening, if you know the history."

She began to read. "The Taino Indians lived in a community south of Adjuntas. Nearby was a river, which the Tainos called Coayuca. Fernando Pacheco founded a town in 1756, bringing growth adding a church, town hall, a plaza and streets. The Taino named it Yauco and Fernando Pacheco became the first Mayor."

"We know the Pachecos!" Celia said.

"That's right. They're a big family," I said.

"Well, many Pachecos are not descendants of Don Fernando Pacheco by bloodline. They carry his name because they were his slaves," Martina said. "The Pacheco name is common around there."

I raised my hand and said, "Last year, leaders of the failed 1868 El Grito de Lares rebellion joined with others to plan a second attack, this time at Yauco. That's what I overheard." I covered my mouth. "Oh, God," I said. "Papa is probably involved too."

"What?" Martina said.

"I overheard a group of guests talking at your wedding. They said they were planning a rebellion in December. I told Papa."

"You think Papa is involved?" Martina said. "Because he and Dino were involved in El Grito de Lares?"

"I talked to Victor," I said. "The day after your wedding. He told me to stay away from Yauco. I have no doubt Victor's involved. I think they moved the date up."

"Dino said one more thing last night," Martina said. "The leaders, exiled in New York, sent thirty thousand machetes for locals, and another supporter offered five hundred rifles. That room filled with weapons? Likely came from those shipments."

"We're living in the nest," I said. "Dino is a leader, and Victor? He's surely in deep."

BY THREE O'CLOCK THE FOLLOWING DAY, word came about those arrested. Messages passed from farm to farm, with the list of missing men. Families anguished over husbands and sons who didn't come home. Others feared capture and the possibility of death for their participation. A rumor floated about a girl who had been shot, and was possibly killed.

We sat in the front room, reading the newspapers. The Spanish newspaper said nothing of the incident, presenting business as usual.

"Why is there nothing about yesterday's uprising?" I turned the pages of the newspaper, scouring for information. "Our men didn't just vanish."

"Spain wants to appear strong and in control," Jorge said. "To report the revolt would show weakness and bring more trouble."

"Where are all the men?" Martina asked.

Antonio shook his head. "I don't know."

✡ ✡ ✡

The next morning, a messenger came to the kitchen door while we were having breakfast. Pedro, the cook, answered then came to the table.

"What is it?" Martina asked.

"The Spanish Military has arrested over one hundred fifty men," Pedro explained. "They're being held prisoner in Ponce, accused of various crimes."

"Oh, no!" I cupped my hand over my mouth.

"The girl was killed," Pedro continued. "A Pacheco. An eight-year-old descendant of Don Fernando Pacheco. They don't know if she was killed in the crossfire, or if a local shot her."

"Thank you, Pedro. You may go now." Antonio said.

"That's terrible news," Martina remarked. "The Pacheco girl is dead? That poor family. Whoever did this should be hanged."

"Our friends and neighbors held in prison right now will be hanged," I said.

"I don't think so," Antonio said. "The Spanish will torture them for information. They want the leaders, and the person who killed the girl."

I looked up and saw Dino on the stair landing. He had heard everything.

JORGE AND I FOUND WAYS to be together whenever possible. I met him at the river on laundry day or at the banana tree. We began to take greater risks and snuck into rooms in the house. Having my room upstairs had become a temptation too great for either of us to resist. When I wasn't with him, I dreamed of being with him. Around people in the house, he brushed against me and my heart fluttered. We tried to be discreet, but soon it was no secret in the house, and it was accepted that we were lovers.

My beautiful Jorge wrote me poetry and slipped it to me on note paper with an illustration to remember each encounter. With his first poem, he sketched a banana tree, the second a river, on the third was a small sketch of our kitchen table and a clock set to midnight. The table was set with a coffee pot, dishes and a plate of pasteles. One night I snuck into his bedroom and spent the night. The next day a poem reflected our time with a candle, burning down to the end.

One night when we lay in bed together Jorge said, "Fina, I have to go to San Juan." He held me as if the news would break me into a thousand pieces.

"For a day?"

"A week. My father wants me to see about a store there."

"Why doesn't he take care of it?

"He's preparing me to take over one day."

"I thought Antonio would be in charge because he's the oldest."

"My father loves his sons, but he knows us. Antonio will be given a job of some importance, but he won't be in charge. He's too impulsive, and hot tempered."

I kissed Jorge on the cheek. "I'm proud of you." I sat up and said, "You probably shouldn't talk too much about your trip to Antonio."

"You know him too."

FRIDAY NIGHTS WERE A TIME FOR FUN and gathering with friends. Dino played cards with his friends every Friday.

Occasionally, they played in Ponce at the apartment Dino owned over the grocery store. On those nights he stayed in town overnight and returned Saturday or Sunday. Martina had freedom to entertain us or go visit Papa. On the evenings when Dino hosted card night at his hacienda in Adjuntas, Martina stayed in her room upstairs. Celia and I had a lot of fun working, cooking and serving. The house was filled with laughter, the smell of Isabella's favorite dishes, and Cuban cigars.

"Hurry, the Alcapurrias tray is nearly empty," Isabella said. "The men will be hungry." She waved her hands to push me out of the kitchen. "Get the food out there."

"Ahh, here it comes," Dino said. "My cook prepared a special fish treat tonight."

Isabella walked in the dining room with us, carrying her prized dish.

"Trunkfish." Dino bragged.

Ricardo Gonzalez said, "I think I'll have the Chillo."

"Oh, don't be afraid; Isabella knows how to prepare Trunkfish." He laughed. "She won't let you be poisoned by the skin."

Celia and I cleared space on the table and served the large platters of rice, sorullitos, mofongo and plantains. Papa's friend, Hector Valdez was there, and I felt my face turn red with heat from embarrassment. It was the first time anyone saw us working as domestics. He avoided eye contact and was very kind. I tried to be invisible and quickly returned to the kitchen.

Dino's guests spoke freely, with no women present. They drank, smoked cigars and told stories not suitable for women. When Celia and I walked in to serve, they interrupted their story and the room fell silent or turned to small talk. We tried to keep from smiling and be quick with service. There was the usual throat clearing and casual conversation until we left the room for the kitchen again. Then boisterous conversation resumed, punctuated by bursts of laughter.

I set a dirty platter in the sink and stepped to the stove where Isabella was cooking. "Isabella, there are packages of meat on the table," I said. "I saw steaks." I pointed toward the dining room.

She laughed and stirred the onions.

"Am I supposed to pick them up?" I asked. "Are we going to cook them tonight?"

"They play for meat."

"What?"

"They flaunt their wealth, playing for meat." Isabella shrugged her shoulders.

"I guess they got bored playing for money," Celia said. "They have too much. I saw a stick of salami or sausage on the table."

"Oh, that's a big bet." Isabella raised her eyebrows. "That comes all the way from Italy."

My eyes widened. "I hope Dino wins that one."

Voices roared from the dining room. "Somebody won tomorrow's main course," Isabella said. "They're calling out Rueben's name. Sounds like he took the pot. I hope we're not cooking chicken stew again tomorrow."

Celia faced the kitchen door to the dining room, waving her hands upward to the sky as if to propel energy into the next room. She whispered, "Come on, Dino."

"Let's get the rest of these platters out," Isabella said. She let a tobacco-stained smile slip out. "Then we'll get our card game started in the kitchen."

I looked over at the table and saw she had a deck ready, along with three full plates of food. "Isabella, you're taking care of us too. What are we playing for?"

"Loser washes the dishes."

SUNDAY WAS MY FAVORITE DAY of the week. Celia and I were included in family day, as sisters to Martina, and indulged in all the luxuries that Dino's hacienda afforded. Cooks prepared the meals and I didn't have to help, as it was my day off. I looked forward to it all week.

Dino worked six days and rested on Sundays. The day centered around the dining table. We started with a big breakfast after church, and finished the day with an early supper. When we returned from morning Mass, the cook started service immediately knowing we were hungry. Each week we enjoyed a different menu.

Dino and Martina took their seats at the head of the table. Jorge, Antonio, Celia and I sat quietly.

"I smell Mallorca,"—a sweet pastry bread. Celia leaned over and whispered from the corner of her mouth.

I tried to hide my smile. It was her favorite breakfast bread. Dino took a deep breath and exhaled.

He tucked his napkin in his collar. The servants started the parade of food, lining the center of the table with delectable dishes. They set a bowl of fresh fruit in front of me.

"You can put the cremas—a porridge— over here," Jorge said with a laugh.

Dino served himself a heaping spoon of revoltillo— a Spanish style scrambled eggs with bacon. One Sunday the cooks used vegetables and Dino had a fit. He insisted that with his money, he could afford meat. We never had vegetable revoltillo again. The mallorca was set in front of Celia. I turned around to see which servant did her that favor. It was Pilar. How sweet, I thought. Her arm reached in once more, to set down a bowl of jam. We sat around the table, ate, talked, drank coffee and picked at mallorca until Dino was full and excused the table.

We went to the front room to read newspapers or books for most of the day. A mist of rain cast across the sky in the distance. Dino often caught up on sleep after a busy week and napped on the sofa with a book or newspaper propped across his face. Jorge and Antonio usually went to see Victor and Lolo and had their own get together in the afternoon.

Dino laid back on the sofa, with the latest July 1897 newspaper, which was a day old. He folded the paper in half and read aloud. "Gold Rush. People are immigrating to Alaska by the thousands." He held the paper closer and read on. "Jesus, they're digging up gold!"

"Gold?" Martina said. "Gold what?"

"Gold nuggets." Dino sat up and shook out the paper. "They're panning for gold. Pulling nuggets right out of the rivers." He chuckled. "Santo cielo."

"Where is Alaska?" Celia asked.

Dino looked up, over his newspaper. "Alaska! The Klondike. Canada."

"Canada. Is that in America?" Celia asked.

Martina looked at Celia and answered, "North of the United States." She turned to Dino and said, "Don't tell Papa. He'll say, 'This is my chance,' like he always does." She laughed. "Then he'll sell something to go to Alaska."

Dino laughed and wiggled his finger in the air. "He is a dreamer."

"Dreamer?" I said. "I'd rather be picking gold nuggets than coffee beans."

MARTINA GAVE BIRTH to a baby girl in January 1898. They named her Maria Francesca Cesari y Paoli. Martina had hoped to name her after Mama, but Dino's family won the day and he selected the name, even though he already had a daughter, Juliana, from his first marriage. A reminder that Martina had little choice about anything in her life. The birth of our first niece delighted my sister Celia and me, and living with them became more precious. Martina was careful to not treat us as servants and allowed us to do our work mostly unsupervised. Pilar took on the duties of assisting with Francesca and picked up the nickname Nanny Pilar.

Dino and Martina hosted family dinners, usually on Saturdays. Servants spent the entire day preparing a small feast, with platters of roasted chicken, pork and smaller portions of beef. Young children were served in the kitchen with the help, while the adults gathered around a formally set table for dinner, during which many business matters were resolved.

Dino's children from his first marriage were now grown. There were no children roughhousing, and everything was in its place. I noted that their table had none of the scars of battle that our family table had. Dino's first wife was the queen of her household. Children were put to bed early and were seldom allowed in the formal living room. They had a playroom for rough housing. I remember visiting when I was young, and our parents disappeared into the living room while the servants took care of us. We didn't mind, because we felt we got away with more.

With no small children, the gatherings were all adults and when Juana's family came Celia and I were not guests. We served those nights.

Francesca would be a new beginning for Dino, and he was excited about being a father again. With Martina as his wife, the house was warm, and we used the once formal living room, previously reserved for Sundays. Celia lay on the floor, reading a book. Dino sprawled out on the settee with the newspaper, while Martina and I took the overstuffed chairs beside Antonio and Jorge. The baby joined us, in her cradle, completing the family. Martina insisted she not be kept in the nursery, or with the Nanny, as Dino's other children had been. Francesca looked like her father, with his warm, caramel eyes and soft, wavy dark hair. She was beautiful.

The house was vibrant with color. I'd never seen so many vases of fresh flowers. Each room of Dino's house had a colorful, fresh arrangement.

Papa's land was nearly barren of flowers. Vases lined up on the shelf in the house like dutiful soldiers ready for service. Lolo brought flowers home to Mama often.

When the afternoon meal was over, Antonio and

Jorge played guitar while Dino played string and accordion. Music filled Dino's home with joy. He was always in a good mood when they entertained. Martina was relaxed and having fun. When she laughed, she threw her head back and her body giggled in laughter; usually a signal the wine was taking effect, and a reminder to hold my glass back. It had been nearly a month since the Cesari family had gathered for a meal. The end of coffee growing season was a very busy time.

* * *

Dino and Martina enjoyed trips to Ponce for the theater or dinners with friends. On February 9, 1898 Governor General Manuel Macias gave town councils complete control in local matters.

"Martina, why don't we entertain guests here tomorrow?" Dino asked. "Have Isabella prepare Chicken Paprika. I like that dish."

"Is Ponce cancelled?"

"The Governor has no authority in civil or political matters, unless authorized by the Cabinet," Dino said. "The town councils are assuming control. I think we need to stay home for now."

"Why did the Governor do this?" Martina said. "He knows the town councils are corrupt." Her voice raised. "This is dangerous."

"Martina, there is nothing we can do for now," Dino said. "The town council and corrupt town police will wield their power. We must not be in their path."

* * *

Dino and Martina entertained friends for dinner, to celebrate the end of the coffee season. There was always plenty of good food, good wine and good cheer on these occasions. Celia and I served that night. We'd grown accustomed to being full-time domestics. It allowed us to be with Martina and to be out of Papa's house, where we would surely be facing a pre-arranged marriage. We gave most of our salary to Papa, to help him, and it saved our own skin.

Dino sat at the head of the festively dressed table, with Martina in the first seat of ten chairs. Jorge sat across from Martina, and Antonio was seated beside her. The candles were lit, blue and white patterned china was set with silver goblets, and silver flatware. Martina didn't own her own china, and I always wondered if she was bothered using the set from Dino's first wife. It had been a gift to her from Dino and came all the way from Corsica. Each plate reflected the light with a warm glow and the silver sparkled like a jewel. A huge bowl of fresh fruit served as a centerpiece for the festive table set for twenty.

Dino's daughter, Theresa and her husband Norberto brought two friends along.

"Arelia, have some more pork." Dino offered a platter heaped with juicy, roasted meat. "You are not eating tonight," he said.

"I had plenty, thank you." Arelia sipped on her glass of wine.

"Where are you from, Arelia?" Antonio asked.

"Cabo Rojo."

"Oh, yes, my Papa knows about Cabo Rojo. The red headed village of romance," he laughed. "Right, Papa?" Antonio looked down the table and continued.

"He took my mother there once, and the pink colored water from the salt flats captivated her to the extent that when she returned home, she wanted the whole house painted pink," he laughed.

"Many men have professed their love at the shores in Cabo Rojo and proposed marriage," Arelia said.

Martina took a drink of wine.

"Antonio, why don't you tell everyone about your day?" Dino said.

"Yes, I'm sure they would like to hear about it," Jorge gave a wry smile.

Antonio glared at Jorge. "Nothing special."

"Ha, ha!" Jorge laughed. "I heard you were chased by Ricardo's pig! Guess there won't be any bacon for Antonio tomorrow." He laughed again.

"It's not funny, Jorge! It was a wild boar and I'm lucky I wasn't gored!" Antonio said. "I'm going to kill that boar!"

"Oh," Arelia shuttered, "those are terrible looking monsters. Have you seen one Martina? They have tusks and hairy snouts ..."

"Forget it. Just forget it." Antonio said. "I don't want to talk about boars."

"Martina, what have you arranged for dessert tonight?" Dino asked.

"Los amantes de la torta, Lovers Cake." Martina laughed. "One bite and you will not be able to resist me, my darling!"

I served cake to each guest. I dropped a fork on the floor and Jorge reached down. He squeezed my hand as he looked deep into my eyes and smiled. He was the most handsome man in all of Puerto Rico, and I was the object of his affection. My cheeks flushed with heat, and I felt my heart beat faster. I wanted to run my fingers through his thick black hair, combing every wave. I'd never felt like this before and I only wanted to be alone with Jorge.

Celia looked at Antonio who stared at his cold, empty dessert plate.

Dino called out, "Celia, coffee please!"

There was a knock at the front door. The guests continued laughing, while Dino's servant, Julio answered the door. A moment later, he returned.

I watched the blood drain from Dino's face as Julio whispered into his ear. Dino, who seconds earlier was jovial, was now solemn. He dropped Martina's hand. He checked the time on his pocket watch, pushed back from the table and snorted angrily as he rose to his feet.

"Ladies and Gentlemen, I apologize but a matter calls for my attention," Dino said. "It seems our evening has come to an end. Julio will see you out. Martina, see that Francesca is asleep. Jorge, Antonio come with me." He turned and briskly walked to the study.

I looked to Jorge who was on his feet. "Fina, go to your room — now!" Jorge placed his hand gently on my shoulder.

Martina thanked her guests and rushed up the stairs to check on her baby daughter.

Celia sat, bewildered, looking to Antonio who was halfway across the room, walking toward the study. He had no instructions or words of comfort for her.

"Come, Celia," I said. "Let's go upstairs." I stood on the stairs and watched for a moment.

Julio ushered the final guests out the double

wooden doors. He closed and bolted them and slid the iron rod across for extra security.

Dino motioned for Jorge and Antonio to come to the study. He closed the door behind them.

I quickly ran across the foyer and listened.

"Don Rafael has come with news," Dino said. "Spain is closing in, the Government is intent on finding the men involved in The Intentona de Yauco barrio incident," Dino's voice raised, "Damn it! Now that the Governor has given authority to town councils to handle civil and political matters we are in greater danger. Tell them, Don Rafael."

"Yes," Don Rafael said. "The leaders of the Spanish Government have the names of some of the men involved at Yauco and local Police are hunting for them. I received word that three men have been arrested and put into prison. They want the man who killed the Pacheco girl."

"What names do they have?" Jorge asked.

Don Rafael shook his head and said, "I don't know all of them, but witnesses saw you. They claim you killed the girl."

"Father, you know it wasn't me—"

"They will come for you, Jorge," Dino said. "If you give up your brother, he will be hanged. The men they capture will be tortured until they speak and give up names of others, your name will come up as a leader. There's no protection from this." Dino checked his pocket watch. "Spend your life in prison or escape to Cuba."

"Jorge, listen, they are searching for the organizers," Don Rafael said. "They want the leaders. The men they put in prison were only rebel soldiers. They will not be as kind to the leaders. They will kill you; I am certain."

"Thank you, Don Rafael. You must go now." Dino said as he extended his hand.

Don Rafael embraced Dino and kissed him on the cheek. He hugged Antonio. As he gave Jorge a hug he said, "You can have a good life in Cuba." Then he left the room.

Dino shouted orders like a General. "We have little time! Antonio, ready the horses. I'll prepare the papers," he paced the floor and combed his beard with his fingers. "We were prepared for a rebel attack on our home, but we cannot stop this. Tonight, we lose a family member in exile." He looked at Jorge. "In one hour, I'll take Jorge to Guanica Harbor for a boat to Cuba. You'll need a disguise. Use your mother's clothes in the wardrobe closet." His voice slowed, "They won't be searching for a woman tonight."

I snuck up the service stairs to my bedroom before they opened the doors to the study. It was all I could do to hold in my screams. I couldn't let Jorge go. Why had I not stopped him from getting involved in Yauco? I knew about the secret meetings. I'd heard the men talking at Martina's wedding. I knew there were plans, but I had no idea what the cost of freedom would be. Now I would pay.

Jorge raced upstairs to his mother's old bedroom to prepare for his escape.

I sat on the bed, curled up in blankets. Tears washed down my cheeks. "I don't understand why this is happening. Jorge, why can't you take me with you? You can't leave me here. Will you come back?"

"Fina, listen to me." Jorge lowered his voice.

"In '68 my father was a part of a major revolt against Spain. He and a group of hundreds of rebels took control of Lares and they moved on to take over the next town. The Spanish militia surprised them in great numbers, and the rebels retreated back to Lares. The Governor ordered the Spanish militia to round up the rebels." Jorge circled his hand in the air. "Over 450 rebels were held in prison. A military court convicted them for treason and sedition and sentenced all the prisoners to death." His hand cut the air. "The incoming Governor granted a general amnesty early in 1869 and all prisoners were released. Many were sent into exile, and those who stayed never forgot." He paused. "We are the sons of those men."

"I know about the Grito de Lares," I said. "And I know about Yauco." I paused.

"We've never succeeded in our efforts for full independence. But some of the men who were exiled moved to New York City and formed the Puerto Rican Revolutionary Committee. They recruited men and gathered weapons for a major coup to begin in December. They secured the use of a steamship with 200 men from Cuba. When the committee from New York heard that the Spanish militia knew of their plans they feared arrest and our group here in Puerto Rico needed to act. Rather than wait for December, we took action in March."

"Wait a minute. We? You were there? Victor never told me that. I thought it was him and Antonio."

"Yes, I joined the rebellion."

"Why are they after you?"

"We attacked the Spanish militia's barracks to take over the ammunition and get a stronghold. Once again Spain was prepared and ambushed us. Just like twenty-nine years ago, at El Grito de Lares. We retreated and sent in a second group to attack a barrio at Yauco, but you know what happened."

"You were involved at Yauco? That was a year ago. I thought they arrested everyone they wanted."

"They want the leaders, the organizers."

"I know what the papers said. They reported the arrests of rebels and described how it failed. But tell me what really happened."

"My involvement in the Intentona de Yauco should have gone smoothly. I was in charge of a group of about 50 men, and we were supposed to take over a barrio I was familiar with. It was a quiet barrio, where there were no soldiers around. I know the families living there." Jorge cleared his throat. "Bullets were flying. One ball skimmed my shoulder. My chest pounded. I pulled the trigger, held my breath then fired again. I reloaded and continued, firing as fast as I could. The fire battle lasted only about twenty minutes before the soldiers swarmed in and began rounding men up. I saw my friends being captured and beaten with rifles. I escaped down the narrow streets. Thankfully, I knew my way." Jorge paused. "I came upon Antonio and Victor, hidden behind a house."

"What happened?" Fina asked.

"The Pacheco girl was in the street. What a horrific thing. Antonio had collapsed into tears on the ground."

"Oh, God."

"Victor pulled him together, and we got out of there," Jorge continued. "But I was seen. I've been watching over my shoulder ever since. The Spanish Militia arrested over 150 prisoners that day. You know the story. They accused them of various crimes, convicted them and took them to prison in Ponce.

Mattei Lluberas, our leader, went into exile in New York City and joined the Puerto Rico Commission. In December, those who participated were granted clemency and released from jail, but not me. I was never captured. Because a witness saw me, they believe I was the killer."

"Tell them," I said. "Tell them that you didn't do it."

"Give up Antonio? They'll still want me for being involved. I have to go."

Tears streamed down my face. "I overheard the conversation at the wedding that rushed the plans at Yauco. Someone from the Spanish militia also must have heard that day and alerted the Spanish government," I said. "What could I have done to stop this?"

"Nothing, my love." Jorge wiped my tears. "Our leader has been trying to convince President William McKinley to invade Puerto Rico for some time," Jorge said. "Now, if I don't go to Cuba, the Spanish Militia will come for me. And they will not go easy."

"You will receive clemency too. Like the others."

"No, my darling. They will surely make me suffer in prison or I will be hanged."

"Oh, no!" I gasped and sat up. "Jorge, please don't leave me here. Take me with you."

"Women aren't included in such things." Jorge moved quickly about the room. He placed a bible, a shirt, one pair of pants and a wallet of money in a satchel. He slipped his mother's black satin dress over his head and wiggled his shoulders through. He pushed his arms into the puffed sleeves with gathered black lace trim. Fortunately for Jorge, his mother had an appetite that was satisfied by her wealth. Jorge was the shortest of the sons, at five feet seven inches. The dress fit, with gathered satin fabric crossed at the waist, which bloomed into a full skirt and flowed to the floor, covering his boots. He placed a brimmed mourning bonnet on, which I tied under his chin. His slender frame was feminine enough to pass in the silhouette of darkness.

"Take me with you," I begged.

"Jorge!" a rap on the door alerted him to quicken his pace. "Coming along in there?" Antonio's voice was impatient.

"A few minutes!" Jorge called out.

Jorge turned and looked at me. He stepped to the bed; his dress swished with each step. He reached for me and I scooted to the edge of the bed. He kissed my forehead and my tear-streaked cheeks. He held me and kissed me the way he knew how to make me his.

"My sweet love. I will write and when it is safe, I will return for you."

"When?" I could barely speak.

"Be patient."

"But the—"

"I planned to marry you—" Jorge hugged me, then placed his hands on my shoulders. "I wanted to—"

He leaned in and kissed me once more.

Another knock on the door. "Father is waiting!" Jorge reached under his dress and pulled out his pocket watch. He checked the time; it was midnight. He placed the watch in my hand and said, "I'll write soon, and I will send for you."

I watched him walk out of the room, dressed in his mother's clothing, and felt my heart beat to the hollow sound of his boots clapping on the stairs. The echo left me cold, as if the life had drained from my body and gone with him. I ran to the open bedroom window, just in time to see Dino and Jorge ride off under the cover of darkness. I watched them ride past the gates and disappear into the night.

Time stood still and silent, but for the ticking of the pocket watch clutched to my breast.

DINO DROVE THE HORSES HARD. If the Soldiers caught up to them they would surely kill them both. It was a warm night and Jorge was sweating under the disguise. The wine from the evening sloshed in his stomach and nauseated him.

They were getting close to Guanica Harbor, and it was now safe to remove his mother's clothing. Dino and Jorge stopped along the roadside, and Jorge tossed the dress and bonnet into the bushes. He vomited the toxins. They arrived at the dock by 3 a.m. where they woke Dino's cousin, Hector, the captain of a fishing boat. From there, they would get Jorge to another boat headed for Cuba.

Hector would not question Dino's papers and would protect Jorge should the Spanish Government officials arrive.

Jorge was about to board when he turned and said, "Father, I'm sorry. I know you are angry. Antonio was supposed to be in my charge. He refused and followed Victor that day. We were ambushed immediately. Antonio panicked. Now, I am accused of the girl's murder. Antonio's crime, but if I defend myself, I betray my brother. So, I am left with no choice. I lose my country, my family, and the woman I love."

"Rebellion is a dangerous business. You should have never become a part of it. I was not a good father to have allowed it," said Dino. "I will get you to Cuba where you can live safely but you can never come back. You must understand." He reached out and held Jorge's arm with a firm grasp. "You can NEVER come back here," he repeated looking into Jorge's eyes. "They will put you in prison or kill you."

"I know that father. But Fina—" said Jorge.

"You will find another," said Dino. "I will write to you," Dino hugged his son and kissed him on the cheek. "You must go."

Jorge turned and walked down the dimly lit pier to the boat. His head hung low. Dino stood with the two horses in the moonlight. The tide was receding and the sound of the waves softly crashed onto the rocks calling for Dino's beloved son. Dino watched as the boat left the dock and sailed out of sight.

26

HORSES' HOOVES POUNDED the brick pavers, announcing to all that the local police and their volunteer brigade were inside the gates. Martina rose from her rocking chair with her daughter in her arms. She rushed to the window to see a group of men with rifles dismounting from their horses. Her long hair swung loose at her waist and she ran to her sister Celia's room. She opened the door "Celia! Wake up, the police are here. Quickly! Come to my room!"

Celia sat straight up in bed. Antonio popped up beside her. Martina, surprised, looked away and closed the door. She stepped into the hallway, leaned over the banister and listened as the servant answered the impatient rapping at the wooden door downstairs. He started to speak. "Good evening, Sir—"

The uniformed policemen pushed the doors open and entered the house, not waiting for the servant to finish his greeting. Martina quietly raced back to her daughter's room and closed the door behind them.

She could hear the men downstairs.

"Where is Don Bernardino Cesari?" demanded the officer. His voice was stern.

"Senior Cesari is out for a ride," replied the servant.

"At nearly midnight? Does Senior Cesari often ride at midnight?"

"It calms him for sleep," answered the servant.

"You seem very calm. Let's see who else is here to talk to us tonight," said the officer.

Martina heard the beat of footsteps up the stairwell and throughout the house. They are coming, she thought and looked around the room for a weapon. The banging from the kitchen signaled that the search continued. The sound of pots and pans crashing to the floor heightened the sense of fear. Fear and intimidation were part of the interrogation process.

Downstairs, the interrogation continued. She could hear the booming voices of the police officers in the dining room. "Where are Senior Cesari's sons tonight? Jorge and Antonio?"

"They're on a ride with their father," whimpered the servant.

A door slammed and Martina looked out the window to the courtyard below. Two police officers grabbed the servant by the arms and dragged him outside. The officer in charge followed, walking tall and proud, with his sword at his side. He ordered the servant tied to a post and with the wave of his hand, a man began to whip him. Martina retreated and listened from her hiding position in the corner. She could hear everything from her opened window.

After four lashes, the officer asked "Where is Dino Cesari? Where are his sons?"

The servant only wept.

Martina was crouched in the corner of the bedroom, with her infant daughter when the man barged in the door. He was scrawny and reminded her of a bow-legged donkey they once had. He slammed the door behind him, and Martina felt a tingle of fear as she took a breath and held it.

✡ ✡ ✡

Celia was curled up in the closet in her bedroom when the man opened the door. His face was sweaty from climbing the stairs and searching under beds. He grabbed her arm and hurled her with such force that she flew across the bed. Celia looked up to see his eyes had shifted from anger to menacing determination. She jumped up and moved toward the door. He stepped closer to her and began to reach for his trousers. He grabbed Celia and began to kiss her — hard. She fought with him but he would not stop. She tasted the cigar on his breath and bit his lip. He slapped her, knocking her back onto the bed. Celia cried out then she felt his hand over her mouth and nose. He pressed on her face so hard it shoved her head deep into the pillow. She smelled the cigar on his hands and clothes as she fought.

"You are a lively one," said the sweaty local as he straddled her.

Celia struggled for breath or even to move a muscle, the smell of his cigar permeated her nostrils. The man's weight was heavy on her slender body. Celia felt the steel blade of a knife on her neck.

"Do not move or make a sound."

The sweaty volunteer pushed Celia's nightgown up, exposing her breasts. He sliced her undergarments and pulled them off her body. Celia lay nude under his legs. He loosened his trousers, pulled them to his knees and with one thrust Celia felt him inside her. He used her as an animal attacks its prey. Licking, biting and devouring her face as he pumped himself into her. All the while, she felt the blade of the knife at her neck. As he ran his rough hand over her body, she wondered if she would be better off if he sliced her neck with the knife.

Finally, he finished and dismounted her. He took his time straightening his blue and white striped uniform, and replaced his cap.

Then he left the room.

✡ ✡ ✡

Martina felt helpless as she listened to the servant's cries from her window. What would this night bring? She thought. The scrawny man set his rifle down and moved closer to her.

"Stand up. Put the baby there," he ordered, pointing to the crib.

Fearing for her new baby daughter, Martina complied. When would Dino return? She needed him now! She thought.

The volunteer policeman opened the wardrobe closet and placed her daughter inside. Martina's fingers began to tremble. She thought of reaching for his rifle or a nearby heavy vase. She had to be successful. If she only banged him on the head, he would kill her daughter. She knew she would have to kill him or knock him out.

She turned to see the volunteer waiting for her. His eyes, black and cold, trained on her. His mustache was thin and failed to cover his upper lip which curled into a grotesque scar. It was him. The bandit, the man from the Perez attack, she thought. Terror shocked her body and she felt dizzy. She stepped sideways, away from the closet when he shoved her onto the bed. Martina began to cry as she felt his weight upon her.

The door burst open and a second man stepped in, dressed in a linen uniform with blue and white stripes. Martina looked to the door, frightened to think what was coming next.

"Recruit!" the second man ordered, "Report downstairs. Pronto!"

The bow-legged volunteer got up, grabbed his rifle and scurried out the door.

Martina sat up and released her emotion in a flood of tears. "Paulo! How did you get here?" Martina stuttered. "What are you do — doing?" She jumped up and raced to the closet, opened the door and picked up her baby.

Paulo stepped closer, and whispered "Martina, are you all right?"

She nodded, "Yes," and pulled back. "What are you doing here?"

"After the Governor made his proclamation, I thought I'd better check on you. Giving full power to local police means trouble in this area. I've heard some things," Paulo hung his head. "I can't talk too long. Be careful. And they cannot know about our past friendship."

"I don't understand." Trembling, she touched his hand.

"I work for the Governor," he explained. "Listen, we have no authority here," he waved his hand around the room. But I can stop them from doing certain things."

"Thank you, Paulo." Their eyes met for a moment, just as they did at the dances in San Juan. "I won't tell a soul."

"Were you harmed?" he asked.

"No." Martina shook her head and wept.

"Are you going to be all right?"

Martina nodded.

"Listen, if you ever need help, contact me." Paulo turned, walked to the doorway and said in a loud voice, "Sorry to disturb you, Señora Cesari," and closed the door.

Martina exhaled and kissed her daughter.

She listened to the sound of boots pounding on the tile floors as the search party made their way out, taking Paulo with them.

Francesca softly sobbed. Martina stood and held her close. She ran toward Celia's room and stopped in the hallway to peek over the railing to see the servant sitting on the tile floor below. The volunteer's whip had opened up gashes that poured a river of blood down his back.

Martina opened Celia's bedroom door and found her rocking on the floor, cutting her hair with a bread knife. Martina laid her daughter on the bed. "Celia, they're gone."

Celia's face was vacant.

"Did you hear me? They're gone."

She said, in a numb voice, "He raped me."

Martina pulled Celia's nightgown down to cover her legs and wrapped her in a blanket. She asked, "Where is Antonio? He was with you." Martina looked around the room for him. "Celia, where did Antonio go?"

Celia rocked, saying nothing.

Martina asked again, firmly, "Where is Antonio?"

Celia stared at the wall and mumbled, "He jumped out the window when the police arrived."

Martina's body began to shake.

"They were not the police."

Photo: Brian Shea

27

PAPA AND I MADE IT BACK from our ride to Guanica Harbor without coming across any police or locals. We stopped briefly at the bottom of the hill before returning to the house.

"Take a moment to catch your breath," Papa said. "They will be full of questions. The less you say, the better." He held up a finger. "We searched, but didn't find Dino."

"I've got it."

"Check yourself. Dust off any dirt, and wipe your hands." Papa tossed me a handkerchief. "Clean any dirt from your fingernails."

My hands shook and I began to cry.

Papa brought his horse along side mine and reached over. He took the handkerchief and wiped my hands, then folded it over and wiped my cheeks. "They will think you're upset over Jorge leaving. Say nothing else." He tucked the cloth into his pocket. "Are you ready?"

I nodded.

He turned his horse and I followed. We arrived back at the Cesari hacienda and found the gates were opened. I assumed they'd left them open, awaiting Dino's return. My mind played tricks on me. I couldn't clear the image of Dino's dead body on the ground. How would I ever forget what just happened? How would I keep this terrible secret?

Papa and I hitched our horses to the post and approached the quiet house. Papa stopped and took notice of the bloodied ropes tied to the post. He drew his pistol, looked at me, then took the porch in three large strides.

"Dear God," he whispered.

ONE WEEK LATER, on February 16, 1898, Isabella burst into the front room, breathless. She waved a note in the air and rushed her words. "Where is Señor Antonio?"

"Isabella, slow down. What's the problem?" I asked.

Martina asked, "Is it Dino?" She cupped her hands over her mouth. "Oh, my God."

I grabbed the note from Isabella while she muttered, "No, no. They blew up the American ship in Cuba!"

"What?" Martina gasped.

I read the note aloud. "Telegram received. American ship exploded in Cuba."

"The messenger just came. I was fixing breakfast," Isabella said as she paced back and forth. "Where is Señor Antonio?"

Martina and I locked eyes. We knew what this meant. The Americans were now engaged.

THE FIRST WEEK OF MARCH of 1898, Antonio called everyone to dinner. His sister Juliana and her husband Norberto came, along with Auntie Juana. Antonio took Dino's seat at the head of the table, which made us all feel uncomfortable.

"I received a letter from Jorge today," Antonio said.

"Oh, dear God!" I burst into tears.

"Any word from Dino?" Martina quickly added.

"Hold on," Antonio continued. "Jorge is fine and working at the sugar company in Cuba."

I exhaled and finally took a breath.

"He said to give his love to our father. I'll let you read his letter. But this confirms that my father is not in Cuba, as we had hoped. He's been missing for three weeks now." Antonio poured a glass of red wine from the decanter.

"We knew he didn't go with Jorge," Juliana said,

"because you spoke to our cousin, the boat captain, right?"

"Yes, but I thought perhaps he turned back after seeing the posse and took another boat. Or maybe traveled to another port. I imagined all sorts of things, like him going to Fajardo or someplace," Antonio shook his head. "I think he's in hiding, at a safe house."

"Hiding from what? He wasn't at Yauco. He'll be home soon," Celia said.

I looked at Auntie Juana for a reaction. she looked down, her face was stern and set. Old people no longer held onto hope the way young people did. They'd had lived through too much. I felt like she saw right through me and I turned the conversation.

"Antonio, you were here that night. What did you see?" I asked.

"My father and Jorge rode off, then you took off shortly after. Running after Jorge I suppose. I was upstairs when the locals arrived and I went for help."

"You went for help?" Martina said.

"I went to your Papa, Guillermo's house," Antonio said. "He raced off on his horse to help my father and Jorge. He thought the posse would be after them."

"Antonio, what about you and Victor?" I asked. "That left you two at Papa's house, right?"

"We gathered weapons and went after the local police too," Antonio said.

Martina cocked her head. "They were here, at our house. You didn't come back here until morning."

"They came for my father, my brother and me," Antonio said. "But we weren't here so the Police were out looking for us everywhere." Antonio looked around the room, presenting his case. "I knew they would be searching for Victor too. They have our names. We couldn't come back."

"Did Victor know my sisters were here alone?" I asked. "Did he know the locals were here?"

"Don't argue," Celia said.

"I told him the local police came to our house, looking for my father and Jorge, but they had left. The police would be on their way to your Papa's house, and out searching for us. They were going to round everyone up."

"You told Victor they had left?" I said. "But they hadn't left—"

"Enough," Auntie Juana interrupted. "Let us know when you hear from Jorge again. Give me the letter," she reached out her hand. "I want to read it. If you hear from Dino, message me immediately."

Antonio handed the letter to Juana.

I realized that my brother, Victor, had no idea that Antonio knew the town police were at Dino's house, and that my sisters were left alone. In the three weeks since the attack on my sisters, Celia wouldn't sleep alone. She slept with me most nights while Martina slept with Francesca. The first few nights, we all slept in the same room. During the daytime we kept to our usual routine, dinners were uncomfortable with Antonio and as the evening grew later, our nerves became more frayed and tension heightened.

After a few weeks Celia returned to her own bed. I was relieved, feeling exhausted. I needed a good night's sleep myself. If only I could occupy my mind and keep my thoughts from Jorge. I lay awake wondering what he was thinking, where he was in Cuba. Would he send for me soon? Sometimes I watched the sun rise after a sleepless night of imagining his life and his thoughts. My future was tied to him, and I was powerless over it.

✡ ✡ ✡

After a dinner of awkward conversation, Celia took me aside. “Fina, please don’t tell Victor about Antonio.”

“What do you mean?”

“Don’t tell him about Antonio leaving when the police were here.”

“Oh, you mean don’t tell Victor that Antonio escaped out the bedroom window? Leaving you and Martina all alone with the local bandits here? Don’t tell him that?”

“Fina, please.”

“Celia, he left you defenseless. He should answer for that.”

“We’re together now. Victor would ruin everything.”

“Together?” I shook my head.

“At least he’s here, not in Cuba.”

Her words landed on my cheek with a slap. “Have it your way, Celia.”

WE WATCHED THE NEWSPAPERS carefully. The following week, in March, 1898 I read an article that took my breath away:

LOCAL MAN FOUND MURDERED

A body was discovered by a worker in a field. The man had been tortured, burned and suffered stab wounds. The victim has not been identified and is described as white, black hair, in his twenties, with a scar on his lip.

"Martina, look at this," I handed her the paper.

"How awful," she said. "When will it stop?" She pushed it back across the table.

"Read it again," I pointed at the paper. "The last line. He had a scar on his lip."

Martina paused, then said, "You think it's him?

The man who came to the house, and tried to attack me. Maybe the same man who was at the Perez farm?"

I asked her, "Do you think Victor found him?"

"This man was tortured! How could you—"

"Don't be naïve. Victor's involved in plenty," I said. "You don't think he'd take revenge? He's doing things he doesn't talk about."

Martina's body quivered. "I'm not sure about this." She read the article again. "What do you mean, he's doing things he doesn't talk about?"

"Do you remember when Dino was having trouble with thieves stealing his coffee beans?" I said.

"Yes."

"He had Victor take care of it."

Martina furrowed her brow.

"Victor did special jobs for Dino," I said. "Outside of being his steward," I shook my finger. "Nobody stole from Dino again."

"I never heard about that," Martina said. "I knew plantation owners had their own ways, and the police hired locals to back them to run the law their way. But Dino never told me that Victor did anything like this for him."

I rose from my chair and walked to the dining room window. "He may not have," I said, "but it's changing, now that town councils are taking over. People are looking out for themselves. We can't trust anyone and we sure can't trust the local police or government."

Martina sat back in her chair and said, "Antonio is thinking of running for town council. He says if we don't get involved, then Ponce will be run by corrupt politicians, like many other towns. The Police are corrupt in some places." She folded the newspaper. "We don't want that. King Alfonso of Spain is finally allowing Puerto Rico some independence. Maybe this is our chance."

"You sound just like Papa. This is our chance," I said. "It's already corrupted. The businessmen want to run things, but there's still many old thinkers, loyal to Spain."

"If Dino were here, he would run for Council, and people would follow him." Martina's face grew sad. "Fina, I don't think Dino's coming back. Antonio's been trying to ask around town. To see if anyone from the posse knows anything. We think the police found Dino that night and killed him."

"I'm sorry. Do you think they're going to tell you? No, that's impossible." I began to pace the room. "I don't think he's coming back either." I stopped and stared out the window. "Tell Antonio, thank you for bringing the newspaper home," I said and walked out.

I had to see Victor. I was determined to walk every inch of the property until I found him.

* * *

I forgot about fear until I reached the bottom of the road to our house. Stories of bandits roaming the night had haunted me and going home brought back memories of Mama being attacked. When I looked around and found myself all alone it sent a chill down my spine. The once tranquil property was now eerie and danger seemed to loom everywhere.

There was no one in sight and the quiet reminded me there was no sound of Dino's mill running. Nerves on edge, I kept looking back, over my shoulder. I quickened my pace, placed my hand in my skirt pocket and rested my fingers on my pistol. Walking up the hill to our house, I passed by six abandoned shacks made from dried palm fronds with thatched roofs. They stood as ghostly reminders of days when Papa's farm was a thriving business. He had many workers back in the days, to tend the acres he owned. When we were children the coffee from Adjuntas was considered the finest in the world. Papa, and other local coffee plantation owners exported their coffee to Europe. We had a good life, with servants, private teachers and we had Mama. Now, Papa had only a small piece of his land and was barely making a living with a few hired hands.

It was a short trek up the hill to the barn. A broken donkey cart sat unattended. Papa wasn't in the barn and I didn't see him anywhere outside. Then I saw his donkey, roaming loose. Where is Rio, I thought. My mind raced and I began to panic.

I approached the house cautiously, and walked through the kitchen door. My heartbeat slowed down and I took a breath. Isabella was busy chopping vegetables and dropping them into a large pot on the stove.

"Fina, I didn't expect you today."

"I've come to see Victor. Do you know where he is?"

"He's working on a broken fence on the north parcel," Isabella said and wiped her brow.

"The North parcel. Way up there?" I picked up a carrot and ate it. "Where's Papa? There's a broken cart outside."

"He was working on it, but needed a part. He went to town to see the blacksmith."

"Oh," I turned to leave and Isabella started chopping meat. "Did he take the dog?"

She nodded, "Yes."

"Isabella, you're cooking steak? Papa is living the good life."

"It's only stew."

I knew Dino Cesari's house had just received a delivery of steaks at the house. "Isabella, did you take this from Dino's house?"

"He always said I could have the leftovers. Don Cesari does not like stewed meat. He prefers fresh cooked steak."

"There's plenty here." I stepped closer. "You could feed a large family. Dino was a wasteful man." I stuck my nose into the pot and sniffed. I smiled and looked at Isabella from the corner of my eye and said, "You are a resourceful woman."

"Was?" Isabella looked confused and said, "He will be back. Don Cesari has not tasted my beef stew." She let out a giggle. "It's better than steak night."

"Well, keep feeding Dino chicken stew and bring Papa the leftover steak." I gave a nervous smile. "I'll be over for dinner anytime." I said and headed for the door. "I may come back in for a bowl before I leave. First, I've got to see Victor."

Isabella shook her wooden spoon at me and said, "Don't you tell my secret now. I want to keep getting the extras, child."

"I'll see you later." I waved and walked out the door.

Victor would be working up there, I thought. "Make me walk the steepest grade on the property," I muttered to myself. My two layers of linen were hot and

I lifted my skirt to allow some air circulation. Sweat beaded on my forehead and pooled between my breasts. I felt a trickle of sweat drip from my neckline, run down my back, and soak into my undergarments. Now I would have to wash this entire ensemble, and take a bath. How I disliked to sweat. I trudged up the hillside, through the coffee trees and found Victor. Rio lay comfortably in the dirt beside him. The true Mayodormo.

"What are you doing up here?" he asked. Victor was repairing a broken fence at the north end of the property. He was wearing pants held up with a rope tied at the waist, and a shirt that looked like he'd worn it all week. Covered in dirt and sweat, he lifted the brim of his hat and wiped his face with a rag. Victor could throw a glance that was like looking at Mama's face, and he had that look right now.

I was grateful I'd seen Isabella and didn't have to walk the entire farm to find him.

"You know I always wondered, why do we have a fence here?" I asked. "If someone wants to steal a few coffee beans on this section of the plantation, let them. They'll probably fall off the edge, into the river anyway."

"Did you come to help me?" he asked.

"I read the newspaper, about the man they found tortured."

Victor continued wrapping the wire fence post.

"I need you to be honest with me," I stepped closer. "Tell me if you had anything to do with it." I placed one hand on my hip and the other shaded my eyes.

"Did you know him?" He squinted in the sun.

"No, but I wonder if he's the man who came to the hacienda the night Martina and Celia were attacked. The newspaper said he had a scar on his lip," I said. "The man who attacked the Perez', shortly after Mama was robbed, had a scar on his lip."

Victor put his tool down and removed his gloves. "There are things that are handled best — let's just say, in ways you don't need to know about. Know your place, and let men do their job."

"Listen brother, our place has been to do whatever is asked of us for the family. Martina sacrificed the love of her life to marry Dino for the family. I lost Jorge and now we're all living at the Cesari house to earn money for the family. I'm working as a servant, for heaven's sake." I could feel my face grow hot with anger and my voice deepened. "You don't have to worry about being sold into marriage, do you?"

"Stop." Victor raised his palm. "Don't get angry with me. I'm not ignorant about what's been going on and I've been working to protect you all along, to keep the bandits away from here. Do you think I was happy to see my sisters going off to live with the Cesaris? It's safer for you there. He can hire men to protect you." He laid his gloves on the fence post. "Listen, Dino treated Martina well, but I wasn't happy about Jorge and Antonio getting close to you and Celia."

I felt my cheeks blush. "Jorge was good to me," I said. "We're in love."

"And why aren't you in Cuba with him?"

"What about the man in the newspaper? Are you trying to avoid answering my question?"

"I asked around. The distinctive scar on his lip wasn't hard to track down," Victor's voice grew quiet. "When I found him, we talked."

"You talked?"

"I had a few questions. He answered."

"I see."

"Fina, don't push. He said some things I can't repeat."

"Try."

"He said, 'the three virgins weren't home, but I had the Queen Mother'. It made me sick to hear him speak."

"The Reina Madre," I mumbled. "Mama." I cupped my hands on my cheeks. "My God, I never—" Tears filled my eyes and the pain rolled down my cheeks. "And the Perez'?"

"I won't go on further. It was him and several of his friends."

I wiped my eyes and said, "Thanks for telling me."

I decided not to tell Victor about Antonio leaving Martina and Celia alone the night the local police and their posse came. The night Paulo appeared and saved Maria from the man with the scar on his lip. I was afraid of what Victor might do. I wasn't sure if I was protecting Victor from going to prison for doing something stupid, or if I cared about Antonio's life.

April 25 - Aug 12, 1898

MARTINA TOOK CELIA AND ME ASIDE. She said, "I can't believe it's April. It's been two months since Dino went on the midnight ride to take Jorge to Guanica Harbor. Nobody has seen him or heard from him and we're all desperate with grief. I want to believe he's in hiding, but something feels very bad." Martina's eyes welded up with tears. "I can't watch my own sisters serve in my house as domestics."

"You're sending us home?" Celia said.

"I'm asking you to stay with me, as my sisters. You are guests in this house, not servants."

"Oh, Martina," I looked around to be sure we had privacy. "How will Antonio take this?"

"It's my house. I'm Dino's wife."

I looked at Celia and felt nervous excitement. I took a deep breath and exhaled. "Let us help you with

Francesca or with the cooking."

"You can do whatever makes you happy. You can crochet all day or make baskets. I'm sewing. I just finished a dress. I'd go crazy if I didn't have something to work on." Martina raised her finger. "But Pilar's job is to nanny. I don't want to take that from her. You can assist her, but find other things. Help in the kitchen if you like."

"Thank you, sister," I said.

"Let's set a few days each week to resume our studies," Martina said. She smiled for the first time in months. "I can continue as your teacher. Let's all practice our French with letters to our cousins in Corsica. Papa would like that."

We looked at each other as if the idea should have come long ago.

ADDITIONAL GUARDS WERE PLACED around Dino's property twenty-four hours a day, working in shifts. Papa, Lolo and Victor lived alone at our house with no hired guards. Dino's guards crossed the road periodically and checked in on them.

Dino had an apartment above his general store in the town square in Ponce where he often stayed. Martina, Celia and I were at breakfast one morning, when Martina took a sip of coffee and made announcement. "I'm going to start going into Ponce, to look after the store."

"Really?" Celia's face lit up.

"I could use the company, and I'm sure you'd like to see friends in town."

"That sounds lovely!" I said. "We can tidy up the store. I can arrange the fabrics."

Celia's face dropped.

"I'll be taking care of the books," Martina said.

"You can watch Francesca and visit friends. No need to work in the store."

Celia smiled. "I don't mind helping a little."

"I want to give Pilar a day off," Martina said. "You can watch Francesca and stroll around town."

Dino had stayed overnight at the apartment anytime he had late business, a card game or when he and Martina attended a social event. I envied the opportunities she had with Dino, going to concerts and dinners with friends in town.

Now, it would be the three of us. Ponce had a wonderful outdoor market on Saturdays, and a few times I stayed overnight in the apartment with Dino and Martina. It was refreshing to get away from the big house and from domestic work. We bought fresh produce, and Dino took us out for supper. It made me feel special.

"I can't wait to go again," I said.

"This time will be with an armed driver," Martina said. "Maybe two. One driver and one on horseback."

We began making trips to Ponce with Martina. She decided the Saturday market day was busy in the store and doing the books after the weekend was best. Our trip day was set for Mondays. The retreat made me feel invigorated once again, and got me through the week. Each week, we came home with some small trinket or memento of the day. A bag of candy, candles or fabric for a new dress. Celia bought more candles than any of us which surprised me.

"Are you worried about a hurricane or something?" I laughed. "Goodness, Celia. You can open a candle store in Adjuntas."

"Worry about your own shopping list," Celia said.

"How much candy do you have in your bag?"

I popped a chocolate covered coconut cluster in my mouth and walked away.

* * *

Victor was nervous about our trips and made sure we were each armed with a handgun and a rifle was in the wagon. We had grown up around guns on the farm and my sisters showed mild interest. I followed my brothers around more than my sisters and was more practiced at shooting. Since the bandit attacks, we all went with Victor into the fields and trained. I felt fairly confident that I was a better shot than my protectors by the time we were finished with Victor's training.

It was Celia's job or mine to stay in the apartment with the baby while she napped; then we could take her out and see the town. We took turns going downstairs to the store and bought things at a family discount. Martina worked all day, and when she finished, we spent the evening together. The next morning, we always went to church and then paid a visit to Aunt Lottie before returning up the mountain road to our home. A few times we stayed in town for two nights. I found out later that was because our driver had too much to drink the night before and needed the day to sleep it off.

Our secluded and charming country life in the mountains had faded into an illusion. An image I had painted in my mind. Our new reality was being painfully, urgently presented in the newspapers.

Everyone was on edge after the United States lost a battleship, the U.S.S. Maine, when an explosion sank it in Havana, February, 1898. I was eager to go to Ponce with Martina, just to get my hands on a newspaper or hear from someone who'd heard anything.

"Has anyone heard from Jorge?" I asked. "I wonder what's happening in Cuba."

"This war between the Americans and Spain is going to get worse, and Spain is prepared for an invasion here," Martina said. "Did you hear that most of Spain's military has left Adjuntas? They're sending their soldiers to San Juan to fortify the entry point. El Morro will face battle once again."

DAYS SEEMED TO DRAG, but the calendar flew by. It was already July 1898. It had been five months since the Spanish soldiers stormed Dino Cesari's hacienda, attacked my sisters and tortured Dino's servant. Nearly half a year since Jorge escaped to Cuba and Dino went missing. His family presumed he'd been killed by the soldiers that night. I could not reveal the truth of what really happened to Dino that night. If I did, I would risk life in prison or death for what I had done. I wasn't sure they would hang a woman, but I had no doubt I would face a prison sentence. It was a predicament I could not escape. A secret I was finding impossible to live with.

Martina looked exhausted from sleepless nights, mourning the loss of her missing husband. Guilt and memories of Dino's bloodied corpse tortured me. I had nightmares and began to suffer headaches. How could I live with the knowledge of what happened to Dino and never give my sister the answer she so desperately sought? The story I held within boiled and churned in my stomach. I'm going to explain everything, I thought. I will tell Martina what happened to Dino.

"Where's Celia?" Martina stopped by my bedroom doorway, holding Francesca wrapped in a towel. They were headed to the kitchen for a bath. "I need to see if she's going to Ponce on Monday."

"She said she's not interested," I said. "She wants to finish an assignment for our studies, but I'd love to go."

"All right." Martina shrugged. "I spoke to Victor. He said he can take us."

I followed Martina downstairs to watch the baby have her bath. "Here, hold her a minute." Martina placed a large tub on the sink and filled it with hot water from the kettle on the stove. She filled it with cold water and stuck her elbow in it. "Just right. Come, Mejia." She reached for naked little Francesca and placed her in the water. She splashed and cooed.

"Da, da."

Martina looked at me and her eyes filled with tears. "Very good, sweetheart." She looked at me, "She's been saying that for a while now."

It occurred to me that Francesca would ask about her father one day. The day had come sooner than I hoped.

"Celia didn't want to come to the city? To study?" Martina said. She washed the baby's face, neck, and ears.

"No. Do you think she is afraid to leave the house now because of the threat of invasion? Or do you think she wants to stay home because of Antonio?" I waved my hand in the air. "Have you noticed the way she looks at him?"

"Uh, huh," she nodded her head. "They think they're being so coy, but I know what goes on in my house." Martina snorted. "He — oh, I'm so angry at him for leaving her that night. He jumped out the window to save himself from the police and left her all alone."

"He's a pig," I said. "I keep asking him for a letter from Jorge. Antonio says Jorge hasn't written to me, but there are letters to everyone else. It's strange."

"Watch over Celia," Martina said. "Antonio can be very charming, but if you cross him, he's ruthless." She finished washing Francesca and rinsed her.

"But I never did anything to him. Why don't I get word from Jorge? Is Antonio cutting me off or has Jorge forgotten me?" I began to cry.

Martina picked Francesca up out of the water and wrapped her in a towel. "Fina, we both have broken hearts," she said. "I know how it feels—"

"I'm sorry." How could I complain about missing Jorge when Martina's husband was dead? I couldn't tell her. I had to change the subject. "I understand. I'll watch out for Celia. He could take advantage of her, but she's going to do what she wants."

MARTINA WALKED INTO THE KITCHEN cradling a book. "Celia, what are you doing?" she asked. "I'm writing a letter." Celia looked up from her thin writing paper with three tears in it.

"Celia dear, you can't mail a letter with torn paper." Martina picked up the letter. "This paper is too flimsy. I'll get you some thick paper. She took the pen from Celia's hands and placed it in the well.

"I don't want to start over again," Celia complained. She slumped on the table with her head down.

"And where's the blotter?" Martina walked around, behind Celia. "You need to put a blotter down on the table before using ink."

Isabella stood at the kitchen sink, and looked over her shoulder.

I got up and went to the desk in Dino's office for a blotter and returned to the kitchen. I placed it on the table and put the ink well on top. "Better?"

"I'm sorry," Martina said. "Let's finish the letters then I want to do another lesson."

"Please finish your lesson soon ladies, or the lesson will be a cooking lesson," Isabella said. "I need the table to roll out dough."

"Yes, Isabella," Martina said.

We knew who really ran the house.

We wrote our letters to Corsica, in French. Addressed them to our cousins and set them aside. I put my study book down on the kitchen table. "When is the United States going to invade or send help?" I asked. "Spanish troops are everywhere now. They didn't all leave for San Juan."

"The Americans have been talking about Puerto Rico or Cuba being their prize for decades," Martina said. "I thought they would invade right after their ship exploded in February."

"They declared war with Spain in April, and the U.S.S. Maine continues to be in the news. Now it looks like Cuba will not be theirs because it sounds like Cuba will be independent," Martina said. "Do you know what that means for us?"

"They want our homeland?" Celia asked.

"That's right. The United States sees Puerto Rico as the perfect asset. Our location offers something valuable to them. They want to position themselves in the Caribbean, as a military strategy." Martina nodded her head. "Watch and see."

"How do you know this?" I asked.

"What they didn't teach us in school, I learned from others or read about in the newspapers. It may not be in our newspapers, but you need to read what's in the European or American papers. Papa taught me that. I used to get old European newspapers from Gertrude White, the grocer in town."

"The English woman?" I asked.

"She was in touch with family in England, who sent her news. When she finished the newspapers, she gave them to Papa. I read them all. Before I went away to school, she talked to me about life. In the world, not just here."

"What do you mean?" I asked.

"She knew I was leaving for the big city," Martina said. "She gave me a lovely teacup and talked with me about being in a strange new place. She moved all the way from England with her husband to Adjuntas many years ago and knew what it would be like for me to be away from home." Martina waved her hands in the air. "Anyway, when I returned home, I talked to her anytime I went to town. She knows what the news is around the world."

"I never talked to her about anything but groceries," I cocked my head and thought for a moment. "But I used to see Victor talking to her."

Celia sat with a look of confusion and her mouth hung open.

"Open your book to a world map, Celia. I'll show you England." Martina pointed to Great Britain. "Now, find Spain."

Celia struggled, but located Spain.

"Very good," Martina said. "Spain owns Puerto Rico. The United States is interested in taking it. You know, not too long before the revolution, during El Grito de Lares, in 1868, the United States tried to buy some of the islands in the Caribbean. They tried to purchase our beautiful little island of Culebra."

I interrupted. "No wonder Papa and the other local men were so incensed. Do you think El Grito de Lares was inspired in part by the United States threat? They fought for independence because the United States was going to take us from Spain?"

"Perhaps," Martina said. "What we are witness to now is very important. Our path to freedom from Spain has been slow and uncertain."

"It's very complicated," Celia said. She rested her elbow on the table and placed her chin on her hand. "I thought we have Spanish blood from Mama?"

"Spain offered land to people in Corsica and Italy so they could occupy the island, and they wanted Catholics here. That's when Papa came over, along with many others," Martina said. "Spain saw us as a possession for themselves. They needed our island because of our location for shipping and military position."

"Mama's family has been here forever," I said. "They have stories of pirates and slave trade. She always said her family came from Spain. On her father's side."

"That's right, she did," Martina said. "How do we separate ourselves from a country that lives within us? In our language and in our blood? It's been a struggle with Spain. They don't treat us as their own. They use us. The United States offered to buy Puerto Rico from Spain after El Grito de Lares." Martina nodded her head. "Spain refused, and the first political parties were organized here."

"So, this may be the only opportunity for the United States to have their prize," I said. "They're going to take it."

"Spain is prepared for an invasion, with soldiers in place in San Juan to protect the port of entry." Martina shook her head.

"This is a terrible problem," I said. "Spain wants to use us for goods and taxes. They don't educate our children or offer what they do for citizens of Spain. It's like we're servants for Spain.

Celia sat up and looked out the window. Her eyes darted back and forth. She said, "What about us? I don't want to be a servant to Spain. Are they going to fight over who gets us?"

"Don't worry, Celia," I said. "There is no fear of fighting in our little mountain town of Adjuntas. We're far away from San Juan."

Celia paused, then finally asked, "Then why are the Spanish soldiers all around? Everywhere we go I see them."

"They're all over the island," Martina said. "But the fighting will occur at San Juan. And, the United States is going to fight for our freedom from Spain. So that we can be independent, like Cuba."

"Right, everything will happen far from here. You've seen the fort in San Juan, El Morro," I said. "It's been through battles before. That's where the United States will invade. Don't worry, Celia."

Tiple

WE GOT UP EARLY, on July 25, 1898, and planned to go to Ponce and return the same day. We were nervous to be away from the house. Victor drove the carriage. Martina sat in the middle, beside Victor and held six-month-old Francesca on her lap. We didn't pack a food basket because we planned to go straight to Ponce. Martina would do a little work, then we could eat something and return home. Victor drove slowly and gave us a smooth ride for the baby. She had learned to say "da, da, da," and was making lots of noise. She was going to be a talker, like her mother. I was in love. She had learned to roll on the floor to get where she wanted and we had to watch her more closely. I planned to take her for a walk while Martina worked.

"What do you plan to do in the city today?" I asked.

"I'm going to pick up a new tiple," he said. "Santiago said he'd have one ready for me."

"That will be nice," Martina said. "I love guitar music."

"I don't know why, but I didn't get Mama's voice or Papa's talent with musical instruments," I said.

"Whoa," Victor pulled on the reins. A cloud of dust appeared ahead.

"What is that?" Victor pulled our carriage to the side of the narrow road. He drew his pistol and hopped out. "Get out," He whispered and motioned for us to get behind him.

"My God," Martina said.

The sound of feet pounding the dirt road echoed across the mountains delivering an ominous, eerie sense of fate. I pulled my gun from my dress pocket. "There's probably fifty of them," I noted.

Victor reached into the back of the wagon for his rifle, then crouched down beside the wheel. There was nowhere for us to go.

We sat and watched the Spanish military march up the main road. "There's more than fifty. They just keep coming," Victor said. "Look, they're filling the road."

"That's the end of them," Martina stated. "There must be over one hundred soldiers."

"I think more like two hundred. Looks like they're going to San Juan," Victor said. "They're headed for the military road. They've been pulling back from towns all around here," Victor put his gun back in his holster.

"I wouldn't want to be in San Juan," I said. "It's going to be a battleground."

36

WE ARRIVED IN PONCE with a degree of relief, although the local police were reckless and inexperienced. Mostly untrained volunteers, the men patrolled back and forth, carrying pistols with rags hanging from the barrels. We didn't rely on them for law and order; most of the men had never shot a gun before. One day a crowd gathered, and they shot their pistols into the air over the people's heads frightening everyone and scattering people in all directions. Politicians escaped punishment, going about their business riddled with criminal activity. Our beautiful city of Ponce was now unsafe and lawless.

The United States threatened military action and we took it seriously. They had already taken over Hawaii on July 8, 1898. Many Puerto Ricans didn't see it as a threat, but rather a rescue. It was the bloodshed we all feared.

Getting a newspaper was our first priority when arriving to town. We knew the Spanish military had posted additional soldiers at the entry points in San Juan. Since we were far from there we would have plenty of warning and time to get home should there be an attack.

We went straight to the Cesari general store. The street was bustling. I scanned the crowded street, looking for a friend. An ox cart blocked the front of the store, so we stopped behind it and got out. I made a quick stop at the telegraph office for my newspaper. The clerk sold me the current copy, July 25, 1898. He folded it in half and handed it to me. I tucked it under my arm and rushed out the door to join my sister at the store. Martina's clerk, Fernando manned the sales counter while he made a weak attempt to sweep. The cobwebs hanging from the ceiling told the story of his routine. Papa always said Fernando had the brain of a bird. When we failed at something we called each other Fernando. But not Martina. She was caring and nurturing to him. When she married Dino, she hired Fernando to work in the store. "Even a stupid man could sweep and carry boxes of stock", she said. Papa argued that Fernando was too skinny to carry enough stock to earn his pay. She didn't care and handed him a broom. I could see he wasn't earning his pay with that either.

Martina handed Francesca off to me and went to the back room to work on the ledger. I spotted a half-smoked cigar in an ashtray on the desk. Dino's? Or had Martina taken up the habit? No, I thought and shook my head.

"I'll go outside for a while," I said. Carrying Francesca in my arms, and a pistol in my skirt, I walked past a large, clear glass candy jar filled with candies wrapped in assorted colored papers. "What are these?" I asked Fernando.

"They came from Italy," he said.

"Take one," Martina called out from her table in the back. "I like the yellow ones. They're lemon."

"The woman has ears." I pulled on mine.

Fernando smiled, revealing his tobacco-stained teeth.

I took a pink candy, unwrapped it and popped it in my mouth. A burst of strawberry flavored delight saturated my tongue. "Mmm, delicious! Thanks." I carefully placed the lid on the jar.

Boom! I jumped and we all turned toward the door. I covered Francesca's head and held her close. A huge ox had forced his enormous head through the swinging wooden doors to the store and was trying to get inside. He knocked over a shelf and collapsed a table, spilling bags of rice and dried beans all over the floor. His handler, a skinny man, held tight to the rope around the ox's neck and pulled hard. Martina grabbed Francesca from my arms and crouched down behind a display.

Outside, a woman screamed, and a man yelled obscenities. The wild-eyed ox snorted and wailed. His usual cow-like moo sounded panicked. He screeched and made a high-pitched noise I had not heard before. I looked around and saw no other way out. If that ox gets loose in the store and stampedes, we're all going to be killed, I thought.

Fernando was not much bigger than me. We were in deep trouble. He approached the ox with the confidence of a bull fighter and threw a cloth over his eyes. He took hold of the rope around ox's neck and backed the beast out to the wooden walkway. Then he turned him around into the street, creating a cloud of dust, where he tied him to a post.

Fernando walked back in, folded the cloth and dropped it on the counter. He said, "Stupido. He doesn't know how to handle an animal; he should stay home."

I remembered to breathe again and looked at Martina, who was holding Francesca. "You were right," I said. "You do have everything in your store."

We burst into nervous laughter. "Fernando, you are a hero," I shouted with applause.

Martina grabbed a fan from the neatly organized display and was frantically cooling herself while swaying with Francesca in her arms.

I grabbed my newspaper and took Francesca. "We'll go outside so that you can finish your work." I looked at Fernando, "Do you need some help?"

"Take the baby outside," he said. He grinned like a matador who'd gored the bull.

I sat on a bench out front with Francesca, ready to comb through the paper for news or gossip. She was wide awake after the excitement of the ox, and I desperately needed fresh air and an opportunity to see old friends. It was a quiet, sunny day in town and a gentle sea breeze drifted through, keeping the temperature comfortable. Men were picking up supplies, with ox, horse, and donkey carts. Women stood and talked with friends; a dog scurried to keep up with his master. I was feeling especially nostalgic, thinking of Jorge. I remembered his words, "I will send for you." Was he as miserable as I was? My heart sank and I thought I'd ask Antonio once again if he'd received a letter for me.

My eyes glazed over and I found myself staring in the distance, up the hill at Cerro del Vigia, the cross overlooking the town of Ponce. Early settlers stayed watch there, on the lookout for merchant ships and pirates. The cross was beloved and precious to us, in its simplicity. Two intersecting tree trunks served and a loyal watchman stood guard twenty-four hours, seven days a week, with only a hut for protection. He alerted the town to incoming ships by raising a flag. If they didn't recognize the ship, no flag, a military brigade was sent to investigate.

The Cerro del Vigia served as a refuge for citizens in times of despair, after a storm or earthquake. It was thought to be a holy and protected place. Mama's cousin was one of the watchmen and I always gave a silent salute when in town, whether it was him on duty or another faithful servant. I said a prayer that my miserable life would change course and Jorge would send for me.

The spirit of the watchmen was within me that day. My eyes followed locals as they came and went. A scrawny farmer rode by with his dog following behind, and a rooster ran up and down the street clucking. Next week we must come on Saturday for the market day, I thought. How I missed it. My eyes drifted across the street to Catedral de Nuestra Señora de Guadalupe, our beloved church. Today I would light a candle for Jorge before we go home.

I unfolded the newspaper to see the headline.

UNITED STATES INVASION

Advance Guard expected to reach Puerto Rico any day.

Troops may be landed at once. San Juan on guard.

I jumped to my feet and ran into the store. "Martina!" I waved the paper. "It's happening any day."

"What?" Martina walked toward me and took the paper. "We'd better go home earlier than planned." She turned to look at her desk. "I'll pack up my ledgers and bring them home. You find Victor. We need to leave now!"

THE SOUND OF POUNDING HOOVES turned our attention outside. We walked to the door and looked down to the far end of the street. A cloud of dust raised alarm. The farmer's dog barked as if he was our patrol mascot.

The scrawny rider was a local. "The Americans are coming!" He galloped down the street yelling. "The United States landed at Guanica Harbor! They're here!"

I stood on the walkway and listened with Martina. A small crowd had gathered in the street. Everyone was looking around. The rider stopped and dismounted. He waved his arms and pointed. "They attacked at Guanica and they're on their way to Ponce!"

Cheers broke out, with a few rebel yells of protest. I held Francesca close and ran inside.

"They're coming!" I shouted. "The Americans came in at Guanica Bay!"

"Calm down," Martina said. She dismissed Fernando, locked up the store and we hurried upstairs to her apartment.

We heard gunfire and loud boom noises not far off. A shiver of fear ran through me like electricity. I looked out the window. "I was watching the Cerro del Vigia. There wasn't any warning."

"They didn't come in from Ponce," Martina snapped. "Get away from the window!"

I jumped back and almost tripped over a chair. "I have to see what's going on."

More gunfire and what sounded like cannon fire in the distance. A pounding on the door startled us both.

"Who is it?" Martina asked.

"It's Victor! Open up!"

Martina let him in.

"They offloaded their ships at Guanica Harbor!" Victor was out of breath. "The United States. They're here."

"We heard," I said and peeked outside.

"They took Yauco and they're arriving now," he said.

"We've got to go! I have to get home!" Martina began to grab things and stuff them into her bag.

"Martina, you're not going anywhere," Victor replied.

Francesca began to fuss on the floor.

Martina sobbed and then tried to catch her breath, "I can't — I can't stay. We have to go. We have to go now." She grabbed her hat.

I placed my hands on her shoulders. "Martina, you can't go out there; it's not safe. You're safe here. We have Victor with us and your baby needs us." I looked at

Victor and pulled a gun from my skirt. “Can we get out before they arrive?”

Victor looked at the gun in my hand, “I’m glad you remembered your training, but they’re marching up the street right now,” he said. “Listen, it sounds close.” He stepped to the window and looked out.

The sound of gunfire triggered all my senses. “Oh, my God. It’s happening right now.”

Victor kept his gun holstered. I put my gun in my bag. “We’re not going to be able to leave this apartment,” I said and I peered out the window. “Here they come.” I saw a platoon of soldiers march up the center of town. “This is was not what I expected. I imagined men lurking behind buildings, firing at Spanish soldiers from rooftops in a bloody battle.” Freedom for Puerto was unfolding before my eyes, but I wasn’t sure that it was real. I realized I was holding my breath and remembered to exhale and take a deep breath.

“Look at them,” Victor said. “The American military is on horseback and on foot. They’re looking all around, as if curious about us in the same way we are curious about them.”

“Wait, they’re carrying the United States flag,” I noticed.

Martina sobbed uncontrollably.

“Why is she crying?” Victor said. “We’ve been waiting for the Americans to come. Hoping they would come. She should be happy. Thank God there wasn’t much bloodshed. That was my fear.”

“I’m relieved, that is certain.” Martina took a deep breath and exhaled slowly. “What are they doing?”

I peeked out the window, “They’re raising an

American flag," I said. "They marched right up the center of the street."

"What?" Martina said.

"Well, what did you think they were going to do?" Victor said.

"I thought they would give us our freedom," I said. "We would fly our flag."

"We need their protection," Victor said.

Martina and I grew excited and wanted to scream in celebration but remained concealed.

"Listen," Victor placed his finger on his lips. "The people are yelling 'Viva Americanos! Viva Puerto Rico libre!' There's a small crowd gathered. Their general or commander is about to speak."

Martina stood back with Francesca in her arms. We all listened.

"He said they are here to give us a banner of freedom, and I believe him," I said.

"You know our flag was first flown at El Grito de Lares," Martina said. "If they're giving us independence,"— she cocked her head — "where is our Puerto Rican flag? Why not place their flag beside ours?"

"Did you hear Victor?" I asked. "They will restore order. Finally, the rebels and corrupt political leaders will be driven from our lives. The American soldiers will protect us."

"I carried our flag at Yauco," Victor said. "Believe me, I've fought for our freedom. Spain must've been caught off guard. I don't understand why they were met with no resistance."

"I think Spain sent their military to San Juan," I said. "They weren't protecting Guanica Harbor."

"Well, somebody's been paying attention," Victor remarked.

* * *

We made it back up the mountain to Adjuntas before the road was cut off. Then the wait began for the Americans to arrive and take our town over from Spain. Spanish soldiers ruled the area, and we had to be careful.

The road between Adjuntas and Ponce was closed and communication was cut off with the telegraph line being cut.

Martina entrusted Fernando to run the store in Ponce and take the deposits to the bank. The ledger would have to wait.

I ate from nerves, while Martina grew thin and her eyes looked hollow.

Latest Cablegrams

August 3, 1898. New York

Anarchy in Puerto Rico!

Gen'l Stone says Guerillas Plundering and Murdering

The latest dispatch from Ponce, P.R. reports that Gen'l Stone, who just returned from the vicinity, claims a state of anarchy exists in the country districts. The withdrawalof Spanish troops gives the guerillas free play.

A force of irregulars sacked and burned a large plantation near Adjuntas. Gen'l Stone claims that the people are terrorized, and they are praying for American protection.

He described the natives and Spaniards as "cutting each others throats" .

THE AMERICANS SET UP a command post in Ponce but had not yet taken control of surrounding towns. Spain positioned a small group of soldiers to hold Adjuntas. Women rarely left the property and never went out alone. Men moved about in pairs, only going out when necessary. Newspapers were hard to get, but when we got one, we devoured it. Mrs. White's grocery store news of the world was cut off.

Antonio's voice boomed through the house when he walked in the front door. "Come quick! I have news!"

Martina, Celia and I rushed in to get the latest news. Victor and Antonio laid a newspaper out on the dining room table. Antonio pointed to an article and said, "The Spanish Military's Colonel San Martin has been tried and sentenced to be shot in San Juan for allowing the Americans to take over Ponce without a fight."

Martina let out a yelp.

"He was a good man, a good soldier," Antonio continued, "but Spain is cruel and if you disappoint, or don't give the result they expect—" he ran his finger across his throat. "Colonel San Martin's second in command, Lieutenant Colonel Puig committed suicide at Utuado, on the road between Adjuntas and Arecibo."

"Spain's military is falling apart," Victor said. "We need to be very careful."

"They're forcing locals to serve as soldiers under the threat of death," Antonio said. "Things could get more dangerous around here. With the telegraph line on the mountain road cut off, we're isolated."

"I have a communication plan," Victor said. "We'll create a messaging system. Spanish soldiers will be watching plantation owners and businessmen closely, but we can use laborers and servants to send the messages," he looked at Pilar and the cook. "I mean no disrespect, but most of you are illiterate. The military won't suspect you. You can pass more freely about town, for work or delivering supplies. I will deliver messages too."

"I will too, but where will we deliver these messages?" I asked. "From plantation to plantation?"

"We can pass them from house to house all the way down the mountain, to Ponce. And return news back up here," Victor said. "I already talked to the grocer. They will be our central connection."

"Hmm, the grocer." Antonio rubbed his chin. "Victor, you place your trust in this man?"

"Yes, I talk to the grocer and his wife about things beyond our little island. They give me newspapers and tell me about what's going on in the world. What our newspapers aren't reporting. But since the invasion, newspapers aren't coming in. I think They would be very helpful."

Antonio raised his eyebrow. "You can't believe everything the American newspapers are printing."

"I understand," Victor said. "I'm talking about American newspapers, European papers and books from all around the world. I've been reading what world leaders are saying."

"I will send the first message," Antonio snapped. He looked at Pilar and said, "Have a laborer prepare to go to town with you." He walked into the study and closed the door.

"Victor, what if we are captured by a Spanish soldier with a message?" I asked.

"This is dangerous and only for those who volunteer." He looked at Pilar. "You don't have to do this. I will talk to Antonio."

"I want to," Pilar said.

"Me too," Celia said.

"I can't," Martina said. "I have to think of my daughter." She looked around at the faces in the room for approval.

"Don't worry, it's not as if we're going to be the local telegraph office," Victor said. "A message now and then is all we need. I think we can handle it."

Antonio came back into the room with a two-page, hand written note.

"We'll disguise it, wrapped like food and pack it in a basket," Victor said.

I wrapped the message in a banana leaf and tied the ends, in the same way Isabella taught me to make pork pasteles. Pilar placed the savory-looking note in her basket of fruit and flowers.

"This will be fine," Antonio said. "Give the message to the grocer in town and don't speak to him. Only to say this is from Antonio Cesari."

Pilar nodded. "I understand."

We continued our new messaging system with notes wrapped as food items, or hidden in laundry baskets, sometimes using the grocer as a connection. Word of mouth was spread from neighbor to neighbor. We reported the activities of the Spanish military, or if any news of the Americans trickled up to Adjuntas, we passed the information along.

At the end of the first week, Antonio sat in the living room in front of the picture window. I'd never seen him alone in the big room, quiet and contemplative. He held up a message and offered me a rare smile. "Our little underground newspaper," he said with quiet satisfaction.

"News? Shall I call for Pilar?"

"I will take care of it. General San Martin is alive," he said. "The newspaper reported he was shot, but the order was not carried out. He negotiated and will return to Spain to face his sentence."

"Is he fiercely loyal and wants to die in Spain?" I asked. "Or is he hoping for sympathy once he's back on home soil?"

"I don't know, but we can't rely on what's printed in the newspapers. I think our messaging system, person to person, is more trustworthy."

"And Puig?" I asked.

"He's dead. But now I heard he committed suicide on the beach, not on the road to Utuado. I don't know which is true, only that he's dead."

"I'm going to the kitchen. Can I send Pilar to see you?"

"I'll walk with you." Antonio stroked his moustache.

We found the cook, washing a chicken in the sink. Antonio walked through to the back bedrooms where domestics were housed. I heard him knock on Pilar's bedroom door and enter. My eyes met the cook's and I quickly diverted my gaze. I took a piece of fruit and walked out.

Sending a messenger to Ponce was rare and riskier but we were able to send word when a supply wagon was dispatched. The word back was disheartening. The Americans wanted to take Adjuntas, but kept pushing back plans because of the difficult approach. Access to our town was by a narrow, one-lane mountain road. We would have to hold on.

Martina and I sat in the spare bedroom, now a sewing room filled with craft projects. The bed was covered with fabrics, threads and half-finished crocheted pieces. We even learned to make straw hats while secluded at home. A special project was our first priority and we talked about everything in the world, while we worked.

"I'm tired of this isolation. How long will we have to wait before they get here?" I pulled a stitch and tied a knot.

"I pray each night the Americans will come. But God isn't answering," Martina said. "Four months have passed since the start of the war, and a month since they took Ponce. We're damned on this mountain." Martina shook out her fabric piece. "While we wait, the criminals for Spain attack our plantations. You know they leave the laborers alone. They beat the owners and rape their women. Maybe we'll have to take on the Spanish military ourselves."

"The attacks are so close. They're working their way up the road. The Tirado house burned completely before anyone could come to help them." I shook my head. "They said the burnt bodies of the women couldn't be identified." My voice rose. "They called them 'the women'. The bodies of Inez and Petra. Call them by their names. You think Spain will punish those soldiers? I don't think so. They punish those who don't kill for them."

"The Americans can't come soon enough," Martina said and patted the gun in her skirt. "This will always be at my side. And you won't get me to leave this house."

"Victor sent a messenger to the Americans in Ponce to let them know about the attacks and that Spanish soldiers are murdering women," I said. "It's terrifying. With the rainy season near, I'm afraid they've given up plans for an advance on Adjuntas."

"The Americans will find a way. Until then, I'm here with you, and we can fight." I put my hand on my pistol pocket. "Pass me the thread."

"Don't forget, we have the key to Dino's ammunition room." Martina looked up from her sewing. Our eyes met and she placed her finger over her lips. "Antonio and Victor are nearby." She continued. "I miss the days of going to town with Papa or the boys." Martina sighed.

"You know what I want?" Martina said. "Rope sandals."

"What would Mama say?" I laughed. "I know what she'd say. You're going to join the common women now?"

"I'm quite serious," Martina replied. "I want a pair to wear at home. I've always envied the women who wear them. They look comfortable. I'll wear my leather shoes in public."

"Well then, I want to smoke," I said. "Do you remember prune faced Aunt Juana smoking in the wagon? I was shocked, but have thought about it since and want to try smoking."

"Cigar or cigarette?"

We giggled nervously. "Perhaps a cigarette," I suggested. "It looks more delicate."

"It can be arranged." Martina smiled.

"Victor goes to town and can get your sandals," I said.

Victor appeared in the doorway of the sewing room. "How's it coming along?" He came to visit Antonio often. They had private conversations about plans for an independent Puerto Rico.

"We're almost finished." I fluffed the large red, white and blue sewing project. "Celia's working on the stars and we have to add the last row of fabric."

"I can't believe you ladies are sewing an American flag." He raised his fist. "I'm proud of you for your courage. We will raise it soon."

"We weren't sure how many states there were currently," Martina said. "We determined there were forty-five. I hope we're right."

"I wish they'd get here," I said. "Spain has withdrawn nearly all of their soldiers. How can a group of a dozen Spanish soldiers keep the Americans from taking over?"

"Unfortunately, they'll have to come in by single file," Victor said. "The road is too narrow to march in a platoon. The Spanish military can shoot them from the trees. It would be easy to pick them off one by one."

"I wish that wasn't the only way into town," Martina said.

"Can't we help them?" I asked.

"Believe me, we are ready," Victor said. "Just waiting for them to come."

I tied a knot in my fabric and said, "Pass the scissors."

PAPA WAS FILLING A BUCKET at the water pump when a rider approached fast on horseback, leaving a cloud of dust behind him. Papa squinted from the sun and adjusted his hat. He released his hand from his pistol. The rider was the boy from the grocery store in town. He served as messenger often. He stopped and rushed his words. "Ernesto sent me. The Spanish soldiers are leaving. Many." He panted and tried to catch his breath. "Hundreds arrived and now they are all leaving."

"They arrived? Or they're leaving?"

"They came through town." He caught his breath and waved his arms in the air excitedly. "The soldiers from our town are joining them and they're all leaving."

"Are they going to fight the Americans?" Papa dropped his bucket of water. "Thank you. Go to the Cesari Hacienda and give this news to Antonio Cesari.

Papa turned and ran toward the house. He pulled the whistle that hung on a chain around his neck and blew it in loud short bursts.

Victor came running from up the hill. "What is it, Papa?"

Papa gave Victor the news, that the Spanish soldiers were on the move. They grabbed their pistols and ran to the barn, They added a machete to their arsenal and saddled their horses. Not wanting to alert the soldiers, they rode in silence, forgoing the customary whistle blowing. Adjuntas was about a ten-minute ride from Papa's farm. Upon arrival, they discovered a quiet town. They tied the horses and entered the grocery store. The usually busy store was empty.

"We got your message," Papa said.

"Four hundred Spanish soldiers rode through earlier, but they left. Maybe one or two hundred remain," the grocer said. "Americanos can handle them."

Victor looked at Papa and said, "They're retreating and pulling back to San Juan."

"I don't know, San Juan is about forty miles." The grocer scratched his cheek. "Ponce is about twenty miles. We got a message from the American leader, General Stone," the grocer said with a smile. "They're making their advance."

"Finally!" Victor smiled wide for the first time in months. "Let's get some men and show them the way," he said. Victor strapped a machete around his narrowing waist and tightened the leather strap. He would need to make another hole. He'd lost too much weight. He pulled up his pants and tightened the rope holding the waistband. "This had better be the last time we have to do this," he said.

Images of Yauco flashed through his mind. Soldiers on horseback, his men shooting and fleeing, a girl lying in thc street, blood. He took the handkerchief from his pocket and wiped his face, then walked into the street to rally the local men. He raised his machete in the air and called out, "Viva Americanos!"

Papa and Victor sent locals in every direction to get the word out. They gathered a group of armed men with machetes and headed out of town to guide the Americans and assist in the fight against the Spanish soldiers.

The Americans understood that going up the narrow road single file was a dangerous position, and they risked being shot by the Spanish soldiers. They would be sitting ducks, clustered in a small group. They needed to appear as if they were a large platoon, so they spread out in a long line of soldiers. It was a risky strategy. When the enemy saw Americans, one after another coming up the road, it would appear as if the line of soldiers never ended. In fact, the group was small, assisted by Victor and a small group of locals armed with machetes. General Stone and his soldiers met little resistance from Spain. Most were skinny, tired soldiers or locals made to serve and they laid down their weapons or surrendered almost immediately. A few were held as prisoners, while others converted to the American side, grateful to be free from Spain's rule.

When Papa and Victor returned to Adjuntas with the Americans, they saw a flurry of activity. A crowd gathered in the square and the air was filled with the buzz of voices.

One phrase was repeated: "Viva Americanos."

* * *

At the hacienda, a bang on the kitchen door alerted Antonio. "Hey, where is everyone?" he yelled impatiently as he walked through the house in his bare feet. Celia followed dutifully in her nightdress and wrapped a shawl around her shoulders.

The high ceilings and plaster walls echoed Antonio's words. "Why does nobody get the door?" He opened the kitchen door. It was a messenger. "What is it now?"

"I came back to tell you that the Americanos are coming," he said. "We're meeting in town to welcome them. Some men went down the road to help fight and guide them in."

"Thank you." Antonio closed the door on the messenger.

"Martina! Fina!" Antonio called out. "Celia, get the flag."

"Oh, my God," Celia squealed. She stood in the kitchen doorway with Martina.

"Get the flag. Let's go," Antonio said. "Hurry." He put on his freshly polished shoes.

Martina knocked on Nanny Pilar's bedroom door in the back hallway. "Pilar, I'm going to town. I need you to watch Francesca."

Antonio made sure a handful of men stayed for security of the property. I wrapped the flag in a blanket and placed it in a basket, covered with laundry. I prayed the Spanish soldiers wouldn't stop us, for their sake and ours.

Antonio drove the carriage fast. Martina and I held our pistols at the ready in case we encountered trouble. I gave Celia a nod and she pulled her pistol from her pocket. We nervously watched every tree and held our breath at every turn. Thankfully, there were no soldiers to be seen along the road.

We turned down the street into town and saw the jubilant crowd in the square. People stood waving their small, homemade American flags. Women carried armfuls of flowers. Adjuntas was a town of roses, vibrant and colorful. For one brief moment my mind captured it as if it were a painting. I exhaled and tucked my pistol in my skirt pocket.

Antonio pulled up as close as he could and stopped his carriage. We hopped out and I reached for the laundry basket in the back. Celia knocked it over and I quickly unwrapped our huge flag. "Let's go," she said.

We wiggled through the crowd to reach the Alcalde's Office. People commented, "Look at what they made," or "it's an American flag," as we walked by. I felt as though we did something for our whole country, not only for our town.

Our Alcalde, or Mayor greeted us with a smile. "My goodness, ladies. What do we have here?"

"We've made an American flag and would like to present it to the American General," I elaborated.

"Let's see it," he said.

Martina and Celia unfolded the flag and held it up. The crowd roared.

"Your American flag is beautiful with the stars and stripes in red, white and blue," the mayor said. "Stitched with Puerto Rican hands, from fabric in Adjuntas. It is a true honor."

Tears welled up in my eyes. I looked at Martina and Celia. They weren't holding back their emotions. I nodded my approval and we gave each other a little smile.

"I will present your flag to General Stone when he

arrives," the mayor said.

"Thank you." I stepped back with my sisters. We turned to see the Americans arriving at the end of the street. The crowd surrounded them like a parade. Women carried armfuls of flowers and kissed the hands of soldiers on horseback. They tossed flowers into the sky, letting them fall down like rain onto the procession. The horses trotted on a flower covered street, muting the sound of their hooves. The locals shouted, "Viva Americanos and Viva Puerto Rico libre!" Women presented their hand sewn flags and I realized we weren't the only ones who'd made one. The procession slowly made its way into the square. I reached up to wave at the American General, who smiled at us. His hand touched mine and I realized it was the first time a male stranger touched me without a gloved hand.

The American leader went inside the Alcalde Office. Locals brought milk, liquor, fruit and gifts for General Stone.

"Look at that one." Martina laughed. She pointed at a fat American soldier on a horse. "The poor pony has a hard job."

I looked around at our skinny men and realized they didn't have enough food to be plump. I paused for a moment to look at Martina and Celia and saw just how thin we were. These men had full faces. They must come from wealthy families to have such rich diets.

"Victor! Papa!" I cried out and began to weep. My father and brother marched at the end of a line of American soldiers, along with other brave locals, who carried nothing but machetes. I'd never seen Victor smile so broadly and his chest was puffed out like a proud rooster. They approached, covered in dust. I threw my arms around my heroes and kissed them on the cheek.

"We made it," Victor whispered in my ear.

"How did you get here?" Antonio asked. "Was there a battle?"

"Thankfully, no," Victor said. "Instead, it rained flowers." He looked up and smiled.

"What about the Spanish soldiers?" Antonio asked.

"We met no resistance. The Americans took a small group of prisoners. The rest were locals who surrendered their weapons or ran off. People came out of their houses to greet us as we came up the road, and when we arrived to town, this welcome is what we got."

"This is the way of Adjuntas," Antonio said.

General Stone came out of the Alcalde Office and made a speech to the crowd. It was followed by great cheers and applause.

"General, we have a very special gift for you," the mayor said.

The General smiled and rocked on his heels. "Oh?" He looked around.

The mayor waved his hand to his assistant, who brought out the flag that we had made. "General, we have an American flag. It was made by women in our town, and we would like you to raise it."

"Oh, no," General Stone said and waved his hands. "I couldn't. That is your honor."

The crowd cheered and the mayor insisted. "We insist. Look at the people. They want you to do the honors."

"Very well," General Stone agreed.

The crowd cheered.

General Stone waved to his men and two soldiers snapped to. "Men, raise the flag."

The American soldiers prepared the flag and General Stone placed his hand on the rope to raise it. The crowd watched and listened as the ceremony was foreign to us. The men placed their hands on their chests and projected their voices in unison. I wished I knew what they said, but the ceremony itself was very symbolic.

A sense of order and calm came over me as I watched the flag raising. We had lived in chaos, disorder and terror for so long. The Spanish soldiers were angry at their weakened position against the Americans, and they were taking it out against us. Punishing us with attacks, rapes and murders. The Americans brought order, discipline and law. Finally, we might have peace and safety.

I took a breath of fragrant air and listened to the nearby river in the background. It flowed, like applause to welcome the Americans. I drank in the moment and knew I would remember it forever.

The Americans might very well have been met with anger or been attacked by the Spanish soldiers. They could have been ambushed while in town, but they were not. Instead, they were treated as heroes. After the flag raising, we danced and sang in the flower covered street.

I looked around and realized I was not alone in my joyful tears.

Days later I cried tears of relief and joined many Puerto Ricans in celebration when they achieved a complete takeover from Spain by August 12, 1898. Finally, free from Spain's stranglehold, we had hope that we could live freely and prosper. We hoped that Puerto Rico would be independent and have the protection of the laws of the United States.

Dinner hour was relaxed and I began to feel hope that our old life might return after all.

✡ ✡ ✡

"I'm running for Town Council," Antonio said.

"Oh, so fast? I didn't know that the Americans had organized a government in Adjuntas yet," Martina said.

"Ponce Town Council."

Martina stiffened. "I see."

"You're not going to wish me luck?"

"Of course, good luck. I'm sure you'll win," she said. "And you'll do good things for Ponce." Martina gave a weak smile.

Antonio became empowered by the new opportunities afforded him, as the head of the Cesari family and with the United States protection, Puerto Rico was headed toward independence. Local businessmen stepped into political leadership roles and Antonio controlled the Cesari business. He ran for Ponce town office to help reform our government and wanted to establish his position as a prominent business owner in town. He won and was our first hope of positive change.

"Martina, do you remember when the local police came that night?" I said. "Antonio escaped out the window and left Celia defenseless."

"Why bring this up?" Martina asked.

"When the messenger brought news that the Americans were making their way up the mountain. Papa and Victor joined others to fight. They walked on foot, with no rifles, only machetes. Antonio got the same message and joined the women to bring the flag to the town square."

Martina shook her head. "Are you just figuring this out now? Antonio is a coward and would push his grandmother out front to save himself."

"Our hope for the future of Ponce," I said.

MY INFATUATION WITH the United States faded into bitterness and resentment when Martina brought the newspaper home.

"Fina, Celia! The United States signed the Treaty of Paris and annexed Puerto Rico." She held up the paper.

"What does that mean?" Celia pulled up a chair at the table.

Martina handed me the paper. "Well, the treaty ended the war," she said. "I'm grateful for that, but many will see it as a takeover. I talked to Antonio. The U.S. dollar will take over as our currency. Hopefully that will stabilize our economy."

"Did you read all of this?" My voice raised. "It says they're going to change our country's name from Puerto Rico to Porto Rico. Are they trying to Americanize the spelling, or Americanize us? What happened to our independence?" I felt my face flush with heat.

Antonio walked into the kitchen, stone-faced. I

expected news of someone's death. "They passed a law," he said. "It's now a felony to fly the Puerto Rican flag."

"They finally got their island in the Caribbean," I sighed. I walked out before I exploded and directed my anger toward Antonio.

I went to my bedroom and slammed the door. I folded my homeland's flag, wrapped it in a tear-stained linen sheet and placed it carefully in my trunk. I would never give it up.

Martina quietly opened my bedroom door and came inside. "Fina, don't give up hope. Change comes slowly, but it comes."

"Antonio laid down for the Americans when we needed him to be a leader for Ponce and for our independence," I said. I shook with anger.

Martina sat next to me on the bed. "Freedom is not ours yet. The American military will govern our country, but we need them for now. The children's orphanage is being organized; the troublemakers were run out of town or recruited."

I wiped my tears. "Really? You think it's going to work out for us?"

"Yes, give it a little time. Town leaders have been meeting with the Americans. They are making lists of our needs and communicating with the government in the States. Plans are being made for things that we couldn't do without them."

"I've held onto nothing but hope. It's all we have left. I guess I can't give that up too." I gave Martina a weak smile.

✡ ✡ ✡

Four days later, Celia walked into the living room and dropped a newspaper on the sofa. "Antonio brought the paper," she said.

I picked it up and read aloud, "It says in December 1898, members of the Porto Rican committee in New York were in meetings to discuss education. They were fighting to get public schools for the children, like they have for children in the states."

"Look at that," Martina said. "Spain held us as a colony, with little support or education for our people. Look at all the illiterates. We asked for more from the U.S. and they're delivering."

"It also says we're only to be a territory as a temporary measure." I stood and read on, "The article says they hope for statehood, once we learn the ways of American government."

We cheered and jumped around the kitchen like children.

Antonio

EARLY ONE OCTOBER MORNING in 1898, I was helping the cook with breakfast when a rapid bang on the kitchen door startled me. I turned off the stove burner and answered the door to see a ghostly-faced messenger who pulled a note from his shirt.

He was panting from his run up the hill, and didn't need to say a word. The panic in his eyes said it. I took the note and ran upstairs to Antonio's room. I knocked on his bedroom door.

"Who is it?"

"I have a message," I said.

Antonio opened the door a crack and took the note from me. I went to Celia's room to wake her. Her bed was empty. My heart sank and I knew why Antonio hadn't open her door.

I started down the stairs and Antonio flew out of his room, yelling. "Everyone, come downstairs!"

We gathered in the dining room. Antonio held the note and said, "There's been another attack at a farm." Veins bulged in Antonio's neck. "They killed Rueben Soltero."

Gasps filled the air and one servant, Yasina, burst into tears. She had worked for the Soltero family.

"There were twenty gang members this time. They were cruel and took their time at the house." Antonio swallowed hard, then continued, "The brutes forced his daughters to dance around their father's dead body."

Moans echoed in the room. Martina said, "Are the women okay?"

"I don't know anything more," Antonio said. He tucked the note in his pocket. "I'll increase the number of guards. And listen, I want everyone to have a gun."

"But the Americans require us to have permits now," the cook said.

"I will get a permit," Antonio said. "Everyone in the house will have a gun." He looked at the cook. "The Americans. Ha! They just raised their flag two weeks ago and offered us protection. I think we need to protect ourselves."

"I have a gun," I said. "The city women in Ponce used to say we were country folk up here in the mountains, but I'll bet they wish they could shoot like us now."

"Don't tell people you have guns," Antonio said. "Start practicing in the fields. And you'd better be good."

I gave Martina a half-smile. "No problem,"

✡ ✡ ✡

We lived in terror. Papa wouldn't let us come to

visit, believing Dino's house was the safest place for us. Even behind the walls of the Cesari hacienda, we kept a pistol in our apron pockets. We doubled up in our rooms at night. We sisters slept together, or Celia slept with Antonio. I began to slip into Jorge's empty bed when I was alone, wanting to feel closer to him. Each night I wished he would send for me.

Weeks passed and one day Martina walked into the dining room, where I was stitching a project at the table.

"My God, did you hear the news?" Martina asked. "They arrested the gang members from the murder," Martina said. "They're going to trial. One of them worked here."

"Here?" I stopped sewing. "Who was he?"

"Antonio said he was a man hired for one season. He found him sleeping in the fields and let him go."

"Well," I said. "He might have been tired from his night raids."

"He was not someone who was ever at the house. Never served as a guard."

"Still, he worked for the Cesaris'?"

Martina nodded yes. "I know, this is very bad. The enemy was right here."

"Oh, God." My hands began to shake. "He was across the road from our house." I started to cry. "Mama!"

* * *

We were glad when the gang members were sentenced by Spanish law. They were garroted in December.

Lolo

BY JANUARY 1, 1899, we followed news of events in Cuba. We'd heard that Spanish forces left Cuba. She was now independent. Many of us felt betrayed that the banner of freedom promised by the Americans had not become our reality. Some loyal to Spain remained a threat and a peaceful life in the mountains eluded us.

My mind filled with thoughts of Jorge. I hoped that he was safe and that he would find his way back to me.

The United States maintained their headquarters just outside Ponce, the second largest town in Porto Rico. They had built a depot at Comercio Street for storing gunpowder, equipment and explosive weaponry. People in local barrios were concerned about so much flammable material being stored in one place, but it was a necessary part of war.

I remembered seeing rooms filled with weapons at Dino's house during the time of rebellion, so it didn't bother me too much. I trusted the American soldiers, and felt they could guard it properly. There was a stable nearby for horses and mules used to haul the equipment, and it was stocked with hay.

On January 25, 1899 the town of Ponce was once again threatened. "Did you hear the news?" Victor barged in through the kitchen door at dawn. "There was a huge fire in Ponce last night."

Antonio set down his cup of coffee. "What?" He rose from his chair. "Why was I not notified?"

Victor slapped the back of Antonio's head and said, "I'm notifying you." He scooped a mouthful of eggs from the skillet. "Let's go!"

"What fire?" Martina asked. "Is it out?"

"Yes, it's out," Victor said.

Antonio grabbed his hat, gun and holster and walked out the door with Victor.

I realized my mouth was hanging open and closed it. "Oh, my God," I looked at Martina. "Did you see that?"

"I know. It's scary, but I'm glad to hear the fire is out."

"No, did you see what Victor did?"

"What?" Martina looked around the kitchen.

"Victor marched in here and ran the room. He just slapped Antonio on the back of the head the way he did to us kids at home. He talked to Antonio the way he talks to the hired hands."

"Oh, my," Martina's eyes widened. "He did. I saw it too."

"We grew up together, but I've never seen Victor boss Antonio around before. I've never seen anyone boss

Antonio around."

⁂

Antonio returned late that night and we peppered him with questions. "Hold on, I'll tell you all about it." He removed his suit jacket and placed it on the back of the kitchen chair. He took a seat.

"Where's Victor?" I asked and sat down.

"He went home. He's fine." Antonio loosened his bow tie.

Martina asked. "Is the store okay?" She pulled her shawl around her nightdress and stood beside us.

"Yes, the store, hotel, all of our businesses are safe. It sounds like the fire started in the stable. Probably in the hay, but it threatened to spread to the ammunition storage depot. The animals were running loose and that's how they noticed something was wrong." Antonio looked around. "Is there anything to eat?"

"I'll get you something," I said. I brushed my stringy hair away from my face and looked in the cupboard for some bread and fruit.

Antonio cleared his throat. I need something to drink. "A group of firefighters tried to put out the fire," he said. "But the military ordered them not to."

"What?" Martina put a glass and a bottle of rum on the table.

I added a bowl of fruit and bread, with a glass of juice. Antonio drank down the juice and set the glass down. Then poured the rum.

"I don't know what happened. Maybe they thought it was too dangerous or maybe someone started the fire and didn't want it extinguished." Antonio continued. "The men disobeyed orders and fought the fire, putting it out. Lucky for them, the Pump Park was nearby and water was available," Antonio said. "But they were arrested for insubordination."

Martina sighed. She grabbed two more glasses, filled them with golden rum and drank hers down.

I served Antonio a plate of leftovers from supper and picked up a glass of rum and swallowed it. He ran his fingers through his hair and coughed. "We're back where we started."

✡ ✡ ✡

The next morning, I went home to talk to Papa and Victor. I repeated what Antonio had told us and Victor confirmed everything.

"I'm tired," Victor said. "I can't fight the United States for Porto Rico's freedom. We barely broke free from Spain," his voice raised. "We'll never be independent. It's like we're eating our own children for power." Victor's shoulders slumped and his face hung, like an old farm dog. "Our little slice of heaven, here in the mountains has become hell."

"Who started the fire?" Papa asked. He scratched his beard.

"Nobody knows." Victor shook his head. "It started in the ammunition depot. Their commander ordered everyone to evacuate because he worried the fire would spread and cause an explosion."

"I heard they said to let it burn itself out. To let Ponce burn. Is that true?" Papa asked.

"But the firemen ignored the orders and saved the city," I said. "Saved everyone, and now they're in jail. Is that true?"

"Who knows what's true anymore? The Americans said they were here to give us freedom," Victor said. "Was that the truth?"

"We're organizing to protest the arrests," Papa said. "We will fight this."

"How, Papa?" I asked.

"Patience, Fina," he said. "We Paoli's have patience. And persistence. We will make our voices heard. Believe me, we will not let this go."

I watched my father and other experienced organizers protest. The public outcry was so loud that soon the firemen were pardoned by the United States Congress and they were recognized as local heroes.

My brother Lolo announced that he had made the decision to become a firefighter. It came as no surprise, as he was always a helper to others and always made us proud. He wasn't accepted because of his limp. They told him he wouldn't be able to carry the heavy load, or carry people. They didn't know my brother.

Lolo didn't come home the night he got the news. He drank rum from every farm in Adjuntas. We all felt his disappointment and hoped that bitterness would not find a safe harbor in his heart.

Victor went out at four in the morning to find Lolo. He discovered him lying on the roadside. Victor brought him home and we never spoke of it again.

SET ON A NEW COURSE, we were all changed in ways my mind struggled to comprehend. Puerto Rico was being torn apart by loyalists to Spain and those wanting independence. Our family was being torn apart by loyalty, and the quest for riches. Port of Riches. The place for dreamers, my father.

Always the optimist, Papa's favorite line, "This is our chance," usually rang hollow, but there was a grain of hope, that the United States setting us free from Spain's stranglehold would be our chance.

Papa had plans to continue exporting coffee to Europe without Spain's heavy taxation and fines. The United States support was taking shape, but still there were forces at work against merchants and businessmen. Trouble makers, loyal to Spain, robbed stores, burned books and harassed store owners. Many of us grew impatient and were becoming agitated thinking relief would have been immediate when the Americans landed.

"This banner of freedom the Americans offered? It feels like they've wrapped us up, and we're tangled in it," I said.

"It's squeezing us to the point of suffocation," Martina said. "My store was ransacked. The trouble makers are the only ones free. Free to rob and loot."

I prayed in the morning, at noon and every night that the United States could enforce laws to calm our situation.

Our system of passing messages from house to house continued. Getting a newspaper was rare, and newspapers didn't tell us what was happening in our own backyard. The English woman grocer, Mrs. White, filled us in on any news from Europe about our situation in the world's eyes. Mail was even harder to get in Adjuntas. The telegraph was our lifeline to Ponce. Word also trickled up from them by messenger.

I was in the kitchen when an excited messenger came to the door one afternoon.

"What is it?" I held the door and wiped my hands with a dish towel.

"The American soldiers tracked the bandits. They opened fire from a distance, with their long-range rifles." He nodded. "They got them."

We cheered when we heard the news. "They are no match for the Americans," I said.

The cook waved her spatula in the air, and said, "I hope the cowboy American soldiers can drive all the bandit troublemakers away!"

I CARRIED THE PAINFUL SECRET of Dino's death in the year since he went missing. I remembered that terrible night in vivid detail and re-lived it every day. It was my life sentence.

I remembered riding that still night, my path illuminated by the moonlight. I was searching for Papa and Jorge. Certain if only I could catch up, I would be able to convince Jorge to take me with him. Riding as fast as darkness would allow, I reached the crest of a hill, and in the distance, I saw Papa in the moonlight. But there was someone else. The silhouette of a man holding a gun on him sent a bolt of terror through me. The man looked bulky and had another, riderless horse with him. Oh, God I thought. This man is a bandit who will shoot Papa and steal his horse.

I jumped down from my horse, pulled my rifle from the saddle and drew a bead on the bulky man. Thankful I had the chance, and he had not already shot Papa, I fired. He fell to the ground and I approached.

It was Dino Cesari, my sister's husband.

There is no forgiveness for someone like me.

IT WAS FEBRUARY, the end of the coffee growing season. The Cesari family was prepared to accept the fact that Dino was not alive. Antonio was eager to take the reins of the family business. He pushed for the reading of the Will, but first he needed the declaration of death, which he handled with little emotion. There would be insurance and the distribution of property.

Martina was in discussions with Papa and Victor in preparation to take over Dino's huge enterprise, now that the family would soon have him declared him legally dead. She would require the support of her family, but would continue with the laborers already on hand. A widow might inherit her husband's property, but it would be difficult to run a plantation or manage laborers. Antonio would no doubt oversee the large plantation.

On February 10, 1899 the Cesari family gathered at the house for the reading of the will. Martina looked drawn and pale. Her once smiling eyes were dark and shadowed from sleepless nights. The months since

Dino's death had aged her. Her black dress, usually crisp, hung on her and beckoned for laundry day.

Dino's vibrant tropical flower had become a wilted, black rose.

Antonio stopped us in the hallway before joining the family downstairs. "Martina," he said. "My father never updated his will after his marriage to you. He left everything to his children by my mother. You are not mentioned, and no provision was made for your care." His cold, dark eyes glared at Martina. "I have a copy of my father's will." He held up a paper. "Francesca will not receive a peso, until she reaches adult age." He poked at the paper with his finger. "I'll manage the funds until that time. We will, of course, assist with appropriate housing." He looked at me and Celia. "Perhaps you will want to live near your sisters?" He turned and walked down the stairs.

I swallowed hard and thought Martina might faint. I grabbed her arm.

Antonio was throwing us all out.

We went downstairs and found the entire Cesari family in the living room. It was a large enough space to accommodate a group, with high ceilings, heavy chestnut brown wood beams against cream colored, rough stucco walls. A huge fireplace centered the room on one side. A portrait of Dino's father hung above. He was a handsome man with light hair. I always wondered what Corsica looked like and what the people were like. I wondered if Dino's father knew my grandparents. Somehow, I felt like this portrait followed me and knew what I was thinking, knew what I had done to Dino.

My mind flashed with scenes of Papa and Dino in the moonlight, the night I rode after Jorge. I quickly shifted my thoughts and pushed them away.

We stepped into the sitting room and took a seat on the settee. I nervously fidgeted with the hand crocheted doilies on the arm rests. Pilar served coffee and breads. Voices filled the room, as if it was the theater lobby and they were about to enter for a performance of a great opera. Martina looked across the room, and started to say hello to Juliana, Dino's daughter and Auntie Juana. They looked away, ignored her and continued their own conversation. Juana held her nose a little higher in the air than usual and the message was clear, that Antonio had previewed the will to them. I wanted to leave and spare Martina this humiliation, but it was too late.

Dino's attorney and close friend, Don Carlos Jiménez arrived and joined us. Dino had amassed a fortune, owning several businesses in Ponce and San Juan in addition to the coffee plantation. Antonio sat across from us, flanked by his sisters. Señor Jiménez pulled up an armchair and began to read the will.

Antonio seemed nervous, got up and stood near the window. I imagined the many hours Dino must have spent, standing at that window, admiring his property and the lush, tropical setting. The window, like a seasonal painting, was a feature of the room. Bright red coffee berries, ready for final harvest, green mountains and banana trees filled the frame. At our property, the prime view was from Isabella's back porch. Papa built our house up high on the parcel, with no view. He wanted to be close to the barn. Papa had a strategy; Dino had vision.

Martina sat with her head down. The room fell silent. Antonio's sister, Juliana stared at the floor. Señor Jiménez opened with a warm welcome to the family. He talked about his friendship with Dino and told the story of how they met as young men. They had shared stories, secrets and plans for the future.

I knew Dino trusted him as a friend and as his attorney. Señor Jiménez began reading the will. Small bequests were made to the Church and a few loyal employees.

Señor Jiménez cleared his throat, looked up at Antonio, and said, "Your father updated his will. He realized that he had been remiss in not updating it after his marriage to Martina. He came to my office the day after Francesca was born."

I looked around the room and saw a startled look on Antonio's face. He whipped his head around and stared at Señor Jiménez."

"I hereby bequeath—"

I was so busy watching Antonio's head spin that I had trouble following the words.

"—As long as she is my widow and until she remarries —"

"Wait a minute," Antonio said after Señor Jiménez finished. "I've never heard of this change. You mean my father left the plantation to us children and Francesca? And he left the general store and hotel to Martina?"

"Yes. The plantation, and other businesses, except the general store and hotel, which he left to Martina. He knew Martina would need the income from the general store. He also left her money to buy a house for herself and Francesca. You, the children of Dino Cesari from his first wife own this hacienda. All of you children will share the plantation ownership, including Francesca."

Antonio's mouth hung open.

Juliana looked at her Auntie Juana, whose face

was contorted into a scowl.

"I'm sure you will need time to digest this information. I'll be available in my office next week."

Señor Jiménez tipped his hat, said, "Good day," and walked out the door.

✡ ✡ ✡

I followed Martina to her bedroom. "That nearly turned into a disaster," I said. "Did you see the look on Antonio's face?"

"I have no intention to gloat about it," Martina said.

"I understand, but I did see your eyes brighten." I grinned. "I had to hide my smile."

"It was a great burden lifted." Martina gave me a side glance. "That is certain, but Antonio is not to be crossed."

"I always knew he was a scoundrel," I said. "Be careful. For some reason, he and Victor have always worked together. I wonder what business they could possibly be up to."

"I know all about what they're up to. They were involved in the rebellion to free Puerto Rico, and of course they work on the plantation together," Martina said. "But forget that. Listen, before we walked out of the room Antonio approached me."

"What did he want?" I was afraid to hear.

"He's concerned that since he no longer has an interest in the general store or hotel in town. He may not be able to continue to serve on Ponce Town Council."

"I hadn't thought of that. With the coffee plantation and other business interests in shipping, he has plenty. Let him buy something in Ponce on his own. Don't let him take advantage of you."

"He will come to me with an offer for the hotel. I'll keep the store and the apartment."

"The store and the apartment are attached to the hotel. Are you sure you want to sell the hotel?"

"If he's on the Town Council, he could make it hard on me. I can keep the store and apartment and sell the hotel with the casino. I don't want to run that anyway. It's more his style. I could use the money to buy a house in Ponce or pay off Papa's loan," Martina said. "I have a lot to think about."

"I wonder if it's enough to pay off the loan? Papa's plantation is under fifty acres now. I heard Papa and Victor talking. A good picker can get maybe fifty pounds of berries a day and fetch a cent and a half per pound. Papa is down to ten pickers, and he pays the young girls twenty-five cents a day." My mind was spinning with ideas. "Even if Papa paid off his loan and wanted to expand, where would he find more land? What have you heard about other plantations around here? Are the Spaniards going to sell and go back to Spain?"

"No, they figure values are going up, now that the Americans are here. They're hanging on. Even pledging allegiance to America."

"Are you going to ask Papa?"

"No, he would tell me to sell it and give him all the money. I need time to think about it."

I rubbed my tired eyes. "I'm not sure the plantation is going to recover. Nobody's buying our coffee. I'll give credit to Spain; they were good for our market. The Americans buy coffee from Brazil, so we lost the European market when they took over."

"Yes, I see it at the store too," Martina said. "Everything is down. The United States broke us free from Spain, but they're not doing anything to help support our economy. They aren't interested in our coffee: they think sugar is the gold here. Everything is about sugar cane. We are on our own and I've got to figure some things out. Let's see what the Americans will do for us."

"Antonio's not going to wait long for an answer. When he comes to you with an offer, you need to be ready."

"I realize that, but Papa left his family behind in Corsica for this land." Martina plopped on the bed. "It's more than land. It's our family legacy, our livelihood and it's at risk. The plantation is how our family stays connected. Look, already you and Celia are gone and living here as domestics. That's not how we grew up. We had servants and private teachers. Losing our plantation is destroying us."

"Martina," I said, "Papa can't sell us off in marriage one by one to get his plantation back."

"He wouldn't."

"I'm not giving him money anymore. I'm not working anymore. He has two cards to play." I held up two fingers. "Celia and Fina."

"Oh, God."

Later that week, Martina sold the hotel to Antonio and loaned the money to Papa. "Save our family," she said.

August 1899

Victor

VICTOR STOOD IN THE COFFEE FIELDS, rich with the first showing of dark red, cherry-colored berries. A bright contrast against a threatening sky. He picked a berry and squeezed it between his fingers. The cherry would be hulled, dried and the seed inside would then be roasted for coffee. It was time to begin the first harvest. Looks like a good season, he thought. Time to have the Jibaros arrange the drying racks. Better clear the storage area too. The racks will need to be brought under cover if it rains.

He fastened the new fence post on the southern corner of the small plantation. Intruders had been stealing coffee berries recently to sell on the black market. A new fence would help to keep trespassers away. He would place armed guards on duty to put an end to the thieving. He placed the hammer in his saddlebag and mounted his horse for one more inspection of the rails and posts. He stopped to rest his horse and wiped the sweat from his forehead. Strange, the usually cool climate of the mountains was stagnant. "We could use a little rain," he muttered.

Antonio

Antonio Cesari finished his day in the coffee fields, where he supervised the workers. It was payday, and he distributed the wages to the stewards and checked on production.

The coming storm must be bad. Humidity is hell today, Antonio thought.

He stared out to the horizon, gave his horse a nudge with his heels and headed for the house.

Papa was waiting.

Celia

Dinner was served promptly at 7 p.m. in the Cesari residence. Antonio always sat at the head of the table. Martina anchored the opposite end with Dino's empty chair beside her. Relieved of our servant duties, Fina and I took our seats in the high-backed, carved mahogany chairs. I wonder when Antonio will announce what he plans to do about us living here, I thought. Did he still intend to have us move out? Meals had been tense, but Fina and Martina did their best to set their feelings aside. I feared that my chance at happiness with Antonio was at risk because of everything that happened. I wanted to stay. Francesca was an owner of the house along with Dino's other children, and Antonio was showing interest in me. Of course we will stay, I thought. But, the attention he gives me is uncomfortable for my sisters for some reason. I don't know if it's because I'm the youngest, but I sense they keep an eye on us. Why can't they be happy for me as I had been for them?

"Antonio, did you get the news over the wire?" Martina said. "The hurricane missed us and was headed for Florida, but it turned back."

"Yes, but it will be out of steam by the time it reaches us," Antonio said. "And we may not be in its path."

"We're in wait-and-see mode but be ready for a strong storm just in case," Antonio said.

Fear replaced the smiles on our faces.

"Please, can we have no further discussion of hurricanes at dinner," Martina's voice was firm. "As I said, the hurricane has passed us, and this brick house has weathered many storms." She smiled and picked up her soup spoon. "The tomato soup is excellent," she said nervously. "I asked Isabella to make it special for us tonight."

"Production is up this week," Antonio chimed in. "Victor's crew is picking up, but I think we pay him too much," he snorted.

"Your father never spoke about business at dinner," Martina said. "He was a gentleman."

"My father!" Antonio slammed his wine glass down. "My father has been gone for a year and a half. Just when do you think he's coming back? Do you expect him to walk in that door any minute?" He pointed to the massive, wooden double entry doors. "Should we tear up his death record?"

Martina looked away from Antonio, ignoring his outburst and turned toward Fina and me. "How was your day, ladies?" she said with an awkward smile. "I started a new sweater for Francesca."

I placed my hand on my Martina's and gave it a squeeze.

Outside, the winds whipped the palm fronds and blew the curtains in a ghostly swirl.

"Oh, here it comes!" I looked toward the window.

"Finally, a breeze!" Antonio loosened his collar.

"Celia, this is just a rain storm," Fina said. She always tried to calm me, but didn't she see that I was grown up now?

We looked up at the ceiling and listened to the howl outside that was growing louder.

After dinner, Antonio excused himself to the study. He was brooding and I really wished he would ask me to join him. The servants cleared the dishes and my sisters and I found ourselves alone.

A shutter banged against the house, bending and breaking the hinges. Pieces of wood slats from the shutters swirled in the wind. A spear of wood pierced the window, splaying shards of broken glass onto the floor. Martina let out a scream. Fina and I helped her pick up the broken glass.

Antonio rushed in from the study and yelled, "What was that noise? Get away from the window!"

My heartbeat quickened and his voice shook me, like a father scolding a child over a broken vase. I held my emotions back, not allowing others to see that I was hurt. The curtains blew and knocked a picture off a table in the living room. The shuttered window was dark and menacing. A gust of wind sent an ominous chill through the house. We looked up and listened to the roof tiles whistle in wind-whipping notes. The house creaked and groaned. Tree branches snapped and something large slammed the house.

"Secure the windows and doors!" Martina said. "We'll pray, keep things locked up tight and wait it out."

"Put some mattresses over the windows," Antonio said.

I held Fina's hand tight and stood in the dimly lit room. I hated hurricanes and nothing my parents ever did soothed my fears. We tried to remain calm but when the men were frightened, it terrified us. The house groaned and we thought the walls would buckle under the barrage of wind gusts and loud noises from trees. I could see that Antonio was frightened and I wished I could hold his hand.

Martina started up the stairs, "I've got to check on Francesca." She stopped on the first landing, turned and said, "Anyone want to come with me?"

Antonio said, "Let's secure the downstairs. This hurricane missed us the first time. It's come back and it's not missing us this time. Everyone will sleep downstairs tonight." He looked up at Martina, "Get your things. I'll carry Francesca."

"I'll help you." I moved closer to Antonio. Lightning and thunder erupted and I pressed against him on the stairway, but Antonio offered me no comfort. We carried Francesca in her small bed downstairs.

"She didn't even wake up," I said.

I went to the kitchen when a flash of lightning filled the room. Martina walked in and said, "We've had these storms before."

A clap of thunder made me tremble.

Martina wrapped her arms around me and we huddled in the corner of the kitchen. Rain and wind pummeled the house. It seemed no room was safe. We returned to the dining room to see Fina and Antonio standing at the bottom of the stairs. We listened to the winds that sounded like a howling monster, crawling across the rooftop.

"I think we should all stay together tonight," I said.

"Stay away from the windows, and stay downstairs," Antonio ordered as he walked through the room. "I guess it's time for bed," Antonio checked his pocket watch. "I'll see you in the morning," He went to a bedroom downstairs. I wanted to follow him.

"I can't believe Francesca didn't wake up." Martina rolled her crib to a downstairs bedroom.

"Goodnight," Fina and I said. We went to the last open bedroom and cowered under the covers.

ANTONIO'S FORECAST MISSED THE MARK, and there was no further reassurance from him. The storm was not weakening, it was building up momentum and becoming even more powerful. Puerto Rico was already on the ropes and by the time it hit us again, it packed a punch that offered the final blow.

Antonio ordered everyone to stay indoors. "Stop! If you open that door — the wind will rip it from its hinges."

"But, the horses!" I said. Dino had a sizable stable, with horses, ponies, donkeys and oxen.

"I'm worried about Isabella," Martina said.

"She's in her house and your father is close by," Antonio said. "We'll wait the storm out."

"That little house?" I said.

"She's tucked in the trees," Antonio said. "It's safer than being exposed, like your Papa's house."

"Dear God." I looked at Celia and Martina.

"We'll go check on them as soon as the storm passes." Antonio poured a drink of rum and drank down.

"I'll take one of those," Martina said.

"Me too," I said.

Celia stepped forward and put her hand out.

Hurricane force winds wailed for days; at a devilish force I'd never seen before. We listened to tiles rip loose and break on the roof. Martina rocked Francesca and we tried to ignore the terrifying sounds outside through what now felt like wafer-thin walls. If Dino's brick house was being battered by the storm, how was Papa's house withstanding it? Celia stopped looking to me for comfort and I took notice when she walked past me to take a seat beside Antonio in the living room. He ignored her and sat with his head in his hands. Alone, in a room filled with people, poor Celia nervously fumbled with her handkerchief.

Antonio moved closer to Celia and reached past her for a candle. "We'll need these. Want to see if there's something to eat in the kitchen?"

Celia followed.

✡ ✡ ✡

Alone in the kitchen, the usually warm room took on a menacing tone. Darkness cast spidery shadows on the walls. Flashes of lightning heightened Celia's senses, and her nerves were on edge. The usually warm room wore a black and white hue.

Biting into a piece of fruit, Antonio asked "So, what do you think of living here?"

"I like it fine. I don't see Papa as much but I'm

happy to be with my sisters."

Heavy rain pounded the house. The shutters rattled and knocked over a vase that was sitting on the ledge. Celia jumped.

"Whoa. It's all right," Antonio swept up the broken pieces. He put the broom away and looked at Celia.

"Are you frightened? Don't cry."

She nodded and wiped her tears.

Antonio placed his arm around her. "It will pass. This is the finest home in Puerto Rico. Look at these brick walls." He pointed around the room. "These storms pass. It will be over soon."

Celia turned her body toward Antonio and faced him. He placed his hands on her shoulders.

Antonio began to move his hands down her arms then stroked her back. Celia craved the safety of Papa and Mama's embrace. To be huddled in the storm with Antonio would be enough for her. She felt an attraction to him. Antonio's fingers traveled across her hips. He pulled her closer, leaned in and began to kiss her. Celia stopped and pulled back. Antonio pulled her close again and his hands worked their way to her waist. She tasted his lips and squirmed with a new sensation. He caressed her breasts and groaned as he kissed her. His body heavy against hers. Celia wondered if this was what true love was. He kissed her long and hard, breathing heavily. Antonio began to walk Celia backward to the wall. He lifted her dress and she felt his fingers tickle her thighs as he untied her cotton undergarments. Soon she felt the warmth of his bare skin next to hers.

The shutters banged and creaked in the winds outside. Antonio held Celia upright against the cupboard. The lantern flickered. San Ciriaco ravaged the island, howling as it uprooted palm trees and dismantled shanty homes.

In the kitchen, glasses rattled in a crescendo as Antonio and Celia swayed against the cupboard.

SAN CIRIACO PUMMELED THE ISLAND with hurricane force winds for three days and continued with heavy rain. My sisters and I returned to our upstairs bedrooms. I shoved two beds into one bedroom, so we could all sleep together. Francesca slept in one bed with Martina. Celia and I shared another.

I sat up in bed, eyes wide. “Do you hear that?”

I went to the window and opened the shutters.

“What are you doing?” Celia jumped from the bed.

“It’s raining, but the hurricane is gone.”

Martina gasped, “Oh, my God.” She held her hands over her mouth as she caught her first glimpse of San Ciriaco’s devastation.

“Stay inside with Francesca,” I said while putting on my clothes. “I’m going to check on Papa and Victor.”

Martina rushed to the kitchen to prepare breakfast. I knocked on Antonio’s bedroom door. “Let’s go! The winds have gone. We need to check on everyone!”

There was no answer. I went to the kitchen where Martina was cooking breakfast and Francesca sat at the table.

"Mama - eggs." Francesca wrinkled her nose. "No, no. Pastries."

"Mmm, I love eggs." I sat down. "Let's see who eats their breakfast first." I gave Francesca a kiss and looked at Martina. "You give her too many coconut chocolates, Mama."

Martina gave me a dirty look and served us a cup of coffee. Antonio walked in from the servant's hallway.

"Good morning," Antonio said. "It's over," he said incredulously and looked out the window. He stretched and reached for a cup of coffee.

"Are you ready?" I looked over the top of my cup as I sipped. "We need to get outside to see that everyone is all right and see Papa, Lolo, Victor and Isabella."

"I'll get my boots." Antonio walked back to the bedroom in the servant's hallway.

Martina raised her eyebrows. "The Nanny Pilar?

I didn't know they were—"

"Now I know why he didn't answer when I knocked on his bedroom door this morning," I said. "Don't say anything to Celia." I rose from my chair. "I'll get ready." I tightened Jorge's leather boots as tight as I could. I'd claimed them as mine after he left. They almost fit me.

Antonio came back into the kitchen. "Are you ready?" he said.

"Yes," I said. We stepped outside into a hellish world of twisted and torn rooftops. Splintered trees splayed in the mud like toothpicks. It was a scene of total devastation. Banana trees were uprooted, the barn was demolished and small structures had been lifted and blown like leaves in the winds. I worried about the servant's quarters and was especially concerned about Isabella. Dino had about twenty Jibaro's huts on his property. Papa had about ten. These poor laborers depended fully on Papa for everything, which was little. They lived in a small hut-like home with a patch of a vegetable garden. At Dino's plantation they earned tokens, redeemable for food at Dino's store, or took cash at a lesser rate.

I wasn't sure if Isabella was with Papa, or at her house, and couldn't wait to get to her. Hers was the only wooden house. All the thatch huts were poorly built structures and were surely gone from the storm. "I haven't seen anything like this before," I said. "I need to get to Papa's house."

"I'll go with you," Antonio yelled. "We'll have to walk. We can't take a wagon in this mud."

The rains were heavy and moving through the mud was arduous. "Grab that rope!" Antonio yelled as we watched supplies float past in the mud. He tied one end to his waist. "Tie the rope to your waist," he said.

I struggled with the rope. Antonio trudged over to me and tied a knot firmly around my waist. "We cannot get separated. Do you understand? There's a lot of sticky mud, but also a lot of unstable ground. The water creates its own path. There are bodies of water where there weren't any before. Watch where you step."

"Where is everybody? Where are all your laborers?" I looked around.

Antonio's eyes darted around, nervously. He looked me in the eyes and said, "Stay with me. Let's go get Victor and your Papa."

Papa's plantation was across the road and up a hill, not far from Dino's. Papa lived on a hillside where the rains washed everything downhill. The servant's and laborer's quarters were along the road, downhill from Papa's house.

"Oh, my God!" I yelled. The field shack was destroyed. A metal roofed structure collapsed, lying flat on the ground and slowly sliding downhill toward us, in a soup of mud.

"Over there!" Antonio shouted, "In the trees!"

I saw three horses huddled under a canopy of trees. Antonio and I rounded them up and continued.

Papa was walking down the hill toward us. "Papa!" I shouted.

"I'm going to see Isabella," he shouted.

Antonio and I continued toward him with the three horses. The mud was thick and difficult to move through. We could see there was heavy damage ahead, and I stopped cold when I heard a terrible noise. Papa cried out like the ox in Dino's store. A guttural moan, like a wounded animal. He stood; shoulders slumped. Antonio and I got to the top of the hill and could see that the entire back section of Papa's parcel, on the river's edge was gone.

"Papa?" I approached.

Papa took a breath and moved closer to the edge. A large chunk of land had broken off and slid down the mountain to the river, taking Isabella's shack with it. He stumbled and took a step back in the sticky mud. He cried out, "No!"

I felt unsteady and in disbelief. "Papa?"

He turned and walked past us. I was so filled with despair myself; I had no words to offer. I stood in the rain and watched him as he sloshed back toward the house. I could hear his sobs in the rain.

Victor and Lolo stopped him. "Papa!" Lolo called out. "We got the horses. But the barn - it's gone!"

Papa stood in the rain, he remained silent.

"Papa?" Lolo handed the reins to Victor and approached our father.

"The land washed away," Papa mumbled. "The hillside slid into the river." He wiped his face. "Isabella is gone."

He looked up to the rainy sky above. A lone survivor of San Ciriaco flew overhead. "I wish I could fly away too," he said.

IT RAINED FOR NEARLY A MONTH, and I found myself on my knees, day and night bargaining with God. I reminded Him of all the good I had done in my life, what my family had done and what we would do if only God would see us through. I promised to serve him and begged his forgiveness for my sins.

I doubted God was listening when I woke to another day of rain. Rivers overflowed, water found new pathways and the earth gave way, collapsing and sliding down mountainsides. We were witness to our mountain's collapse. The coffee fields were completely destroyed.

Celia grew fearful and nervous. Every creak and noise made her jerk or jump. She began to twist her hair until there was a bald spot at the top of her head.

Martina was short tempered and impatient. She paced the room and repeated herself often.

After about a month, the rain lifted and we got a message from Ponce. It was from Fernando, the employee from Martina's store.

Martina read the note aloud.

"Buildings with roofs torn off or completely collapsed. Rivers overflowed. No drinking water. Flooded with salt water. Hundreds of dead. Bodies floating in the street. Men, women and children. Saw dead animals floating too. Many starving people. Store flooded but it survived."

Martina covered her mouth with her hand.

"My God," I said. "Ponce is devastated. Where is the help?"

Martina nodded and began to cry. "Is there anything left of the island? We haven't had a hurricane like this in fifty years. Can Puerto Rico recover?"

December 1899

The San Ciriaco hurricane destroyed our homeland with its unmerciful power, taking our beloved domestic servant Isabella, along with over three thousand other souls. The entire island was in mourning.

There were so many sick and starving from disease and lack of crops, the best we could do was to stay isolated on our land. Meals were lean and we were all growing thinner by the day. The old days when we smiled and laughed, and cooked a feast for neighbors to share were a faint memory. Now, we counted every vegetable and meat was a rare treat.

Occasionally Papa or Victor brought home something they shot to add to the sauces or stews we cooked. Whenever I complained it tasted strange, Papa said it was always good to add something wild. That was how they cooked in the old country. I learned to separate a small portion for my sisters and me without the wild catch. We sat obediently at dinner without a squabble and Papa was happy.

One evening after dinner Victor came into the kitchen. "We'll never be able to rebuild," Victor said. "We've lost everything and we're deep in debt."

"What does Papa say?" I asked.

"Dino's plantation was heavily damaged but he will recover, although it will take several years to see a healthy crop," he said. "His mill needs to be rebuilt and some of the fields were destroyed, but he still has a small parcel that survived. Papa knows there's no hope here for us. Everything is gone."

"We'll make it, Victor. Somehow, we'll make it."

The specter of death loomed over our mountain, and the body count mounted. Disease spread, killing more each day. Dino's twenty huts which served as housing for Jibaros and our laborers were destroyed by the storm, taking the lives of over one hundred employees and their families. Their bodies were swept away by rising rivers, taken by disease or starvation. One worker was killed by a felled tree that was uprooted and flew into the air, landing on top of his hut. It crushed him, missing his wife and small child. They ran to a neighboring hut, which had the roof torn off in the storm. They all ran into the field, searching for some sort of cover. It flooded and they trudged through the mud uphill where they crouched in the cover of banana trees. When the land began to slide, they moved and appeared on Dino's back porch, covered in mud. There were six hauntingly battered figures, looking exhausted and frightened to death. Antonio let them stay in the barn. Thanks to God, the barn withstood the storm. For the life of me I never understood why Antonio would not allow his own workers to shelter in the servant's quarters off the kitchen. He said that if he allowed them inside, the others would come. Antonio had a cold, black heart that beat only for pesos.

Our sweet brother Lolo had rushed to help our neighboring farmers repair their homes after the hurricane and he worked hard to save what was left of our plantation. He trudged through the mud, working tirelessly for days but there was nothing left to save. Not a tree, bush or berry of life. There was only devastation.

Lolo began to show signs of illness that were all too familiar, and I was frightened that he had caught the disease that was causing many deaths. He grew weary and napped several times a day. He made frequent trips to the outhouse and complained of stomach aches that kept him from work. After about a month we noticed he had the rash of the diseased.

"What are we going to do?" I asked Papa. "Lolo has the rash. Have you seen his feet? Long wiggly, red lines and his toes are infected." I whispered, "It's hookworm."

Papa nodded and took a breath. "He needs to stay in the barn," he mumbled.

"People are dying from this sickness." Tears pooled in my eyes. "He's been hiding it. I think he's been sick a long time. We can't leave him in the barn to die."

"We'll take care of him," Papa said. His eyes reflected the light with a pool of tears that threatened to overrun the rim. "I'll put a bed out there but we don't want to catch it. He must stay out there."

I carried a breakfast tray out to Lolo one December morning and found him. His face was drawn and his eyes were sunken which made him look old and frail, at only twenty-two years old. I nudged him to wake up. He was cold, and his skin was gray. I dropped the tray and ran out of the barn crying and screaming, "Papa!"

Papa raced out the door, "What is it?" He stopped and shook his head. "No!" he cried. "No. Lolo?"

I ran into Papa's open arms. "He's dead."

Papa raced into the barn and I followed but stopped at the entrance, watching from afar. Papa placed his hand on Lolo' head and body, then he held Lolo's hand in his. Papa hung his head low and prayed. I prayed along with him from the doorway, with tears washing down my face. Papa pulled the blanket up, over Lolo's face. He stood and walked to me. He stroked my head. "It's okay, dear one. He is at peace now." Papa pressed his cheek against my head and held me tight. I felt Papa's body shake and we cried together.

We called the family together and gathered around the table to discuss burial plans. "Lolo was our kind-hearted brother," I said. I looked at Victor and realized what I'd just said. "Sorry Victor."

Victor shrugged. "He was."

"What is Uncinariasis?" Celia asked. "Eugenia said Lolo died from a venereal disease."

"Celia!" I snapped.

Papa held up his hand and said, "Eugenia doesn't understand. The doctor explained what Uncinariasis is. Locals call it hook-worm disease."

"Why did Lolo have to get it?" Celia asked.

"He got it from trudging through the mud after the hurricane," Papa said. "He joins over three-thousand others who died from this terrible storm, Celia."

Martina cleared her throat and said, "I'll pay for his burial in Ponce's cemetery."

"Lolo will be buried in a mass grave along with the others," Papa said.

"If he won't have a headstone," I said. "Then we won't have a place to visit his grave or bring flowers."

"There are too many bodies for our little cemetery. Our town is overwhelmed," Papa said. "A mass grave is how they're doing it."

"At least we don't have to endure the uprooting of bodies and watch them stack bones in the corner of the cemetery," Martina said.

"Martina!" Papa said.

"That's why you didn't bury Mama in town," she said. "They uproot the dead and dump the bones in a pile to make room for the new bodies."

"Martina, now is not the time to discuss this," Papa said. "Thousands are dead. Just how do you expect cemeteries to handle a catastrophe of this size? They are burying the dead in mass graves. It has to be done this way."

"Enough," Victor interrupted. "Let's honor Lolo with a ceremony at the tree we used to climb. I'll carve his initials in the tree."

"Thank-you Victor, that's an excellent suggestion," Papa said. "Nine o'clock tomorrow morning. Let's gather here first and walk out together."

That afternoon Martina, Celia and I gathered flowers and filled all of Mama's vases to prepare for Lolo's funeral.

Papa and Victor wrapped Lolo's body in a blanket and loaded him into the wagon. We stood like soldiers and watched solemnly, unsure whether to salute or offer the sign of the cross as they drove away.

They delivered Lolo's body to the cemetery workers in town, who took care of placing him in a mass grave. There was no ceremony or emotion upon transfer of the body. The workers simply took the cargo and payment required.

In the morning we walked together to the climbing tree. Papa led us in prayer. We all cried, taking turns consoling one another. Victor carved Lolo's initials into the tree, along with his birth and death date.

The tree was near the place where Isabella's tiny house had once stood. The property was missing a chunk at the edge where it drops down into the river. It was all gone, swept away in a sea of mud below. She, along with her little house were somewhere at the bottom of the river which was now covered with the quicksand-like mud that was once our mountainside property.

Death became routine.

PAPA'S THINNING HAIR was now mostly gray with a few blonde streaks peeking out. His complexion was sallow and his face was drawn. We leaned on our brother, Victor as our leader. Unfortunately, anger was Victor's driving force. War, rebellion and suffering had left him bitter but it somehow fueled him. He worked hard to feed our family. More than that, he adopted an attitude that he would do whatever it took now. He had become a warrior and a leader. My sisters and I moved to Papa's house. With everyone under one roof again, it was a big responsibility for Victor.

Papa had lost the coffee plantation and regained it through Martina's hand in marriage to Dino. With plans for renovation, Papa took a loan from the bank. Coffee exportation to Europe dropped off after we seceded from Spain and we struggled. Martina helped with the proceeds from the sale of the hotel. Just when the plantation was profitable, the hurricane wiped out the crop and a huge chunk of our parcel slid down the mountain into the river.

Papa owed the bank once again.

Victor and Papa called the family together. Victor began. "We're in financial ruin. A decision has to be made," he said. "We have no favor with the banks, our plantation has no hope of recovery. I heard that the banks are being taken over by the U.S. and our loan will be called. We cannot make good on it without a coffee crop. I met a man in Ponce. He's good. He's a Puerto Rican, works for the Hawaiian Sugar Company. His company is offering jobs for all, with free passage to Hawaii, and no papers required. There is plenty of work on sugar plantations and Papa was offered a job as a Mayordomo." He looked at Papa. "He said I could also work as a foreman with my experience." Victor turned to us. He raised his hands as he raised his voice, "This is our chance!"

Papa said, "It's Christmas," he paused and looked at Celia with her pregnant belly showing. He looked at Victor and said, "What about your sister? Celia can't make the trip in her condition."

Victor's smile disappeared. He said, "The company offers free medical care for the family on the ship or we can go ahead of her and get settled. As soon as the baby is born we'll send for Celia."

"Sell the plantation?" Celia said. "Can't we replant? What about trying sugar? The sugar plantations were making money."

"Celia, stop." Victor shook his head. "It would take five years to grow a coffee crop again, and forget sugar. Everything is destroyed."

"Papa has a loan to the bank. We can't sell it." Martina placed her hand on Celia's. "The bank will own it." She looked at Victor. "I keep hearing about people going on the ships, but I never considered it for us." She looked around the room. "Work in the fields? All of us?"

"Martina, we're out of options and out of money." Victor's voice was commanding. "It's not safe for us here anymore. I can't protect you in the same way — the old way."

I placed my hand on Celia's shoulder and said, "It's a good plan. I need to stay and wait for Jorge. Celia and I will be together." I looked at Martina. "You don't have to go. Martina, you and Francesca have money from Dino, but we've lost everything." My emotions were heightened and I couldn't hold back my tears. "Go ahead, Victor and Papa."

"Celia," Victor said. "After your baby is born we'll send you a ticket to come to Hawaii. We'll say that your husband died in the hurricane and nobody will know about your situation with Antonio."

Celia looked at Victor. "You're a good brother." She stood and gave him a hug.

"I'll talk to the man from Hawaii tomorrow. We'll stay for the holidays." Victor didn't look to Papa for approval. He said, "The next ship leaves the day after Christmas."

Francesca had been tugging at her mother's hair and squirming during our meeting. Martina took Francesca to the kitchen to find something to eat. Victor and Papa stepped outside to the porch. I heard Papa and Victor talking outside.

"Victor, you need to understand," Papa said, "When I was a boy, in Genoa, my parents moved to Corsica. I never saw my grandparents again. When Spain offered us land to settle in Puerto Rico, I was nineteen and left Corsica. I planned to return but didn't; that was the last time I saw my parents. We mailed many letters and photos but I never heard the sound of their voices or felt the warmth of their embrace. You children never knew your grandparents."

"I understand, but we did fine." Victor insisted. "We had Mama's family."

"When we leave this island, we need to leave as a family," Papa said firmly. "We can't leave Fina and Celia behind. And what about Martina?"

"Papa, you can't be serious. We've talked about this for weeks. These men have been working on immigration plans and it's happening now! They'll only take a certain number and the first boat has already left." Victor said. "We need to get on the list now. I'm telling you; this is our chance."

"Yes, I heard you earlier. This is our chance. Now you're mocking my words?" Papa said. "There will be more boats. I say we wait and go together. We can get work on the sugar plantation."

"They're promising you three years employment at fifteen dollars a week and I'll make fifty cents a day. All I can get here, if I can get work, would be fifty centavos, or thirty cents per day. Sugar is only paying a half peso per day. That's twenty-five cents a day. In Hawaii, the girls can make thirty-five cents a day. It's not what we're used to here, but we'll make it. And there's a bonus of seventy-two dollars at the end of three years. Maybe we can start our own plantation there." Victor insisted. "We know how to do this, Papa."

"Victor, enough!" Papa said firmly. "They will always have work in Hawaii. We can go in a few months."

"I don't know if there will be any foreman positions. I'm sure they will fill those jobs with the first boats." Victor said. "If we wait, we'll take what work is available and I'll bet it will be field work. If we stay, we risk disease, starvation and death. Our fate is sealed. Do you want us to end up like Lolo?"

After a pause, Papa sighed and said, "You're right, Victor. Go ahead and take the position of Mayordomo. I'll come with the girls as soon as they can make the trip with the babies."

Victor came back inside and I stepped out onto the porch. Papa was smoking a cigar. He always smoked when he was nervous. "Papa? I heard you talking to Victor."

"It will be okay," he turned to me. "Victor will send money and by the time Celia's baby is born, he'll send a ticket."

"I'm not going. Jorge is going to send for me when it's safe."

Papa put out his cigar and stepped closer. "Fina, my darling girl. Jorge has been writing to his family. Each of his sisters and his brother have received letters. I know this. Even Aunt Juana has received letters." He placed his hand on my shoulder. "If he was going to write you, he would have."

I started to cry. "I knew they had letters from him but Jorge said—"

"Fina, don't do this." He hugged me. "I know you love him and I'm sorry." Papa stepped back and looked me in the eye. "Listen to me, I think it's time we leave here," he whispered. "If anyone finds out about the night you rode after Jorge — and they find Dino's grave—"

I looked around to see if anyone could hear us.

"I told you, it's not safe for us here anymore," he placed his hand on my shoulder. "They could find him.

And then they will investigate. We need to leave."

"I understand." I dabbed the tears from my eyes and we went inside. Everyone was in the kitchen eating pasteles.

Martina wiped the powdered sugar from her mouth and said, "I'm going with you, Victor."

We all looked at Martina.

"Francesca and I have no life here. I'll sell the store back to the Cesari family. Business has dropped since the hurricane. People have no money and now ships are leaving with many of our friends and now family."

"But you don't need to work the fields," Victor said.

"I'll sell the business and the house and move to Hawaii," Martina said. "I'll open a store there. Or a restaurant. We could all work together." She looked at me and Celia.

Celia looked down at her growing belly.

Martina continued, "It will take time for me to be ready. I'll pay off the bank for Papa with money from the store. But I'll keep the apartment. You can move in with me and when the baby is born, we can all go together."

"Well, I hadn't thought of that solution," Victor said. "I'll go ahead of you. The offer of steward won't last."

"I can't accept—" Papa said, looking at Martina.

"There will be no discussion," Martina said. "I'll speak to the bank tomorrow."

"Papa, please," I pleaded. "Please take Martina's offer."

"I will, for Fina and Celia," Papa said. "We need a

place to stay together. But I'll pay you back when we get to Hawaii. I'll get work there."

Victor said, "I'm leaving on December 26th." He walked outside to the porch and sat on a bench.

I followed him out and stood, leaning against a post. Finally, I said, "I don't know who I am anymore. Our family always said no matter what we had each other. Now, we're separating. What must I become to survive here? I've lost all that I hold dear to my heart. My family, my country and my love."

Victor looked up at me with a look I'd never seen from him before. "Fina, you've lost more than that."

"I will die alone, like prune faced Auntie Juana. A bitter old woman."

"She was in love once," Martina's voice joined in from behind me. "She was to be married, but her fiancé died at Grito de Lares."

"What?" I said, "I never heard that."

"Dino told me," Martina said. "He said to never speak about it."

I exhaled a long breath and said, "That changes how I see her."

"Many men have shed blood for our country's freedom," Victor said. "And for what? We've been beaten by Spain, by our own people and by Mother Nature. Puerto Rico will always be my homeland and will hold my heart. But I'm leaving or I will die here. We will all die here. We need to leave."

I turned to Victor and asked, "What did you mean when you said, 'I've lost more than that?'"

"You've lost your innocence."

OUR PAPA HAD BECOME THIN and frail. It seemed he never aged, then all at once, the years caught up to him. He didn't come in for dinner one night and Victor found him in the barn. His face was still and frozen on one side and he couldn't use his arm or leg on his left side. Victor carried our Papa into the house. It was December 1899 and I wondered, who was this old man lying in the bed? He looked so small.

Martina walked in the door. "How is he?"

"Not good," I said. "There's a dark cloud over this house tonight."

We stepped into Papa's bedroom. The small room held two single beds, one dresser and a window with print curtains that I'd made. Papa's tall frame barely fit into the tiny bed. Martina touched the blanket at his foot. He recoiled back. Papa was very weak and he looked boney under the covers. He lay with his mouth open; his breath was labored. Martina covered her mouth and held back her tears.

"Papa?" She leaned in to kiss his unshaven cheek. "It's Martina."

His eyes were sunken and when he turned his head, I noticed his eyes did not follow her.

"Papa, I'm here," Martina said. "Is there something I can get for you?" She offered him a cup that was on the night table and she took a seat beside the bed. "Will you drink some water?"

"They're all here," Papa whispered with a thick tongue, "waiting for me tonight."

Papa's nails scratched at the sheets. His fingers moved quickly, nervously. He seemed agitated. I stroked his forehead and he relaxed into the pillow. Martina offered small sips of water.

"Papa, I'm going to be here but you sleep now. I love you." Martina rose from her bedside chair, kissed Papa on the forehead and we walked to the door.

"Fina, my darling girl," Papa said. "I need to speak to Father Taliaferro."

We attended the small Church in Adjuntas, but Papa was especially close to the Priest in Ponce. I sent for Father Taliaferro, who often spoke Italian with Papa. They would talk about the old country, Italy where Papa's parents were from. Father Taliaferro had a strange, high voice and would laugh, nodding his head in approval when Papa would say something. They used to spend many hours on the porch together. Usually, with a glass of red wine. Father Taliaferro always greeted me with a wide smile and thanked me when he left. His smile often tinged with wine.

Our house was quiet, except for the voices of Father Taliaferro and Papa. Celia took Francesca for a walk and some fresh air. I folded laundry in my bedroom

room. Martina sat on the bed and we listened.

"May I borrow a rosary?" Martina asked.

"In the box, on my dresser," I said.

Martina reached into the worn, painted wooden jewelry box and removed a rosary. She stopped and stared into the box. In the filtered light of dusk, a familiar sparkle appeared as she pulled a long chain from the box. Laying beneath the rosary, trinkets, a cross and funeral cards was a hidden secret and Martina found it.

I set my laundry down, and my heart quickened. She dropped the rosary on the dresser and lifted the pocket watch into the light. I knew she'd not held it in years. She studied her husband's gold engraved watch with the ruby jeweled cross on the cover, then turned to me and said, "Why do you have this? I gave this to Dino for our first Christmas together in 1897. I remember his face the morning he opened the gift. He could have bought himself any watch, but he made me feel as though I'd given him a treasure. Dino carried this every day, never leaving it behind." She closed her fingers around the watch and looked at me, puzzled. "Why do you have my husband's watch?"

I opened my mouth to speak, but words did not come.

"Fina, answer me," Martina's voice raised. "You and my husband?"

We heard Papa's voice echo from the hall. He was talking to Father Taliaferro and clearly mentioned Dino's name. Martina and I paused to listen.

"It was the night he took his son, Jorge, to the dock in Guanica Harbor," Papa said. "I rode after them and met Dino on my way back. We had words."

My heart raced and a bolt of terror pierced my body. Martina stepped into the hallway and crept down the stairs to listen. I thought for a moment about entering the downstairs bedroom to interrupt.

Papa spoke freely, as if sharing an old story with a friend. "Antonio came to my house that night and told me that Dino was helping Jorge escape," he said. "I knew that Jorge loved my daughter Fina, and they planned to marry." Papa coughed, then continued, "I rode after them, but Dino would not allow me to pass to reach Jorge who was already at the dock, or on a boat. Dino had a pistol. I was angry. Two old friends, both pig-headed."

We stood in the hallway, outside Papa's bedroom breathless and listened. Martina clutched Dino's pocket watch, with eyes wide. I peeked into the room. The floorboard creaked and I pulled back. I saw Mama's bible sitting on the table beside Papa's bed. His empty glass was still there from the night before.

Father Taliafero's wooden chair creaked.

Papa took a breath and continued, "I told Dino, 'First you took Martina. Now your sons have taken Fina and Celia. You must allow me as a father to see that these young men honor my daughters.'"

Father Taliaferro answered in a calm voice, "I understand."

"Dino pointed his pistol at me."

Papa was revealing details I'd never heard before, I thought. I felt dizzy.

"Dino told me, 'I cannot, Guillermo.' He was a stubborn man. I knew I would not be able to convince him to let me pass."

Papa's voice was tired and weak as he continued.

"Dino said 'Jorge cannot be a husband or father to Fina's children. If he stays, he will face prison or death. Either way she will be alone. Please understand that I need to help my son live.'"

I swallowed my moans and leaned against the wall. This was the first time I heard what had happened between Papa and Dino that terrible night. I listened. "Oh!" I covered my mouth. Papa was going to tell everything. I stepped back. Martina followed and we stood in the doorway to the living room, where we could hide from view should Father Taliaferro look down the hallway.

Papa coughed and said, "A shot rang out and Dino fell from his horse."

Martina quietly yelped.

Papa's voice was clear, "I jumped down from my horse and ducked for cover. Dino lay beside me, a gaping hole behind his right ear. I was sure the soldiers had come for us. Papa continued, "As the killer on horseback approached from the shadows, a familiar voice called out."

Martina held onto the door jam and stared at me. "The soldiers!" she whispered. Tears flowed down her face.

I covered my mouth and thought, "Oh, my god. My secret! I've got to stop Papa!"

Father Taliaferro asked, "You knew this person?"

I was about to step into the bedroom to interrupt when I heard Papa answer.

He said, "I heard her call out, 'Papa, are you all right?' Then a lantern illuminated my daughter's face. It was Fina." Papa took a sip of water and continued, "I said 'Dear God, Fina. What have you done?' She told me, 'I heard arguing and he drew a pistol on you!'"

Martina's eyes turned dark and she blinked away her tears. She stared coldly at me. She wiped her cheeks, looked one more time at the watch, rubbing her fingers over the engraved initials D.C. on the back, and placed the watch in her bosom.

Cold sweat dripped down my back and I wiped my forehead with a handkerchief. I had a partial view down the hall into Papa's room. Father Taliaferro shifted his feet in his chair. I was afraid he was getting up to come for me. It was too late to stop Papa's confession now. My fingers began to feel numb.

Papa went on, "I asked her, 'Does anyone know you are here?'"

"Fina said 'No,' and she asked where Jorge was. She said she had to go with him. She looked at Dino and her body began to tremble." Papa took a deep breath and sighed. "I told Fina that the soldiers were out that night. They were searching for Jorge. We had no time. We had to bury Dino where he would never be found." Papa's voice trailed off.

Papa's voice perked up again, "Fina stared at Dino's dead body. I had to shake her up. I yelled, 'Fina, are you listening? Do you understand? You will be put to death for this. Let's go!' I ordered her."

When Papa discussed the burial, I stepped out onto the back porch and wretched. I had vivid memories of Dino's body that night. The full moon had illuminated the scene and the puddle of blood at his head. This was my final memory of my brother-in-law. A man who could be kind and generous but who was also so controlling and manipulative that he changed the course of the lives of every member of my family. Dino was a ruthless businessman who used many, trusted few, and ruined those who crossed him. He was the reason Jorge joined the rebellion. Now Jorge was gone. I hated Dino for that.

The clock on the wall ticked and I felt a quiver run through my body. Why, after years of silence, had Papa chosen to speak about this on his deathbed? My crime had become his confession. I had made him my accomplice when he disposed of the body that night.

I belched out the sour gasses and my stomach settled. I went back inside the house.

Father Taliaferro offered a blessing to Papa. They prayed and the priest left the room with his body slumped, head down, and hands together.

I walked him to the door and said, "Thank you for coming, Father."

He said nothing to me as he left the house. And made no eye contact.

A secret that was once between Papa and me was now between me, Martina and Father Taliaferro.

I returned to Papa's room. Martina was in a chair at Papa's bedside. I called softly from the doorway, "Martina?"

"I can't. Not now."

I felt physically drained and dragged myself to bed and waited for her. For the first time, I felt a sense of relief. Finally, I could tell Martina what happened to Dino and explain my tragic mistake. My emotions flowed and all of the pain was released. I turned my face into the pillow, to muffle my sobs and fell asleep.

The roosters crowed and the sun shined in

through the window of my bedroom, alerting me that it was morning. I went straight to Papa's room to check on him and to see if Martina was still there.

Papa's cold, still body was covered in blankets. His face was peaceful, as it was when we left him the night before. I cried out and woke Martina, slumped in a chair.

"¡Dios mío" (Oh, my God!) Martina cried out. "Papa!"

December 1899

MARTINA AND FRANCESCA moved out of the house and into the Cesari apartment in Ponce. She refused to speak to me after the night Papa died. I would have rather had her lash out in anger after hearing Papa's confession than cut me off completely without a chance to explain. I needed her to understand that it was a tragic accident. I felt branded, tried and convicted as a murderer. I tried to talk to her, but she bristled at the sight of me. When I came to her apartment, she wouldn't open the door and I couldn't talk through a closed door. I had to see her face to face.

I saw her through the window one day. I stood outside the door, and I told her as quietly as possible, "Call me a killer! Blame me. Let's get it all out and let me tell you what I saw that night."

She pulled the curtain closed.

✡ ✡ ✡

I decided to enlist the help of Victor, to see if he could approach her. I let him think it was only a spat between me and Martina. I was afraid he would ask questions.

I grabbed one of the last three bottles of Papa's pitorro from the shelf and walked out the back door of our house. I entered the barn and called out, "Victor? It's Fina." I stepped inside. It was dark and smelled a little musty.

"I'm cleaning the horse's stall." He stepped out from behind a short wooden wall. He wiped his brow. "What is it?"

"I thought you might want a break?" I pulled the bottle from my skirt pocket and slowly waved it. "Dinner will be ready in about an hour."

"I'm finished here." Victor leaned the pitchfork against the wall and walked toward me. He slapped his hands together to clap off any dust. "Pull up a seat." He motioned to an old milking stool in the corner. He sat on a hay bale.

We sat in a narrowing stream of sunlight. Tiny particles of hay floated in the air. Victor uncorked the bottle. "I have a feeling I'll need a drink before you start."

I smiled and said, "You know me too well. I only wanted to have a moment with you before you leave for Hawaii."

Victor took a swig from the bottle and wiped his mouth. "You know he always kept a bottle out here, don't you?"

"No wonder Dino was always over here talking to Papa in the barn."

Victor laughed and nodded. "Yes, Dino was a character. He was a good man, you know."

"Of course, I know that. Why would you think not?"

"Fina, I know what happened that night."

I froze.

"Papa told me right after it happened."

I swallowed hard and said, "Why are you telling me now?"

"A trouble shared is a trouble halved. That's what they say, right?" Victor said.

"What did Papa tell you?"

"He came home after being out all night. I'd been out too, hiding from the posse."

"Oh, God." I looked around, to be sure we were alone.

"We were both exhausted, frightened," Victor continued.

"He really told you," I mumbled.

"Papa and I shared everything. The rebellion. Yauco. And he told me that you shot Dino and the two of you buried him." He took another sip of Pitorro.

"It was an accident!" I covered my mouth.

"There were a lot of accidents at that time."

"Victor, it was dark. I couldn't see. I rode up on them and saw a man holding a gun on Papa. I fired my rifle."

Victor offered me the bottle.

I shook my head. "No," I said softly.

"Does Martina know?" Victor asked. "Is that why

she won't speak to you?"

"Did she say something to you?"

"No, but I figured there was something very serious to cause whatever was going on between you two. And she isn't talking about it. Usually if you two have a tiff I hear all the complaints. Martina is quiet, but I can hear the ticking bomb. She's angry and brooding. She's grieving Dino's death like a fresh wound. I can sense she's thinking about him. She talks about him as if he just died."

"Oh, God this is terrible. I came to you for help." I took a deep breath and exhaled. "She heard Papa confess to Father Taliafero."

"What?"

"Yes. I thought you could speak to her. Perhaps you could soften her."

"Soften her?" Victor snapped. "And how exactly do you want me to do that? Tell her that her sister accidently killed her husband. Forgive and forget?"

"I didn't exactly—"

"You'd better look out. She may be out for vengeance. Fina, I know all of it. And I know Papa and Dino were arguing before you rode up. But the Court will see it differently. You will be hung for it; I am certain." He leaned forward. "You have to leave here." He waved his hands in the air. "I have to leave here. Jesus, Father Taliafero knows? Come with me to Hawaii."

Again, I shook my head. "I'm not leaving." Tears flowed down my cheeks. "Jorge said he will come for me. "I'm going to Cuba to be with him."

Victor put the cork in the bottle and set it on the inside support of the barn wall. He turned to me and said, "I told Papa we all have to leave. Hawaii was our best option. Our only option. If we stay, we'll die here. Lolo suffered a slow death. Then Papa died." Victor moved close and got face to face with me. He spoke firmly. "Celia can't come until she has the baby, but she can stay with Aunt Lottie. I'll send money for her." He patted my hand. "You and I have to leave now. We're not safe here. Do you understand?"

"Jorge and I are getting married." My lower lip began to quiver and tears rolled down my cheeks.

Victor rolled his head back. "Fina." He paused and looked at me, sniffing my tears. "I will do what I can for you." He stepped back. "I'll send money from Hawaii."

I held my head in my hands and said, "Thank you."

"Dear God, you're a stubborn woman." He shook his head and his face grew red. "Or stupid." He ran his fingers through his curly hair. "Jorge is gone. He's writing to every one of his family members." His voice raised. "Have you gotten a letter from your lover?"

"Don't be cruel."

DECEMBER 26, 1899, came too fast. Once again, the calendar was my enemy. The last sugar cane ship was leaving and was about to take Victor and Martina from me. Or maybe it was me who refused to go with them. In any case, we were separating for the first time. I wondered what life was like in Hawaii and expected it was something like life in Puerto Rico. Hopefully without the Caribbean hurricanes.

Victor hitched the wagon for our final ride down the mountain together. I knew I would return to Adjuntas, but felt certain he and Martina were leaving our homeland for good. My sisters were already at the apartment in Ponce, getting Celia settled in. Martina had a few things to do before the trip and wanted to sort through her belongings. She set aside a trunk for me to send to her at a later date and would bring only one suitcase with her. I packed up what I could from the house and had to leave more than I wanted behind.

Victor unloaded the last trunk from the wagon

and carried it upstairs to Martina's apartment. "I think that's it. You should have everything you need here." He looked around the crowded apartment.

"You brought the clock?" Celia said with a smile.

Victor groaned and I pursed my lips to send the signal to Celia not to say a word. Victor had bickered with me about bringing too many things from the house, but I was not about to leave precious items behind. Papa made that clock.

Celia walked over and ran her fingers over the smooth, hand rubbed wood clock case. "Do you think we can hang it on the wall?" She tried to lift it from the top of the crate it lay on.

Victor snorted, walked over to a large picture on the wall. He removed it and hung the clock on the nail. "You girls should be able to handle the rest." He walked up to me, standing in the corner, dug in his pocket and pulled out a paper. He handed me a note with a name and address.

Benito Gonzalez

9 Calle Veranda

Ponce

"See him if you get into trouble."

I nodded and tucked the note into my skirt pocket.

"Good luck, Fina." Victor gave me a hug and handed me some money. "That's all that's left. I kept a little for us to get started."

"We'll manage. Don't worry. Aunt Lottie has a few

jobs for me already." I wiped my eyes.

Martina's small apartment was stacked with trunks and furniture from our house. I couldn't leave the rocking chair that Papa had made behind. I saw Martina, alone in the bedroom and stepped in to talk to her. "Martina, I wanted to say good-bye."

She turned around and I saw the pocket watch in her hand. "I can't," she said.

"I want to explain," I stepped closer. "I took it for you. I never wanted to keep it."

Martina put her hand up. "You pretend to care about me, about family, but you are full of lies." Her voice raised and tears pooled in her eyes.

"Martina, please," I begged her. "You heard Papa's story, now allow me to tell you what I saw."

"You mean how you shot my husband? The man who gave you a home?" Martina shook with anger. "Fina, you killed your own family, then dumped his body."

"We buried him."

"Oh, my God."

"Papa was nervous — we were both frightened that the posse would find us any moment. Papa decided we had to bury him. Dino's watch chain captured the moonlight and sparkled. I remembered you gave it to him and I grabbed it so that you would have something."

"So, I would have something?"

"I planned to tell you everything, but when we got back to Dino's house and saw what had happened—" I shook my head, "I couldn't."

"You let it go on, Fina." Martina shook her finger. "I waited for him to return for months. I didn't eat or sleep, worried about my husband. I wondered if he was dead or alive, and you stood by me, knowing all along that you killed him."

"It was an accident."

"I never got to bury my husband. I cried tears in the dark for months, hiding my pain from our daughter. Now, what am I supposed to do? Bury his pocket watch?"

"I thought you would want to keep it."

"Oh, you thought I might want to pass it on to our daughter? A keepsake?" Martina's voice raised. "Here, my dearest Francesca. Here is your father's pocket watch. He wore it the night he was murdered. I think the blood is washed clean. Why don't you play with it?" Martina held it out in the palm of her hand. "Is that what you thought?"

"I wasn't thinking."

"Exactly," Martina said. "You know what I think? I think I'll drop it off the edge of the ship. I'll bury him at sea today."

I nodded and wiped a tear. "All I saw that night was the silhouette of a man holding a gun on Papa. I raised my rifle and fired. When I approached, I saw what I had done. I'm sorry."

"I spared your life by not reporting your crime," Martina huffed. "You would have been hanged for what you did. Dino was a beloved man. If I was you, I'd leave Puerto Rico." Martina walked past me to the living room and I followed.

Victor hugged Celia's round waist. "We'll see you and the baby soon, Mejia." He kissed her on the cheek.

Martina kissed Celia good-bye and turned to walk out the door without looking at me. Celia walked them out and I watched from the window. I waved, but

Martina never looked up. I sobbed and wailed so hard I could hardly breathe.

I wished I was going with them.

AFTER PAPA'S DEATHBED CONFESSION, I stopped going to Mass in Ponce.

Father Taliaferro posed a great threat. He wouldn't look at me and I avoided him in town. I missed the comfort of being in church and felt the accusing gaze of others, who wondered why I wasn't there. My days grew long and I felt it in my body that change was coming. I hated change, and prayed to God for help. The answer came quickly.

It was time for me to leave Puerto Rico. I was in danger. I watched for the priest whenever I walked around town. He was close to the Cesari family and had regular dinners at their hacienda. As soon as Celia's baby is born, we will leave for Hawaii, I thought.

The new year brought loneliness and uncertainty. Victor promised to send money and I looked for work, but with the devastation of local coffee and sugar plantations after the hurricane, families didn't require the domestic help they once did. The only employment I could find was doing laundry and ironing for three families in town.

Celia was sick throughout her pregnancy and I did the cleaning and cooking for us. Neither of us was happy. I tried to bite my tongue. Poor Celia's belly was bulging now and she was beginning to express fear about giving birth. Alone and rejected by Antonio, at only sixteen years old, she would soon be a mother. I had nothing to complain about. Waiting for Jorge seemed like a small problem.

Letters were precious and rarely arrived from Hawaii. By March we got our first word from family. Victor wrote to me and Celia, while Martina's letters were addressed only to Celia.

"You read yours already?" Celia asked, clutching her letter from Martina.

"Oh, yes," I said. "I'm sorry. Victor didn't write much. Here, read it." I handed the one page note to her.

"Our brother, the great lover of books," Celia laughed. "He's not much of a writer, but he takes care of family." She held up ten American dollars in cash.

"Are you going to read yours?"

"I'll read it aloud for you." Celia gave a half smile.

Martina's Letter

March 1900

My Dearest Celia,

I hope all is well in Ponce. It's hard to get letters here. Word from Puerto Rico is slow. Your letters arrive months later. News is shared between others here in camp. We heard that things are bad and food is in short supply. Please write and tell me how you are. I worry about you. Let me know when the baby arrives. Dearest sister, remember my friend Paulo? He told me to contact him if I needed help. I want you to find him in San Juan if you ever need help. His name is Paulo Velez de Rivera.

Victor lives nearby and is well. He works hard in the fields and does some kind of special work for the plantation owners. He arranged for me to take a job as a seamstress and I'm learning to make hats from a woman I met. It got me out of the fields. The work was terrible and the sun gave me headaches. I brought little Francesca along with me. She cried and begged me to go home. Our real home. I miss our hacienda in Puerto Rico.

Dear sister, I know this letter is long, but I want to tell you everything. When you leave for Hawaii, do not take the sugar cane ship. We will send you money for passage. Give us time. Victor will send money and you need to save a little from each letter for a ticket.

I can't imagine getting on a ship again. I don't talk about our voyage. None of us do, but it haunts me and keeps me awake some nights. The ship was crowded and ripe with the smell of people crammed into tight quarters. Food was limited and rotten. I've never seen so many desperate people. Fights broke out and Victor's friend, Armando, beat a man badly for taking food from our basket. Francesca witnessed it and I realized for the first time how ruthless men could be. The thief apologized and begged him to stop, but Armando said he needed to show the others that our family was not to be taken advantage of.

We arrived at New Orleans where we were greeted by armed men. They stood with rifles and acted as guards, directing us off the ship and onto a Railroad train bound for the west. From the West Coast, they told us to get on another ship to Hawaii. The first trip had been so horrendous that many tried to get off and stay in New Orleans, but the men from the sugar company used force and threatened them. We felt like slaves being herded to labor camps. One woman ahead of me had her child taken from her arms by a man with a rifle. She had to make a choice to continue the journey or lose her child. She cooperated and they returned the infant. A man tried to step out of line and was head-butted with a rifle and knocked unconscious. I never saw so much regret and anger, but there was no turning back. I hoped for a better future in the Pacific Islands.

When we got to Oahu, they separated passengers into groups, but I made sure we always stood tightly together with Armando. He told me that when we arrived, Victor would see to it that we would be sent to the plantation Victor had already signed on to, in Maui. We saw families separated and sent to different plantations, on different islands in Hawaii. One woman, who I made friends with, had some spots on her skin, perhaps from poor nutrition or from the sun but they sent her to the leper colony and I never heard if she came back or is still there. This was the most frightening time of the journey for me. I could not survive if I was separated from Victor.

It was our turn for inspection and we received our work orders. Armando was relieved to see he was assigned as an overseer but was being sent to a plantation on Oahu. We were being separated and I was terrified that I was next. Then we got our papers. Francesca and I were being sent to Victor's plantation which made me happy.

We were herded into labor camp housing. I don't know why they call it a house. They're more like huts, cramped and lacking provacy. Through the wall I can hear my neighbor urinate. The smell makes me sick. I dream of my life in a hacienda. I miss our homeland and the sounds of the night. There are no coquis to sing to me here.

One night, Francesca developed a high fever. The medical care they promised was not what I expected. I waited a day until the doctor was available, and then he treated me poorly. He acted like I was ignorant. He has no idea of my education or what my life was like in Puerto Rico. I felt insulted and helpless for Francesca.

A woman approached me as I walked out the door of the building and spoke Spanish to me. She was the American doctor's wife. She was kind and offered help for Francesca. We became friendly but needed to be careful that the others didn't see us together. The woman warned me about the sugar cane company owners and their management. She said the reason the company went to Puerto Rico to recruit was because of labor disputes with their Japanese workers. The workers demanded better conditions and higher pay. The company wants to flood the labor pool and needs U.S. citizen workers. The United States takeover of Puerto Rico made our men prime candidates and the hurricane made us vulnerable and desperate. As non-aliens, we needed no paperwork and no passport. We were easy for them to pick up. Remember how they said "Just come aboard...no paperwork necessary!" All their promises — only to take advantage of us and fill their bank accounts. The Japanese workers are not too happy with us and it's not our fault. Pray for our Puerto Rican laborers.

Victor was hired as overseer which kept him out of the disputes between the laborers. There is a clear division between the Japanese, Koreans, Chinese, and Puerto Ricans. Tension is high and the sugar company's plan worked out perfectly for their profits.

We are saving money to move to the mainland. Victor says New York is nice.

Your loving sister,

Martina

WHEN I CLOSED MY EYES, I remembered- what April was like in Adjuntas. The fragrant white flowers that blossomed on the coffee trees, presenting the opening of coffee season in our picturesque mountain village filled my senses. I blinked the image away. I didn't want to remember the beauty of Adjuntas, because it was taken from us, destroyed by the hurricane. Nothing made sense to me anymore. Jorge, our plantation, Mama and Papa. All gone. Why was I still here?

A letter arrived by messenger in March, 1900. "What is it?" Celia asked.

"It's from Antonio. He's taking over the apartment."

"What?"

"He says it's part of the real estate owned by the family. It's part of the hotel, not the store," I said.

"I wish Martina was here," Celia said. "Did she give you the papers from the sale?"

"No. I'll send a telegram to her." I threw Antonio's letter on the bed. "Bastard. He's not going to take responsibility for getting you pregnant." I saw that Celia was crying. "I'm sorry. After you have the baby we'll go to Hawaii." I sat next to her and put my arm around her shoulders. "We'll all be together again."

I sent a telegram to Martina in Hawaii and she answered.

No papers. Used his lawyer.

I gave the clock and rocking chair that Papa had made to Aunt Lottie in Ponce, while Celia and I moved into a small, sparsely furnished apartment in a poor barrio of Ponce. After growing up in what was considered a wealthy household, with servants and private teachers, our lives were reduced to poverty and I was barely finding work as a domestic. We had only a trunk of clothes, a bible and a few family photos. One morning in early April, 1900 Celia awoke with a twisting pain in her lower abdomen.

"It feels like someone is wringing a washcloth down low, here." She held her hands on her lower abdomen. "It woke me from a deep sleep."

"Oh, dear. How often are the pains coming?" I asked.

"It started slow, the pain intensified, then weakened. They're not regular." She shifted on a narrow, straw mattress. We lay quiet in our beds, waiting. As she drifted back to sleep another pain jolted her awake. It was time for her child to be born.

Celia's fists pulled at the bed sheets. I covered my face, to hide from the pain she was experiencing.

She began to moan louder, "Cramps squeeze my stomach tight!" she cried.

I got up and went down the hall. I paced back and forth, sitting with her and stepping outside for a break. Hours passed and it was hard to watch Celia in such terrible pain. She was so young, only sixteen, and it made me angry at Antonio for getting her pregnant. I heard the neighbor's roosters crowing through the paper-thin walls. Outside the back door of our small quarters was an outhouse. I helped her shuffle out to urinate. I swatted at the flies and walked her back down the hallway. Celia yelled in pain and I realized it was time to send for the midwife.

I helped Celia to her bed and brought a wet cloth for her head. The midwife comforted her and that evening she sent me to get some medicine to ease Celia's pain.

The midwife stayed by her side during her very long labor. Just before the birth, the midwife sent me on another errand to her mother's house, for a special medicine she would need for the baby. It was getting late and her friend Eduardo took me. Her mother lived about thirty minutes away and it took what seemed like an eternity to prepare the concoction. I paced the small kitchen while she boiled, then simmered the mixture in a large pot. The old woman stirred it and talked to me about her cures. She was a crazy old woman and I began to doubt her ability to produce a proper elixir. The mixture had to cool before she could pour it into a bottle. This errand took me over two hours.

While I was gone on the midwife's errand, and after fifteen hours of labor, Celia gave birth to a daughter. I returned to see Celia was very weak and the midwife had wrapped her in a sheet for comfort.

"How are you?" I asked.

Celia was groggy and said, "The midwife wrapped

the baby in a blanket and walked into another room. She didn't say anything to me." Celia's voice trailed off. "I heard a faint cry from my baby."

"Was it a boy or a girl?"

"The midwife came back in and said, 'Your baby was disfigured. I am very sorry but she has died.'" Celia began to cry and wail. "Where is my baby? I want to see my baby!" She tried to get up from the bed.

The midwife gently placed her hand on Celia's shoulders. "You must not get up. You must rest now."

I looked at her, confused. How could this have happened? Why had God cursed our family?

"I want my baby." Celia struggled to get up. "Where is she?"

The midwife pressed firmly on Celia's shoulders. She held her down. "She's gone. It's better you don't see her. Believe me on this. I must take care of you." The midwife reached for a cup of elixir. "Here, drink this. It will calm you."

For the next three days, the midwife continued to offer the elixir. Celia remained in her bed and slept most of the time.

There was no birth registration for Celia to fill out. She was denied the shame of writing Hija Natural, an illegitimate child born to her. She did, however, fill out a death record.

THE BEDROOM DOOR CREAKED and woke me in the early hours. I turned to see Celia standing in the doorway. Her cheeks were streaked in tears and her nightgown was streaked in breastmilk. I sat up, but couldn't find words in my jumbled, sleepy head. She turned and walked away in silence. I hung my head and cried.

As the weeks passed, Celia's breasts no longer filled with milk, but she filled with grief. "I don't know why you won't listen," she said. "I've told you, my baby isn't dead."

I knew it was time to leave for Hawaii. Celia was broken and I couldn't lift her spirits. I was afraid for her. She had lost touch with reality, thinking her baby was alive. "Celia, we've talked about this," I explained. "The midwife told us that your baby doesn't have a grave because it was buried with the poor. There's no marker."

"I've been to the cemetery many times," she insisted. "I want to see where they buried my baby. They won't show me," Celia's face was red with anger. "And I heard my baby cry. She isn't dead!"

"The baby was disfigured and died." *If only we'd had the money for a proper grave.*

"Why won't you believe me?" she screamed.

I WENT TO SEE DR. ORTIZ about Celia the next day. He came to the house and left without speaking to me. Celia was upset and said, "You should stay out of my business." She slammed a bottle on the table and said, "He gave me a bottle of elixir. Said to take one teaspoon every day to calm myself."

"Oh."

Five days later, I came home from the market to a quiet house. "Celia, I picked up some eggs." I put the groceries away and started a pot of coffee. "Celia, do want coffee?" I walked to her room and found her sprawled across the bed. The empty bottle of elixir lay next to her.

The doctor said if I hadn't found her when I did, she would have died. Celia lay in bed for a week and slept most of the time. Dr. Ortiz came to visit daily and I cared for her at home.

One day in early May, as I was leaving the hotel, Antonio and Jorge's sister Juliana approached. She said, "Fina, I'm so sorry."

I nodded.

Juliana said, "We didn't think — He only wanted to—"

"Juliana," Aunt Juana appeared and interrupted. "Let's not intrude on poor Fina. She has a lot on her mind." Aunt Juana placed her arm around Juliana and pulled her away.

At the end of May 1900, I bought a ticket to Hawaii for Celia with all the money we had. It was time for her to leave Puerto Rico.

CELIA LOOKED AT THE ENVELOPE post-marked from Hawaii, then must have seen the disappointment on my face. It was addressed only to her. "Are you okay?" she asked.

It had been almost six months since Victor and Martina left for Hawaii. Celia was about to leave and join them. "I'm going to be alone in a place that no longer feels like home," I said. "I think you'll be all right. You'll be with family."

"But this is our homeland," Celia said.

"It's not what it used to be. What has all the turmoil done to us?" I reached out and stroked her hair. "I remember the little girl who sang in the wagon with Papa, or pouted to get a toy." I smiled. "I guess we both did that. I miss the old life." I looked down at my skinny body. "What have I become?"

"Let's not do this — let's read the letters we got," Celia said. She held up a second letter.

"At least Victor is writing to me," I said. "His is

addressed to both of us. Martina only wrote to you."

Celia handed me the envelope from Victor.

I wiped my eyes and said, "Let's read Victor's together."

"You read it," Celia said. She peered over my shoulder.

"Dearest Sisters "

"He got married?" Celia yelled in my ear.

I jumped from my chair. "Jesus, Celia."

"I read ahead," Celia said. "Read the letter. What did he say?"

I scanned quickly and stopped at the words 'married.' "He met someone, and they married in April. She's from Moca."

Celia stepped back and sat in her chair. "He married a Puerto Rican. Went all the way to Hawaii to meet her. What do you know."

I continued, "He goes on. He says there are many Puerto Ricans in Hawaii and they gather to play music and dance on Saturday evenings. He met her at one of the social events."

"I wonder what it's like in Hawaii." Celia stared out the window. "Do you wonder what their life is like there?"

"I think about it too. You'll be there soon."

"I should be happy about Victor's letter," Celia said. "Happy to hear he got married. Instead, I don't feel anything. I feel sad that I don't have that." She started to cry. "Someone to marry."

"I understand. I wish we could have gone with them, but now you have your ticket." I looked back at the letter in my hand. "I've noticed that Victor's letters were a little warmer. I should have known he was in love." I thought about the money he included in his letters and worried about the cost to continue to support to us. Now that he was married, would he continue? I needed to leave for Hawaii or Cuba soon.

"Can we read Martina's letter together?" I asked.

Celia handed it to me. I read it aloud. Martina wrote about life in Hawaii. She was making friends and going to the dances on Saturday nights. "Martina always loved to dance," I said.

"Yes, she insisted they have music every weekend." Celia sniffed and wiped her face. She managed a smile and said, "I remember Dino never moved so fast. He danced and danced, to keep up with her."

I nodded. "She goes on. Oh, dear. The housing they promised is like labor huts here. She complains that she can hear the neighbor urinate through the thin walls. Oh, Celia. They're living in very poor conditions."

Celia left the next morning for Hawaii. I was now alone.

The letters from Martina stopped once Celia arrived in Hawaii. Soon, Celia's letters began to arrive. My dear sister's letters were full of love and encouragement. She sounded better and I was happy that she was with family. Victor's letters carried the scent of his cigars but something else. He was sentimental and had become a father figure to us. Love had softened him and he sounded less angry. I sniffed the cigar scented letters and held them like a warm embrace. He asked me to come to Hawaii in every letter, and he sent money. Even with the money, I was having a hard time and existed on meals of rice and beans with an occasional invitation for chicken stew on Sundays at my cousins' apartment. It was time to find more work or move to Hawaii and join the family. But, I had not yet given up hope that Jorge would return or send for me.

After re-reading Martina's first letter to Celia I was worried for the family. She said their living conditions were poor and her heart was full of despair. It was a life of prejudice and fear for Puerto Ricans in Maui. It was important to know the truth, but it made me afraid to join them. I let two more ships leave port without me while the family waited in Hawaii. It was easier to stay in Puerto Rico, even though I watched friends and loved ones suffer and die from disease and starvation all around me.

I grew bone thin and prayed for Jorge to come for me. My unanswered prayers left me empty, spiraling in a dark place in my mind. I shuttered people out, choosing solitude. After a while, I was afraid to stay and too frightened to leave. Sleep eluded me and I lay awake for hours at night. There were no sounds of the coqui frogs. Instead, I occasionally heard a neighbor arguing or a local drunk in the street.

If Jorge wasn't going to send for me or return to me, I wished I would just die. I read Martina and Celia's letters again and again, searching for some new grain of information.

All I got were tear-stained letters and a confused mind.

In early June 1900, I sat outside the hotel. A daily walk was part of my routine, when I wasn't working doing laundry. If I could sit outside all day I would. Anything to get out of the apartment. Jorge's Aunt Juana approached with her usual prune face. I kept my head down in hopes she wouldn't make conversation.

She greeted me warmly, "Hello." Aunt Juana's wrinkles stretched upwards and I saw her toothy smile for the first time. She went into the store. Aunt Juana walked out with a box tucked under her arm. When she turned to walk away, I saw the label read, "Christening gown."

Something wasn't right about Aunt Juana. She couldn't walk away fast enough. Usually, she stopped and quizzed me about my family. And something wasn't right about her purchase of a christening gown. Dino was not a grandparent, and neither was she. My mind clicked. I spent the day thinking about it. The next day I visited my Auntie Lottie.

"That's strange, why would Juana buy a christening gown? That's a baby gift a family member would buy. Just like when she bought the christening gown for Martina's baby." Auntie Lottie said. "Whose baby is being baptized?"

"I know everyone in that family," I said. "The only babies born were Martina's and Celia's."

We paused and stared at each other. Aunt Lottie said, "You don't think—"

"Oh, my god!" I cupped my hand over my mouth. "Celia wasn't crazy? Could her baby be alive?"

"That would be the cruelest thing Antonio could do." Aunt Lottie's soft cheeks trembled.

"After Celia ... got sick, Juliana tried to talk to me. She seemed to have something say but Aunt Juana stopped her."

I lowered my voice. "We're not safe here. I've been saving a little money from each letter Victor sends me.

But it's still not enough for a ticket." I wrung my hands. "The last sugar cane ship for Hawaii is scheduled to leave at the end of the month," I stood and paced.

"I have to be on that ship."

A SENSE OF PEACE settled deep in my soul once I had made my decision to leave for Hawaii. I didn't care about anyone anymore. I was no longer afraid of Aunt Juana or what might happen to me. But I was not going to leave without giving her a piece of my mind. She was going to tell me where Celia's baby was.

I asked my cousin Jose to take me up the road to Adjuntas, to see Juana. I knew he made the trip each week.

"I can take you on Wednesday. That's my day to bring supplies up there. I'll drop you off to see Juana, then go to town," he said. "I'll pick you up and we'll be back to Ponce by dinner."

I agreed and Jose picked me up at nine in the morning after he stocked his cart with supplies. The bumpy ride with his donkey and small cart wasn't like the pleasurable carriage I was accustomed to with Dino and Martina.

We started up the hill and made small talk about the family. Jose was the son of my Aunt Lottie, my mother's sister and was always a chatter box.

We began the twists and turns section of the narrow road. I trusted he was a good driver, but he drove dangerously close to the edge. Jose clenched a whistle between his teeth and held the reins tight. Somehow, he was able to talk from one side of his mouth. "What do you need to see Juana Cesari about?" Jose asked. "She's a little old for you two to be friends, isn't she?"

"I'm leaving for Hawaii as soon as I save up enough for a ticket."

"It's about time." He flicked the reins.

"You're not surprised?"

"Why didn't you go with your family? You should have left with Celia."

"I have business to attend to."

"Juana is that business?"

I shifted in my seat. He asks too many questions, I thought.

"I wouldn't cross her," he said. "She'll cut your head off. I've heard stories about her, when she was a young woman. She is a tough one. How do you think she's living in a fine brick house with servants?"

I began to sense the old, familiar feeling of nerves rattle my bones. Maybe this wasn't a good idea. I was no match for Juana. I took a breath and exhaled. Between Jose's driving and his questions, I was losing my courage to face Juana. What if she brings up questions about her brother Dino? I thought.

"Hola!" Jose yelled to a local, who waved from their porch. The road to Adjuntas filled my heart with love and calmed my nerves. It would always be home.

The lush green tropical growth welcomed me in a canopy of green, adorned with colorful flowers. It truly was paradise.

Jose took the whistle from his mouth. "Here, hold this," he said.

It was covered in his saliva. I let it drop on my skirt.

He lit a cigar.

"Can I take a puff?" I asked.

He looked at me with surprise. "Don't inhale too much. Just a puff." He handed it to me.

I held it between my first finger and my thumb, just like Dino, Antonio, Papa and Victor did. I puffed it just like Martina did.

"Damn! You aren't as proper as I thought," he said.

I handed it back to him and adjusted the pistol in my pocket. "No, Jose I am not."

"You can handle old lady Juana."

Juana

JOSE DROPPED ME OFF at the bottom of the road to the Cesari hacienda. Juana lived at the big house since Martina moved out. She said it needed a caretaker.

I walked up hill I had walked my entire life, and remembered playing in the field as children and kissing Jorge behind the banana trees. Finally, I reached the top. I stepped to the porch and paused to catch my breath before knocking on the massive wooden double doors. Everything familiar, but nothing that feels like home here, I thought. I hadn't been to the Cesari home since the reading of Dino's will, and it was the first time I'd returned up the mountain road that led to our old plantation. I thought about turning and leaving. I took a breath and knocked three times.

Anger overtook my nerves. Prepared to face Jorge's prune-faced Auntie Juana, I was ready to ask my questions. Instead, Pilar the servant greeted me. I knew she remembered me. We'd worked together when I was a domestic for Dino. She had served as a nanny to Francesca. Rather than the usual welcome to the parlor or grand living room, I was directed to the kitchen, my old working quarters. I sat at the kitchen table and gathered my thoughts. I scanned the room and noted the same dishes and cups organized neatly in the cupboard. The same clock hung on the wall. The only change was that people were missing. No Isabella. My sisters were gone. It felt strange to be there. I wiped my palms on my skirt.

Pilar cast her eyes downward and set a glass of guava juice on the table. She backed away and said, "I will let Dona Cesari know you're here."

I gulped down the entire glass of guava juice. *What was I doing?*

Auntie Juana stood in the doorway as if she was too good to enter the kitchen. Her eyes pierced right through me and she said, "Come this way." She turned around and walked toward the front door, her cane clicking on the tile floor. I thought she was about to ask me to leave. "Please sit down," she motioned to a comfortable chair in the parlor. She took a seat across from me.

"What can I do for you?" Auntie Juana had always cut a slender figure, but she'd aged ten years in the last two and she was bone thin. Her eyes were sunken and deep creases carved her face. I'd always feared her, but being alone with her now, I saw an old, frail woman. Was it her who'd changed? Or me?

I wanted to slip out quietly but I needed answers. Words would not come and I searched for what to say.

Juana sat up straight and repeated, "What can I do for you?"

"Thank you for seeing me. I hope your family is well," I nodded with a half-smile. "You know my family is in Hawaii—"

"Fina," Aunt Juana stiffened. "there is no need to play coy with me. Of course, I know where your family is. And I know where you live. Now, what is it girl?"

I cleared my throat and continued, "When I was sitting outside the hotel, you greeted me as you walked outside."

"Yes — and?"

"You were carrying a box."

Juana's dark eyes widened.

"The label read baptismal gown. I wanted to ask you if the gown fit the baby? How did she look?"

Juana adjusted her position in her chair and said, "It was for my niece and I heard the baby looked beautiful. I didn't see her." She looked away. "I sent the gift to my niece in New York."

"Oh, I see. I knew there were no babies in your family and I was bewildered as to why you would purchase a baptismal gown. I thought it might be for Celia's baby."

Juana stood and leaned on her cane. "You thought? Too bad you had no thoughts of my nephew, Jorge. I think I've heard enough." She started to walk toward the door. "I'll see you out."

I stood and turned to follow. Her words echoed in my head. "What do you mean, no thoughts of Jorge? I've been waiting for him. Why do you think I've stayed in Puerto Rico all this time? And not gone to be with my family?"

She stopped and turned to me. Her eyes were fierce and on fire. "You never wrote to him."

"I wrote many letters. I gave them to Antonio.

He said he would send them to Jorge. I asked for Jorge's address but Antonio wouldn't give it to me." I tried to steady my emotions, but tears escaped and ran down my cheeks. "He told me Jorge never wrote me any letters." I looked into Juana's face and no longer saw a prune face. I looked deep into her eyes and suddenly I understood. She was a strong woman who was protecting her family. "Juana, Jorge promised he would come for me."

Juana's eyes flickered and softened. "Fina, I should not have said you had no thoughts of Jorge." She placed her hand on my shoulder. "Thank you for telling me this."

She walked me to the door without another word of explanation. Was I to feel satisfied with her pity? I started to say something and stopped. "Thank you for the juice," was all I could say.

✡ ✡ ✡

The next day there was a quiet knock on my door. I had just finished washing up and was dressing. With my hair unkept and half-dressed, I called through the door, "Who is it?"

"Juana Cesari y Lopez." It was prune-faced Auntie Juana.

I wrapped a robe around me and opened the door. "Please, come in," I said.

Juana stepped in and looked around the small one room apartment. "Sit down," I offered my only chair and I sat on the straw mattress.

"Sorry to interrupt," Juana pointed to the clothes on the bed.

Juana intimidated me, speaking in a formal tone and dressed in her usual plain, black dress. I fully regretted my visit the day before and felt I was about to receive my punishment. Suddenly, she jumped up and began to pace the room. Her cane tapped on the wooden floor and I wondered what she wanted from me. Tap, tap went her cane. Nerves made me feel unsettled.

"It's kind of you to visit today," I said.

Juana stopped, turned to me and said, "Fina, Jorge never got your letters."

I tried to catch my breath.

"He wrote you many letters, which Antonio never gave to you."

My fingers curled and snapped the butterfly hair pin in my hand. "Why?" I said. I stood and tried not to scream. I blinked away the tears and my body shook with anger. "He is pure evil!"

"There's more," Juana moved closer and whispered, "You are a smart girl. The baptismal gown wasn't for my niece. It was for my great-niece."

"What?" I cried out. I dropped the pieces of the hair pin on the bed.

Juana placed her finger over her mouth, "Shhh, these walls are paper-thin. Celia's baby is with Antonio. The gown was for her."

"Oh, my god!" I said and cupped my hands over my mouth. The thought of Celia and her baby was like a weeping wound in my heart.

"Fina," she said in a quiet voice. "It's not easy to tell you this, but I must. The midwife notified Antonio when Celia went into labor and they had someone ready to take the child. When the baby was born, the midwife handed her off to someone waiting and told Celia her baby had not survived. She's alive and being raised by Antonio's sister, Juliana. The baby's name is Adriana."

"How could he," I shook my head.

"He wanted the baby," she said, "but he didn't want Celia."

I wiped my eyes with a handkerchief. "Antonio didn't recognize the birth," I said. "The baby was born heja natural. She's Celia's." I was certain the record would support my statement and Celia would recover her child.

"Fina, remember they told her the baby was dead," Aunt Juana said. "He registered the infant as a live birth and he is listed as the father. He had her baptized, with the gown I purchased."

"I don't feel too good." I sat back on the mattress.

"Antonio is not an honorable man." Aunt Juana made sour face. "It will catch up to him."

I was surprised to hear Auntie Juana speak against her family. I blurted out, "I'd like to catch up to him first."

Juana held up her hand and said, "There is something we can do." She pointed around the room "Look at this place," then she pointed at me. "Look at you, skinny girl. You must take care of yourself. How can you do that here, in Puerto Rico where many are starving and sick? You're living in the poorest barrio. It's time, Fina. Time to leave. Your family has been begging you to come to Hawaii."

"I know, I've been waiting —"

"Waiting for Jorge. I know." Juana patted my hand. "You are a stubborn girl, like your old Auntie Lottie. Go to Hawaii, dear girl."

"What about—"

"Listen to me," Juana clicked her cane on the floor. "I know you are angry. It's time to make a plan." She reached for my hand. "Jorge and Antonio are meeting in Cuba for business. Antonio departs on Tuesday. I can arrange for Celia's name to be added to the Civil Registry as mother. I think I can also amend the Church record," Juana said. "If you travel alone with a child or have a servant with you, it will be more difficult, and your name will be easy for Antonio to trace in the ship's records," Juana explained. "It's better for you to be married and travel as husband and wife with a child. Under your husband's name. You understand. I will arrange for your tickets."

"Married?"

"I can't go back in time and change things, but I can right this wrong. I have a few favors owed. I'll have a groom ready. He might be a little older."

"I'm only nineteen." I felt my face grow hot with anger.

"Or you can go to Cuba without Adriana. I will let Jorge know you're on your way and he will meet you there." She added, "But the ship leaves next week from San Juan, I'm sorry, but you need to make a decision now.

"I must choose?"

"You're not listening to me." Click, click, Juana tapped her cane. She took me by the shoulders and shook me. "We have to do this before Antonio returns." The ship leaves for Hawaii next week. If you want to take the baby to Celia you must leave on that ship. I will send a telegraph to Jorge. Be patient. You will be with him later."

"Be patient?" I cried. "Marry another man?"

"The marriage can be annulled or you can divorce," Juana leaned in close. "Listen to me, if you want to get Adriana out of Puerto Rico, you need to make it look like she's yours. You don't want Antonio chasing after you. If you travel using your own name you're asking for trouble."

"I know a man who can do me a favor. Cooperate in an arranged marriage. Let me contact him," I said, "What will happen to you when Antonio returns?"

"I'm an old woman and have been through many things in life. My brother Dino was a good man of impeccable character and he would not be proud of his son Antonio. I blame Antonio and Jorge for the police coming the night my brother disappeared. I'm certain they killed Dino after he delivered Jorge to the boat. He must have met up with the local volunteer Police idiots working for Spain on his way home. If I ever have the chance, I'll kill any man who served Spain that night." Juana clenched her jaw. "I can take care of myself, and I will take care of Antonio."

"We're all under American protection now, even those men who chased after Dino and Jorge," I said. "But I know there remain groups loyal to Spain. Many are plantation owners."

"Oh, yes," she looked away as if her mind drifted. "These loyalties are in the blood."

"Why are you helping me?" I asked.

"My mama immigrated from Spain on a ship where illness spread throughout. One morning, my mama woke beside her dead parents. She was only ten years old." Tears pooled in her eyes but were contained like a small pond and shook when she spoke.

Finally, one let loose and traced a crease in Juana's face like water trickling down a rock wall. She wiped her cheek and continued, "Another woman on the ship took her and raised her but my mother longed for her parents. Adriana reminds me of my dear Mama. She belongs with Celia. And this is only one of the cruel things that Antonio has done. Please tell Celia that I wish her well." Her leathered face softened and her voice cracked. She whispered, "Write to me."

I swallowed hard and allowed an uncontrolled tear to escape and slide down my cheek.

"How will I get to San Juan?"

Latest Cablegrams

Ponce, March 3rd, 1900.

Puerto Ricans Starving!

The situation is now more serious than at any time before the hurricane. Manypeople are starving, and the price of rice, beans and codfish have increased from 50 to 100percent. Demonstrations against the delay of support from the United States government are arising. In the mountain region, living conditions are poor and people are devastated. Women cannot leave their huts because they have no clothing. Children are not attending school because they are naked. These are civilized, loving people. They cannot understand the delay. Things are desperate. Even wealthy land owners cannot command ready cash.

MARTINA SAT ON THE PORCH in Camp Number 3, in Maui with her brother Victor. The sound of musical instruments tuning up in the background caught Victor's attention. "It's time. Let's go join everyone," he said.

"Victor." Martina's voice cracked.

"What is it?" He tipped his glass to get the last sip of wine.

"Now that Celia is here and we have Fina's telegram I need to talk with you about some things. Can we take a walk?"

"Fina's telegram, that was something," Victor looked around. "Let's walk."

"Come on you two!" a voice called out from inside the house.

"We'll be along soon," Victor yelled back.

They slipped off their sandals and stepped barefoot into the sand. The sky was awash in reds, pinks and purples. The orange-red sun hovered over the ocean like a fireball. "Quick, it's about to disappear," Martina said. They walked toward the beach and stopped to watch the sun drop into the ocean.

"How is Celia?" Victor asked. "Is she crocheting baby things?"

Martina smiled. "She's nervous, excited and I think in a little disbelief. But she says she knew her baby was alive. I hope the trip isn't too hard for Fina all alone with a baby." Martina leaned against a coconut tree. "I never asked you to reveal secrets about the rebellion in Yauco, but was Antonio with you or in another battalion?"

Victor snapped his head around and gave her a hard stare. "Battalion? Who did you talk to?"

"It's only us here. We're safe," she said. "Living in the same house with Antonio, let me just say I've gotten to know who he is."

"What are you getting at?" Victor huffed and stood back.

"He's a coward who'd sell his mother to save his own life," she said with a snarl. "Was he with you in Yauco? Did he show courage or cowardice?" She leaned in. "That's what I want to know."

"What brings all this up?" he asked in the descending darkness.

"I want to know if you were his leader. His senior in rank," she added.

"Whoa, hold on." Victor held up his hands. "It sounds like you've given this a lot of thought, and you want to discuss it now? After more than two years?"

"He allowed you to speak to him as if you were his

superior. You slapped him on the back of the head, like you did to us as kids," she said.

"Antonio and I were like brothers. You know we were both working to free Puerto Rico from Spain. I was his superior, and yes, he is a coward. He couldn't handle it when things got hot in Yauco. Spain got word we were coming and ambushed us. He cringed in the corner like a whipped dog, and I got him out of there."

"I knew it," she said. She shook her head and wrapped a shawl around her shoulders. A Southwind breeze blew in.

"I do not take any pleasure in telling you this," he said. "There is more. Antonio panicked, and fired his rifle into the street. He shot the Pacheco girl."

"Antonio?" Martina gasped.

"I rode up right behind him," Victor said. "He was crying on the ground. Jorge rode up, and a crowd was gathering. They saw Jorge."

"Jesus." Martina said. "That's why they think Jorge did it."

"The Spanish soldiers were rounding up our men, the girl was laying in the street. It was a disaster. I gave the order to flee, and pulled Antonio to his feet."

"You saved their lives," Martina said.

"Only temporarily," Victor said. "I knew they would come for us. Antonio had no choice. Give himself up, or let his brother escape to Cuba and take the blame."

"About Antonio," Martina said. "The night the local Police idiots came to the Hacienda, and everything happened, you know, to Celia that night?"

"Yes."

"Antonio was there."

"What?" Victor clenched his fists and his nostrils flared like a bull. She had just waved the red scarf and needed to get out of his way, fast.

He stomped and kicked in the sand. Victor demonstrated the new Korean swear words he'd learned since moving to Hawaii. "Why am I hearing all these things now?"

"I thought you knew. I was dealing with Dino missing and taking care of Celia." Martina circled her hands in the air as if she was capturing her world of troubles. "Jorge fled in women's clothing for God's sake." Her voice raised. "With Dino missing, we didn't know if Jorge was safe. And you think I was worried about you knowing if Antonio was sleeping with Celia that night?"

"He left Celia to be raped?" Victor said. Veins bulged from his neck.

"I don't think he thought the soldiers—"

"Don't excuse him," Victor said. "I knew they were seeing each other. And Fina was with Jorge. That's not what I'm angry about. But he should have protected all of you. Stayed at the house, like a man." Victor groaned in anguish. Antonio came to our house that night." He shook his head. "That's right. Antonio came to tell us he got word the police and their posse were out searching, rounding up men. Papa went off after Dino and Jorge, and I took off with Antonio in another direction to escape capture. Antonio didn't tell me they'd been to the house, or I would have gone there."

"That's Antonio."

Victor shook his head. "He came to get me to protect him. He didn't want to be on his own that night."

"Coward," Martina spit her words. "He doesn't care about anyone but himself."

"He couldn't leave Celia alone. He took her for himself." Victor clenched his jaw.

"She was always in love with him," Martina said. "She hoped he would choose her one day."

"He got her pregnant, then denied the child," Victor said with a raised voice. "I couldn't think less of him as a man, but then to learn he stole the baby and told Celia the child died. Now you tell me he was there that night? What's wrong with Celia?" Victor groaned and fired off a string of profanities.

"We tried to talk to her," Martina said.

"Wait a minute," Victor said. "If Antonio was at the house, when did he leave? I mean had the police left or were they still there?"

"He was in Celia's bed, but escaped out the window and left her alone. I thought you knew that." Martina stepped closer. "He escaped out the window to save his own skin."

"I'll kill him!"

ANTONIO STRUTTED AROUND HIS HOTEL casino on Monday morning, inspecting his business for the week ahead. He wore a three-piece, dark striped suit and black leather shoes with a one-inch heel, bringing him to a full 5'7". Satisfied that he had made his rounds, he settled into his desk chair in the back room, lit a cigar, and sure that he was alone, kicked off his shoes and put his feet on the desk.

A man walked into the casino dressed in a worn jacket, one size too small and pants held up with a rope tied around the waist. He stopped at the backroom door.

Antonio dropped his feet to the ground and slipped into his leather shoes.

The man said, "Good morning, I'm Benito Gonzalez. Cesar sent me." He removed his hat. "I'm here to take you to see the plantation."

"I thought Cesar was picking me up for a personal tour," Antonio said.

"He will meet us there. He asked me to show you

around the fields and harvesting operations first. I am the steward." Benito smiled, revealing a missing tooth in front.

"Very well," Antonio said. He thought the man didn't look too smart. His eyes were small and one drifted to the side. Antonio didn't have much patience for dealing with idiots and Benito looked like one.

Antonio grabbed his silver handled cane and hat and walked out with Benito. He climbed into the horse-drawn carriage. They traveled east two miles down a dusty road to Cesar's sugar cane plantation that Antonio planned to purchase for ten cents on the dollar. There was opportunity for those with money to capitalize on Puerto Rico's ruin. Antonio planned to taste the sweet life from the investments he would make.

"Cesar thought you might be interested in seeing the curing process."

"I grew up on a coffee plantation," Antonio said. "Cutting sugar cane can't be that hard, but I would like to see how it's processed." Antonio puffed his cigar.

"It's very different than coffee, I imagine," Benito said. He held the reins easy.

"Of course." Antonio ran his fingers down the lapel of his new suit.

"Cesar anticipated your curiosity in our operations. I have a few things ready to show you." Benito pulled the carriage up to a Mediterranean style stone and mortar building with a terracotta tiled roof. Two lion statues sat atop stone fence posts, serving as guards. Ornate iron fencing surrounded the building grounds. Vegetation had been cleared, creating a large area within the gates for parking carts and wagons.

"Impressive building," Antonio said. "That's a tall

smokestack."

"Yes, and this is considered a small mill. There is a larger mill about five miles from here. That's the one the American company bought. This one was too small for them. Otherwise, the price would be much higher."

"Why build something so architectural?" Antonio said. "It's in the middle of nowhere."

"The original owner was passionate about the business. His home was fairly simple. This plantation was his love. There is a small residence nearby. Cesar will take you there after we are finished. Come in, I'll show you around."

They climbed out of the carriage. Antonio tossed his cigar butt in the dirt, and they walked inside. The almost empty room had a hollow echo. "This building stays cool until they start the burners," Benito said. "It's a little warm because I have everything running today to show you."

Antonio looked across the large room and saw a row of eight enormous caldrons with lit burners underneath each one. "Now, those look interesting."

"If I may, let's start in here." Benito walked into another room on the left. Antonio followed. "After the sugar cane is cut, it's brought in here, where it's chopped smaller and placed in this cooker." He pointed to what looked like a gigantic cooking pot with a gauge on top.

Antonio ran his hand along a workbench covered in freshly cut sugar cane. Machetes and cane cutting tools lay on a table beside the bench. "We use similar tools at the coffee mill in Adjuntas," he said.

"Of course, yes. The sugar cane is cut, cooked and cured. Cesar will explain it to you in detail. He wanted you to have the opportunity to see it first-hand."

Antonio fanned the air with his hand. "It has an interesting aroma."

"Burnt cane doesn't smell like candy." Benito chuckled. "You get used to it. The smelter is outside. Feel free to look around, if you'll excuse me. I need to check on something while I'm here. You understand, labor always needs to be watched."

"Of course," Antonio said. He turned and walked toward the row of steaming caldrons. The first bullet hit him in the right shoulder. The second dropped him to his knees. He struggled to flop on his belly and crawl across the dirt floor. He dragged his body with one good arm and pushed off with his good leg.

Benito stepped closer. Antonio rolled over and looked up at him with confusion and terror in his eyes. His eyes shifted to the workbench, with a full display of cutting tools. Too far out of reach.

"Victor sends greetings from Hawaii." Benito raised his gun. "This is for his sister."

Antonio's eyes widened. Benito finished him with a shot to the head.

Victor's longtime friend, Benito, took off his jacket and laid it on the workbench. He slid a worn pewter ashtray to the front of the bench. He reached into his jacket pocket and pulled out a Cuban cigar, lit it and sighed. After a few satisfying puffs, he set his cigar in the metal ashtray.

Benito removed his shirt and laid it on his jacket. He reached for his apron, slipped it over his head and tied it around his waist. He stripped off Antonio's new suit, and placed all of Antonio's clothing into the incinerator.

His years growing up slaughtering cattle on his

father's farm next door to Victor's uncle had trained him well for the job. He completed the task with the recently sharpened cane knife and an axe at the workbench. He knew exactly where to land his blade to separate the joints with as little effort as possible. Using a long wooden spatula, he disposed of his work in each of the eight boiling caldrons. The body parts would receive the sugar cure.

Nobody would ever find the remains of Antonio Cesari.

Benito returned to town after his day's work and went directly to the telegraph office, where he dispatched a telegram to Victor in Hawaii.

CURED.

IT WAS JUNE 1900, hurricane season. The thought sent a chill down my spine. I laid out my outfit for the morning, brushed my hair and climbed into the unfamiliar bed. The sound of cheerful voices on the street below calmed my fears, but what I was about to do kept me from sleep. Somehow, I managed to drift off to sleep but awoke to the noise of drunks arguing. I wished I could go back into my dream, where I was like a bird. I dreamt I was flying over the trees, headed back to Adjuntas. I swooped down and circled, to land on our house, but it was not there. Isabella's house was gone too. The servant houses were all gone. Our land stood stripped of any buildings, only the coffee trees and roads showed any evidence of our having been there. I landed at the foot of the road and was about to walk up when the drunks woke me.

I lay awake in my hotel room and thought about the hurricane, and the storm of events leading up to it. I wondered what had become my life, my country and its people. There was nothing I could do to calm the feeling of fright inside me once it erupted, so I distracted my mind to thoughts of anything else. What in the world was I doing all alone in San Juan, in a hotel, about to marry a man I've never met?

Martina, I hope this makes things right. And Celia, you're welcome.

The air was still and already getting hot at 7:00 a.m. I missed the cool mountain air of Adjuntas. How people lived in the low lands escaped me. I poured the water from the pitcher into a wash bowl to freshen up. Too nervous to leave my room, I decided to skip breakfast. My favorite Sunday dress was a little worn, but I loved it. The white cotton with delicate embroidery trim on the collar, sleeves and hem was perfect for today. It was more than a dress. It felt like an old friend who knew all my secrets. I'd worn it for every special occasion.

I ate a pastry, wrapped in a napkin from the night before, drank the last of the water from the pitcher and wished I had a cup of coffee. I looked out my hotel room window and saw that Juana was early to pick me up. Her carriage sat across the street and her driver stood on the sidewalk beside. Butterflies began to form in my stomach. I hoped they would fly in formation today, as there was a lot to accomplish. I gathered the last few items for my handbag and looked at the note that Victor had given me.

Benito Gonzalez

9 Calle Veranda

Ponce

I tore the note into small pieces and tossed it into

the waste basket. “Thank you, Victor,” I whispered. “It was good to meet you, Benito.” I recalled my visit across town to the poorest barrio, where I met Benito Gonzalez and told him about my problem with Antonio Cesari. He assured me that his friendship with Victor ran deep, and that he would take care of things. I took a deep breath and exhaled, releasing a shudder from my body. I checked my appearance in the mirror, adjusted my hat and walked out the door.

Juana was waiting in the lobby and greeted me with the warmth of a prison warden. The flock of butterflies in my stomach began to flutter. She was dressed in black and looked as if she was about to attend a funeral. I realized I had never seen her in anything but black and thought she must have a wardrobe closet with nothing else.

I approached. “Good morning, Juana. I can't believe we're here. I haven't been to San Juan in years.” I smoothed my skirt with my hands.

Juana looked me up and down. “This will do fine,” she said. “Let's go, shall we?” She took my arm and we crossed the street to her carriage. Her driver assisted us into our seats and we started our clip-clop way down the cobblestone street. “I love Ponce, but still enjoy visiting San Juan,” she said. “It's a grand city, isn't it?”

“It is,” I said. My eyes were dancing, taking everything in. The man on the corner selling straw hats stacked ten high, the tiny cigar store, restaurants, shops and women dressed in beautiful clothes with their hair styled high on their heads.

I caught the aroma of fresh brewed coffee and breakfast cooking nearby. A few doors down, the wind blew up from an alley and an unpleasant ammonia odor of urine caught in my throat. Juana chattered away.

"Ponce is my home, but the city life revitalizes me. My family is rooted in the farm, now don't get me wrong. I am dedicated to it too. But the ..."

We turned and suddenly I thought, I know this street. We visited my sister at El Convento, where I was planning to attend before Mama died.

"Are you all right?" Juana asked.

"Yes," I realized my attention had drifted and I wasn't answering her. There it was. El Convento. The massive building sat back on the property, hauntingly quiet. I imagined the halls echoing in crying voices. Martina had told me how the young girls begged for their mothers and the sisters scolded them to stay quiet. The girls were lined up for bed inspections and the youngest girls were shamed for bed wetting. Girls as young as five years old stripped their own linens for the wash, while everyone stood at attention. Martina wept when she told the story. It was a painful memory, and I never asked her about it again.

The driver turned the corner and my thoughts shifted again. "Stop here," Juana said. "We can walk."

"We're here?" I asked. Surprised the ride was so short.

Juana and I walked down the narrow street. Juana's cane clicked on the blue cobblestones. I saw him from two blocks away.

Juana smiled and whispered, "Your groom?"

Outside the church stood a man in a white suit, holding a bouquet of pink hibiscus. My first glimpse took my breath away and I felt my cheeks blush hot. The butterflies in my stomach began to fly in formation.

"Yes, a friend. He's Martina's friend from school.

I've never met him, but Martina said I could ask him for a favor if I needed." We looked down the street at the handsome young man in a white suit. He looked different than the photo I'd seen in the letter. He had a boyish innocence about him. He looked too young to have served in the military and Martina never mentioned he wore glasses. He looked more like a teacher than a soldier. A gorgeous teacher.

Juana twisted her wrinkled face in confusion. "A favor as handsome as yours is worth the debt." She gave a half smile, clicked her cane and we continued to walk toward the church.

We approached and I said, "Paulo?"

"Yes. Fina?" He took my hand and bowed.

I tried to cool my warm cheeks and said, "May I introduce Dona Juana Cesari." I turned to see a twinkle-eyed, smiling Juana. Yes, he is very handsome, I thought.

Paulo took Juana's hand and gave her a Queen's greeting. "Pleasure to meet you, Dona Cesari."

"Paulo," Juana said, "Do you understand what is being asked?"

"I do," he smiled nervously. "I guess I'll say that inside, in a few minutes. I mean I do. Yes, I understand," Paulo's face grew serious, "Sorry, I'm quite nervous." He pursed his lips together. "It's time for us to leave, and I have an old friend to see in Hawaii. Fina and I have an understanding."

Juana looked at Paulo then back at me.

"Yes, well, shall we continue on?" I said. "Where is Adriana?"

"First, we need to see the parish priest. He's waiting inside. He will marry you and I'll get the papers."

Juana clicked her cane. "Ready?" She pulled open the church doors and we walked inside. A man sat on the first pew. "Hola, Tino," she said. "Thank you for coming." She hugged the man.

"Of course, my friend," he said.

"Father, this is our witness, Don Bartolino Lopez."

I took a breath and followed the priest's instructions. My hands shook and I hardly heard a word he said. I remember Paulo and I saying "I do," and felt relieved we'd made it through the ceremony. The kiss. I didn't think about the bride and groom kiss. My lips tingled and sent my mind into a confused swirl of guilt and excitement.

"That is all for today," Juana said. "I will see you both tomorrow morning."

I stood for a moment, unsure what to do next. "Go now, girl," she said. "I will take care of the papers."

Paulo looked at me, raised his eyebrow and walked to the door. "Shall we get some breakfast?" he asked.

I followed my husband.

What was his last name again?

✡ ✡ ✡

Paulo and I walked along the port the next morning. The smell of rotting fish nauseated me. I carried one large satchel. Paulo, dressed in fine Italian leather shoes, carried a suitcase and looked impressive in his linen suit and straw hat. Everyone around us looked excited, about to start a new life, full of promise. They were lining up to board, with free passage on the sugar cane ship. It was much too dangerous to warn them about what was ahead. We turned and walked across the dock, toward the ramp for paying passengers.

"Sir, may I carry your bag for you?" a young boy appeared out of nowhere, looking unbathed and wearing dirty clothes.

Paulo reached into his pocket, "Here, this is for you." He handed the boy two coins. "I have no other bags and I'll carry this one, thank you."

The boy ran through the crowd to the next passenger to beg from. "Paulo, you shouldn't have given him money. Now he'll tell his friends and you'll be bothered by other beggars," I explained.

"Fina, he's an orphan. The orphan children live here at the wharf. They work and beg. This is all they have."

I looked around and my heart sank. I'd seen children wander the streets of Ponce, orphaned after the hurricane. The Americans promised to build a home to care for them and I saw glimpses of hope. Still, I felt like I was on a sinking island, about to be swallowed up and couldn't wait to get off. I looked toward the huge ship, when suddenly Juana appeared.

"Hola, Juana."

"Good morning." She gave a half smile. "I wanted to see you off. I heard that Martina has a little store near the camp. Maybe you will work there? I don't know." She pulled a small bundle, neatly wrapped in paper and tied with ribbon from her satchel. "This is a little startup money for Celia and Adriana. Antonio owes it to them." She looked me straight in the eyes. "I trust you will be a good keeper of her money."

"Thank you, Juana. I will see that Celia gets it." I tucked the package into my bag.

"Have a good voyage." Juana clicked her cane, turned and disappeared into the crowd.

Nanny Pilar and baby Adriana stepped into view. I sniffed, choked back my tears and walked toward them.

"Hello," I said and stared at Adriana. "She looks like my sister." Emotion welled up and caught in my throat.

"Please tell Celia how happy I am for her," Pilar said.

"I will." I took Adriana in my arms. She felt heavier than I expected. "Oh, my goodness!" I said as I shifted her in my arms.

"She likes to eat and sleep," Pilar said with a laugh. She paused and held her gaze on Paulo's face. "Have we met before?" she asked.

"I don't recall meeting you," Paulo said while adjusting his glasses. "Have you been to San Juan?"

"No, I live in Adjuntas. I work at the Cesari hacienda." Pilar redirected her attention to me. "Here's her luggage. Everything is in here, blankets, bottles, diapers and—"

"Pilar, thank you," I interrupted. "We'll take care of her. And we'll figure out the luggage. Trust me, she'll be fine and soon she'll be with her mother." I gave Pilar a hug.

"Fina, we really must be going," Paulo said.

Pilar wiped a tear from her eye and said, "Goodbye, dear one," she kissed Adriana on the cheek. "Goodbye Fina. Safe travels." She turned and disappeared into the crowd.

I didn't want to draw attention on the dock. We made our way to the ticket booth. I was very nervous, and thought if there was a problem, we would go to the sugar cane ship, where no papers were needed. That option frightened me more than anything.

"Tickets?"

"No, sir," Paulo said. "We're picking up tickets for Hawaii. They are paid for."

"Name?"

"Paulo Velez de Rivera, Maria Fina Rivera de Paoli and Maria Adriana Rivera de Paoli."

"Oh yes," He reached for a rubber stamp.

"Papers?" the man mumbled.

What papers? I thought. Auntie Juana didn't give me any papers. I twirled the gold wedding band on my left hand. We should run. We should run now. The Sugar Cane ship is leaving soon. We can make it.

"Paper?" the man looked up at Paulo.

"I'm sorry," Paulo said and adjusted his wire rimmed glasses.

"Do you want to purchase a paper for the trip?" He waved a newspaper. "Five cents. San Juan News."

Paulo wiped the sweat from his brow. "No, thank you."

"Your arrangements have all been made." He stamped three tickets and some paperwork that he had prepared and ready, handed it to Paulo and said, "Have a good trip."

I remembered to breathe and said, "Thank you."

Paulo led the way. My trembling hands were calmed by the weight of holding Adriana. We slowly made our way up the gangway and I prayed we'd make our escape. Paulo handed our tickets to the uniformed ship's mate. He smiled at Adriana, returned the tickets and said, "Beautiful little one. Have a good trip, Sir."

Paulo took my hand and helped me step from the gang plank onto the ship's deck, taking the plunge into a destiny already set in motion. I took a deep breath and walked to the rail. "It's beautiful, isn't it?" he said. "Do you know what gives the cobblestones their blue color on the streets of San Juan? They're cast from furnace slag, brought over on Spanish ships."

"I heard something about Spanish ships. I only know that they're beautiful." I looked back at San Juan and longed to follow the footsteps of my family, on the blue cobblestone streets.

"Come, let's find our quarters and put this bag away," Paulo said.

"Don't you want to watch from the deck?"

"Yes, of course." Paulo stood behind me and we watched the crowd on the wharf below. The people looked so small, rushing about. Some were crowed in a bunch, waving to the ship. Pilar reappeared and stood with Auntie Juana. Pilar was very animated, talking and pointing up toward us. I waved. Paulo pushed my arm down. "We don't need any trouble." He whispered in my ear. "I think she remembers me."

I turned toward Paulo, and looked into his face. "Remembers you? How would Pilar know you?"

Paulo looked away. I knew when a man couldn't look me in the eye the truth was not what he was about to tell me. Or the truth was too hard for him to say while looking at me.

"I was there that night," he said. "At Dino Cesari's

house."

I pulled back. "What?" My mind raced. He repulsed me. He was there? One of the men who attacked my sisters, beat the cook and hunted down the man I loved that night?

"Fina, listen," he reached for my arm. "I wasn't with the pack of angry dogs that night. I worked for the government. After power was turned over to the locals, I was sent to look in on things. It just happened that I came to town that night. I rode with them on what I understood was a routine search for bandits."

How could I believe him.

"Because the government could not participate in local affairs, I waited at the bottom of the hill when the local police went up to the house. They said they were checking in. I was at the bottom of the hill when I heard screams. I rode up and went inside. When I burst into Martina's room there was a man. I ordered him out just before—well, I think you know. Martina and I only had a brief moment alone to speak. She never told you?"

"No."

"She protected me."

"It sounded like you protected her."

"But I was too late for Celia," he said. "I'm very sorry. It haunts me, and when you told me about this plan I didn't hesitate for a minute. Maybe this is something I can do for Celia that will take away a little of her pain."

I stretched my neck over, for a peek at the dock. Every hope of getting back to Jorge collapsed on that wharf. I saw Juana's angry face, looking up at the ship. Paulo tugged at my arm and I stepped back with him.

"If Pilar remembers you being at the house the

night the soldiers came for Dino, and now you're with me, Juana will think I betrayed her." My voice raised. "Juana will think I ran off with the Spanish soldier who killed her brother, and stole her nephew's child."

"Fina, quiet down," Paulo said.

I started to cry. We stood against the wall of the ship, away from the crowd. "She will get us removed from the ship." I tried to get a breath, but could not. I looked to Paulo for help and grabbed my chest. My mouth hung open, but I couldn't get air. I felt faint.

"Fina!" Paulo blew into my face. "Are you all right?"

I inhaled a deep breath and realized that Paulo had taken Adriana from my arms. "Yes." I held out my hands. They were shaking. "That was the most frightening thing I've ever experienced."

"That says a lot," Paulo said and raised his eyebrows. "You are a brave girl."

"I can't go back," I said. "What about Juana?"

"She can't stop the ship. Soon, we'll be out to sea." He waved his hand toward the ocean.

"Paulo, what have I become? What's to become of me now?"

"That is up to you."

One of the crewmen came over to check on us. "Excuse me, is the lady all right?"

"Oh, yes sir. Sorry, she is upset about leaving her family," Paulo said. He handed me a handkerchief.

I nodded and wiped my face. "Thank you," I said.

Adriana began to fuss. Paulo bounced her on his hip and said, "Fina, you've got to pull yourself together."

I looked at Adriana and saw my family in her

chubby face. She squirmed in Paulo's arms and seemed delighted in being outdoors, looking all around.

"She doesn't want to miss a thing," Paulo said.

I touched Adriana's leg and felt the softness of her baby skin.

I said, "I wonder if we'll sail past Ponce."

"I think we'll sail straight out to sea." Paulo put his hand on my shoulder.

I walked to the rail and looked back once more to see Pilar and Juana pointing up toward the ship waving their arms in the air with looks of anger on their faces. Paulo took my arm and pulled me back into the crowd of passengers, disappearing from sight of the wharf.

The ship lurched and was released from the dock. I lost my footing, and Paulo held my arm to steady me. We were steering straight out to open waters. A tingle of excitement ran through my body and released through my fingers.

The mountainside farms of Adjuntas that were once heaven sent were now washed away or destroyed by the hurricane. My father and mother did not live to see us sail free. I didn't know if Hawaii would be heaven or hell.

I turned back and said a silent goodbye to my beloved Puerto Rico.

WHAT'S NEXT?

Follow the Paoli family in book two, when Fina travels across the wild west to San Francisco. When she finally joins Victor and her sisters in Hawaii, she finds it's not paradise. Victor doesn't leave things to chance this time. He has plans to restore the family's wealth and return to the lifestyle they once knew.

Made in United States
North Haven, CT
02 November 2022